THE DEAD HAMLETS

PETER ROMAN

FIRST EDITION

The Dead Hamlets © 2015 by Peter Roman
Cover artwork © 2015 by Erik Mohr
Cover design © 2015 by Samantha Beiko
Interior design © 2015 by Alysha DeMarsh / BUNGALOW

Distributed in Canada by
HarperCollins Canada Ltd.
1995 Markham Road
Scarborough, ON M1B 5M8
Toll Free: 1-800-387-0117
e-mail: hcorder@harpercollins.com

Distributed in the U.S. by
Diamond Comic Distributors, Inc.
10150 York Road, Suite 300
Hunt Valley, MD 21030
Phone: (443) 318-8500
e-mail: books@diamondbookdistributors.com

Library and Archives Canada Cataloguing in Publication

Roman, Peter, 1967-, author

    The dead Hamlets / Peter Roman.

(Book two of the book of cross)

Issued in print and electronic formats.

ISBN 978-1-77148-316-2 (pbk.).--ISBN 978-1-77148-317-9 (ebook)

I. Title. II. Series: Roman, Peter, 1967- .

Book two of the book of cross

PS8557.A59346D43 2015   C813'.6   C2014-908378-5   C2014-908379-3

CHIZINE PUBLICATIONS
Toronto, Canada
www.chizinepub.com
info@chizinepub.com

Edited by Kelsi Morris
Copyedited and proofread by Michael Matheson

Canada Council   Conseil des arts
for the Arts   du Canada

We acknowledge the support of the Canada Council for the Arts which last year invested $20.1 million in writing and publishing throughout Canada.

ONTARIO ARTS COUNCIL
CONSEIL DES ARTS DE L'ONTARIO
an Ontario government agency
un organisme du gouvernement de l'Ontario

Published with the generous assistance of the Ontario Arts Council.

Printed in Canada

THE
DEAD
HAMLETS
PETER
ROMAN

ChiZine Publications

THE DEAD HAMLETS

PETER ROMAN

CZP

"Who's there?"

—*Hamlet*

ENTER GHOST

I lost the angel Baal in Berlin during a rainstorm of biblical scale. Some might say the weather was a sign of things to come, or maybe a sign of things past. But if there was one thing I'd learned over the ages, it was that the weather was usually just the weather. Usually. So instead of killing Baal and getting drunk on his heavenly grace, I found a bar on a quiet street and got drunk on regular spirits instead. It wasn't the same, but I'd learned to make do.

Make that drunker. I hadn't been sober in months, not since the Barcelona Incident. The less said about that, the better. Let's just say if I didn't have a reason to kill angels before, I had one now.

If I had been sober, Baal might not have been able to lose me in the crowd at Potsdamer Platz after we got off the S-Bahn train, disappearing like he was just another person on his way home from the office. Sure, he looked like a regular man most of the time, simply another mortal hurrying his life away to the grave. But appearances can be deceiving. Take me, for instance. I look like one of you too, but I'm not. I wish I were. So do the angels. But if wishes were stars, the heavens would be on fire.

So, as sober as I am mortal, I had lost Baal in the rain and the crowd of commuters. Which meant I'd thrown away the money I'd paid to the priest in Madrid who gave me Baal's location. It wasn't the first time drink had cost me dearly. I've lost fortunes over the centuries, thanks to my bad decisions. It wouldn't be the last time either. There's no way I'm going to spend the rest of eternity sober, not with the sort of things that happen to me on a regular basis.

I told myself that it didn't matter as I stumbled out of the rain and into the bar. I'd find Baal again, or I'd find some other angel to kill. There were always other angels to kill. Not as many of them as there used to be, granted, because I'd hunted down my fair share of them over the centuries. But there were enough seraphim left to get me through a few more Dark Ages. God had made a lot of spares.

I sat at a table in a corner of the bar, dripping water on the floor, and told a waitress with a blonde ponytail to bring me the strongest beer she had and to keep them coming. When in Germany, drink like a German, I figured. She smiled like I was the only person who had said that in the entire evening, which I strongly doubted based on the drunken laughter of the people at the tables around me.

I had good reason to drink. Many good reasons, in fact. The one love of all my lives, Penelope, the daughter of an angel and a mortal and thus my miracle, was dead and gone. We had both been killed decades ago when Judas had lured us to Hiroshima in time for the atomic bomb. I resurrected in the ruins, as I always do. Penelope did not.

Yes, the same Judas who had betrayed Christ. The same Judas who was not a mortal, as most believed, but an ancient trickster god who wanted to keep humanity mired in the blood and muck. The same Judas who was responsible for my existence, for if he hadn't betrayed Christ there would have been no crucifixion and thus no dead, divine body in want of a soul so badly it created one for itself. Me.

Then there was the matter of Amelia, my unborn daughter who had died with Penelope. Only she hadn't really died, because she'd recently been birthed by Morgana, the faerie queen, as an act of revenge against me. Revenge for . . . well, she had her reasons. And now Amelia lived with the faerie in the glamour, their world hidden away in ours—if you could say that someone who was still dead lived anywhere.

And if that wasn't enough, Morgana had somehow laid claim to my soul—to me. And I was under her spell, thanks to a bone ring she'd given me that had fused with my ring finger and my mind alike. All I could think about was my longing for Morgana, even though we'd definitely had a challenging relationship before she'd bound me with the ring. The only way I could escape that feeling was to get drunk on alcohol, or high on the grace of angels. The same as it ever was.

Yes, things were definitely complicated. But things have been complicated ever since I'd woken up in that cave all those lifetimes ago, trapped in the body of Christ with no memory of who I was or how I had wound up there. Complicated is pretty much my life.

So I drank beer after beer, and the windows darkened from black to blacker, and the waitress with the blonde ponytail was replaced by a new waitress with dark pigtails. I emptied the latest glass and ordered another, and she worked the subject of the bill into the conversation. There's always a price when you're dealing with the Germans.

I didn't have any money to pay, so I knocked my glass to the floor. When the waitress cursed and bent down to pick it up, I tried my usual trick of lifting the wallet of the man sitting behind me, one of a tableful of men wearing the sports jersey of some soccer team or another. But I was clumsy from the drink, and he caught me doing it and grabbed my hand before I could extract any money from his wallet. He hit me in the face with his beer mug like he'd had lots of practice at it, and then his table-mates joined in with their fists and elbows and feet and whatever else they could hit me with. Even the waitress gave me a few kicks before they threw me outside, back into the rain.

If I'd had some grace, I could have fought them off. If I'd had some grace, I could have ripped their limbs from their bodies and turned their blood into wine that I drank straight from their wounds. But I had nothing.

Yeah, how I had fallen.

I picked myself up off the street and stumbled bleeding into the night, just like usual. Tomorrow would be a new day. Tomorrow I'd get myself sorted out and track down Baal and kill him and drain him of all his grace.

Tomorrow.

I walked the wet, dark streets of Berlin without any idea of where I was going until I arrived there. An old theatre—the kind that still featured live actors on a stage, not its updated Hollywood equivalent. Most of the light bulbs on the marquee were burned out, but there were enough left to see the name of the show that was currently running. *Hamlet*. The lobby inside looked warm and inviting, so I considered ways to sneak in. As it turned out, I didn't have to. The box office was empty, and the doors were open. I just walked inside. Maybe the theatre was desperate for more audience members. Times are hard in the arts these days. But times have always been hard in the arts.

There was no one in the lobby either, but I could hear voices from inside the auditorium, so I assumed the show was already well underway. I thought about stretching out on one of the padded benches against the walls. With any luck, I could get a few hours sleep. But eventually there would be an intermission or the show would end and people would come out and find me dozing there. Then it would be back into the rain for me. Do not go gentle into that good night, but go drunken and pushed. The story of my life. I'd be better off finding an empty seat in the audience and hope the theatre staff missed me when they cleaned up and went home after the show. It was live theatre, so I knew there'd be empty seats. Sorry to any thespians among you, but you know it's true.

I followed the sounds of the actors' voices to a door and slipped through it, into the darkness beyond. And it was complete darkness, not even a light from the stage. I'd entered in the middle of a blackout for a scene change.

I stumbled down the aisle until I tripped over someone's foot and fell into an empty seat. No one in the audience said a thing. I couldn't hear a single cough or anyone breathing. Not even a snore. It was the quietest theatre audience I'd ever found myself in.

Then the lights over the stage came on, and I stopped thinking about the audience.

I've sat through so many productions of *Hamlet* over the centuries that I knew instantly what scene it was, even though the only prop was a translucent curtain near the front of the stage, hanging from chains that disappeared into the darkness overhead. The bed chamber of Queen Gertrude, Hamlet's mother, who was now shacked up with Hamlet's uncle after the suspicious death of Hamlet Senior. The not-so-faithful royal servant, Polonius, stood on the near side of the curtain, his back to the audience. I guessed that to mean he was hiding in the closet, as per the stage directions of the play. Gertrude stood on the other side of the curtain, facing the audience. Hamlet entered from stage right.

"Now, mother, what's the matter?" he said.

"Hamlet, thou hast thy father much offended," Gertrude said, without turning to face him. She was looking straight at me.

The actors spoke some more familiar lines, but I didn't pay much attention to the words. I was too distracted by the people on the stage.

The part of Hamlet was played by the faerie Puck. The actor playing Polonius was human, but when he looked around he had a dazed expression that marked him as one of the fey, the mortals forever caught in the thrall of the faerie and doomed to entertain them until they are lucky enough to get killed in some prank or another gone wrong.

But Hamlet and Polonius weren't the ones I cared about. It was Gertrude who had all my attention. Or rather, Morgana, queen of the faerie, in the role of Gertrude. I didn't know what she was doing up there on that stage, and I didn't care. My longing for her welled up inside me and pushed me to my feet. If there hadn't been the rows of seats between us, I would have run straight to her. I don't know what I would have done then, but it probably wouldn't have been good for my dignity.

I truly, deeply hated her.

"Have you forgot me?" Morgana said and smiled at me as I stood there in the darkness before her.

"No, by the rood, not so," Puck/Hamlet said.

"No," I breathed.

I really needed to do something to break Morgana's enchantment and her hold on me. Maybe once I was done admiring the way the stage lights turned her skin golden. . . .

"What wilt thou do?" Morgana asked. "Thou wilt not murder me? Help, help, ho." She said the words as if they amused her, but the fey played his lines to the hilt.

"Help, help, help!" he cried. Maybe he was just sticking to his part in the play, maybe he was making a broader statement about his fate. Hard to say, really. It didn't matter in the end.

Puck drew his rapier and skewered the poor fey through the curtain.

"O, I am slain," Polonius said, but he sounded more relieved than anything else.

I'd seen enough men killed by blades in my days to know this was the real thing and not a stage death. An observation that was confirmed when Polonius slid off the rapier and proceeded to stain the floorboards with his blood. The stage crew who had to clean up afterward weren't going to be too happy about this turn of events.

"O me, what hast thou done?" Morgana said, raising an eyebrow.

"I know not," Puck said. He prodded the corpse with the rapier and giggled.

"Oh, enough of this," Morgana said, breaking character. She pushed Puck aside and strode to the front of the stage, not bothering to lift her dress clear of Polonius' blood. She glared at me.

"Cross, you know what happens next, do you not?" she called to me.

I wondered why the audience wasn't saying anything about this strange turn of events. None of them so much as turned a head my way. Maybe they thought it was experimental theatre. This was Berlin, after all.

I rubbed the latest bumps and bruises on my face thoughtfully. I wondered if maybe I was dreaming. Or more drunk than I had thought. Well, dreaming or drunk or not, I didn't have much choice but to go along with things.

"The ghost?" I said in response to Morgana's question. "The ghost of Hamlet's father makes his appearance to announce his betrayal at the hands of, well, you." I looked at the crowd some more. They continued to ignore me. Something was not quite right about this theatre.

"Do you see the ghost?" Morgana asked, folding her arms across her bosom. Her ample, perfect bosom.

I shook my head to clear it and looked back at the stage. "No ghost," I confirmed.

"Its absence is notable because it has already made its appearance," Morgana said. "The ghost does not merely haunt the character of Hamlet. Now it haunts our very play!"

"I'm not really following you," I said. Oh, but I would follow her. I would follow her to the end of the world itself and beyond. I would follow her to . . . I slapped myself to focus on what was happening on the stage.

Morgana kicked the body of the fey. "A stage rapier with a collapsing blade," she said. "We tested it. We were certain. And yet." She took the weapon from Puck and thrust it into the body again. The sound of the blade stabbing into the wooden floor beneath the corpse echoed in the theatre. I waited for someone in the audience to react, but no one did.

"The blade was switched," Morgana said. "Supernatural trickery, obviously." She shook her head, as if she had never engaged in any acts of supernatural trickery herself.

"Personally, I'd bet my money it was Puck," I said, not without good reason. Although I already had a feeling it wasn't going to be that simple.

"I am honoured, m'lord," Puck said, smiling and bowing in my direction.

Morgana waved him away. "I was prepared for that," she said. "He was under strict orders and fear of iron not to make any mischief for this performance. As were all my subjects. So it was not any of us."

I rubbed my face some more. I noted her words "this performance."

Which implied the faerie had produced other strange productions of *Hamlet*. Somehow I knew I was about to become involved in something I didn't really want to know about. I was beginning to feel the hangover coming on, and I wasn't even done with being drunk yet.

"Talk to me like I don't know what's going on," I said. "Trust me, it won't be hard."

Morgana went over to the stairs at the edge of the proscenium and stepped down into the audience. A spotlight over the stage moved to follow her. No doubt operated by another poor fey, equally in her thrall as I was. She walked up the aisle to me, explaining things as she went and clearing up nothing.

"You are aware, of course, of the passion the faerie have for theatre," she said.

"Of course," I said. After all, who doesn't know *A Midsummer Night's Dream* was largely based on a real event? Although Shakespeare, crowd pleaser that he was, did take out the parts about murder and bestiality. I guess he was content to leave that to the Jacobeans.

"I'm also aware of the passion the faerie have for chaos and tricks," I added, nodding at the body, which was still twitching every now and then. And I didn't have to point out I knew the faerie had a long history of wreaking havoc with stage productions of all kinds for their amusement. It was their own form of theatre.

"We live in chaos," Morgana said, drawing close now, "and we feed on trickery." She stopped beside me in the aisle and I could smell her perfume. It smelled of dead things in the ocean. It was the most beautiful scent in the world to me at that moment. I had to steady myself on the seat in front of me.

"But this is not of our making," Morgana went on. "And we are not amused by it at all."

I took a deep breath and forced myself upright again, which was harder than it sounds. It was even harder to stop myself from reaching out to her, for just a touch of that beautiful, ivory skin. I managed a shrug instead. "So someone or something switched the fake blade with a real one. What difference does one dead fey make? There's plenty more where he came from." I didn't point out that whoever had killed the fey had probably done him a favour. There was no use in stating the obvious.

Morgana smiled that wicked smile of hers at me. Those lips. . . .

"We would not have invited you to this performance if it were only one dead fey," she said. "But it is not only one dead fey."

She snapped her fingers and the house lights came up. Now I saw why the audience was so silent. They were all dead in their seats. Some had stab wounds like Polonius, others were charred corpses. A couple had split-open skulls and I could see inside their heads. They were mostly fey, but I saw the faerie Peaseblossom among their number. I remembered him pouring me one ale after another when I was a prisoner of Morgana's in that pub in the Irish countryside, both of us laughing as I drank away the memories of the outside world. Now his skin was an odd colour that suggested poison, and the foam that surrounded his mouth backed it up. He wore a dress that would have looked Elizabethan if I hadn't been around for the actual time period. It was stage garb. The other dead all wore similar outfits: period costume of the kind you see in plays but that never really existed in the actual time. They all stared sightlessly at the stage and continued to pay us no mind.

I shook my head again. I had to stop going to the theatre. Nothing good ever came of it.

"Something has been killing my subjects," Morgana said. "Anytime we put on a production of *Hamlet*. Always a seeming accident." She waved her hand to take in the audience. "But this is too great an accident, even for the faerie."

I considered the corpses, as I've done so many times before. They didn't tell me anything. They usually don't unless I raise them from the dead.

"So your plays are haunted," I said. "Or maybe you've got a demon problem. Or some other infestation. What does this have to do with me?"

"We need an exorcism, of course," Morgana said. "Or whatever it is that you mortal types do to rid yourselves of such problems. It's not really the sort of thing with which we have experience. But now that you have become one of my loyal subjects. . ." She smiled that wicked smile of hers.

Now it was my turn to smile.

"I don't think so," I said, although it hurt like hell to say the words. The enchantment wanted me to do anything I could to help her.

Morgana looked bemused, and Puck spat at me, although he grinned even wider. I half expected the dead to turn their heads to look at me, but they stayed dead. The dead are rather predictable that way. Most times.

"You don't think so?" Morgana asked, arching an eyebrow.

"I have no interest in helping you," I said. "Not while I'm under your spell, anyway. Lift it and maybe then we'll talk."

Morgana chuckled, which I wasn't expecting. It's never a good sign when the faerie queen laughs at you. Or, I suppose, whenever any queen laughs at you for that matter.

"I thought you might say that," she said. "So I have prepared an incentive to move you to action."

As if on cue, a young woman walked out of the wings and onto the stage. She wore a white dress that looked as if it had been made from spider's silk. She sang as she walked.

"He is dead and gone, lady. He is dead and gone. At his head a grass-green turf. At his heels a stone."

I recognized the song. Also from *Hamlet*. The character was Ophelia. I recognized who was playing her as well. Amelia. My daughter. She was no longer a babe, like the first and last time I'd seen her. Now she was in her late teens. She had aged unnaturally fast in the court of the faerie queen, but I still recognized her. I saw the combination of features in her face. Mine and Penelope's. Her dead mother's. Just one in the list of so many people I hadn't been able to save over the ages, but the one at the top of the list. Amelia's skin bore the grey pallor of death, as it had when Morgana stole her from Penelope's dead womb long turned to dust and birthed her. Amelia was still dead, like Penelope, yet somehow still living and aging.

"Oh yes, our daughter is older now," Morgana said, as if she'd just remembered.

"She is not your daughter," I said.

"Isn't she?" Morgana said. "I seem to recall bearing her."

"You took her," I said. The words were like ash in my mouth. "You took her from Penelope." And me.

Morgana shrugged, like the distinction was lost on her. Maybe it was. The faerie had always had peculiar ideas about children and ownership.

"She was entertaining at first, as a child," Morgana said as I stared at Amelia wandering aimlessly about on the stage. I tried to imagine her as a child but couldn't. I had seen none of that time. Morgana had stolen Amelia's childhood from me just as she had stolen Amelia herself. I didn't know I could feel even emptier inside until that moment. "But I grew weary of her endless questions and so hurried things along a little," Morgana added.

"What is the meaning of this?" I said. I wanted to run to Amelia, to take her into my arms and spirit her away. But I knew it would not be so easy to take her from the faerie queen and her court. Especially as long as I wore that ring.

"Amelia is going to appear in our performances of *Hamlet* from now on," Morgana said. "She is going to play the part of Ophelia." Morgana put a hand to her lips, like she was trying to suppress more laughter, or maybe something else. Who knew what. "I certainly hope nothing happens to her."

"We must be patient," Amelia said, moving to one of the stage wings now. She didn't look at me. "But I cannot choose but weep, to think they should lay him in the cold ground."

I recognized the passage. The madness scene after she has learned of the death of her father. I waited for her to look at me, but instead she looked at the corpse of Polonius on the stage.

"Poor Ophelia," Morgana said. "Such a tragic fate for one so young."

I would have killed Morgana then if I had been able. Or, failing that, I would have warned her of the wrath I was capable of. But she knew all that. And she knew I couldn't do such things when I was under her spell, even if I had grace. Just like she knew I would agree to anything to save Amelia from another death.

Amelia wandered off the stage, back into the wings, without looking at me. So I turned my attention to Morgana again.

"What do I get in return for helping you?" I asked.

Morgana leaned in and kissed my left cheek. "I will give you visitation rights to your daughter," she breathed into my ear. She kissed my right cheek. "And you will have my gratitude," she breathed into my other ear.

I felt myself nodding, even though I wanted more than that. I wanted my daughter back. I wanted ownership of my soul back. But I couldn't resist Morgana. Damn that enchantment!

Morgana stepped away from me, and the new distance between us physically hurt inside.

"We will call you for our next performance," she said. "So ready yourself."

"I'm ready now," I said and stepped out into the aisle. To my credit,

I was only swaying a little. The events of the night had rapidly sobered me up. Well, somewhat sobered me up.

Morgana looked me up and down. "You are far from ready," she said. She turned and walked away from me. "I can't believe I once took you into my bed."

"It was more than once," I muttered, but I shouldn't have said anything. The thought of those nights made me fall back into my seat again.

"Enjoy your memories," Morgana called over her shoulder. "They are all you will ever have of me now." She went back down the aisle toward the stage. The house lights went out, and the spotlight flickered and spun wildly about the theatre for a moment. When it settled back on the stage, I could see that Morgana was gone, as were Puck and all the corpses in the audience. They'd disappeared back into the glamour.

The body of Polonius still lay on the stage, though. And then Amelia stepped into the spotlight from the wings.

"Good night," she said, looking around at the empty seats. "Good night."

"Amelia!" I cried. "Wait!" I ran down the aisle to her, but it was too late. The spotlight flickered once more and then she was gone too, just like the others. And why not? She belonged to them, after all, not to me. Before she vanished I saw she was marked by the same black ring on her finger that I wore on mine. Black bone. Like the kind that all the fey wore. The bone that bound us to Morgana.

Now it was just me and the dead Polonius. I waited for the lights to flicker one more time and the darkness to take him, too, but that didn't happen. I went over to him to see why he was different. He clutched a piece of parchment in his hand I hadn't noticed before. In fact, I was sure it hadn't been there before. I took it from his dead grasp and unfolded it.

It was a map—a street view like you find online, but hand-drawn in ink with great detail. The forced work of one of the fey, no doubt. It depicted a street with row houses. One of them that looked just like the others was circled with what I was certain was blood. A single word was written on the street outside the place. *Baal.*

I looked back at Polonius, but he was still dead. He'd make an interesting find for the stage crew the next day. He might even become a theatrical legend, like the ghosts who seemed to haunt every theatre that needed some sort of extra box office draw.

"Something is rotten in the court of the faerie queen," I said, but there was no one left to listen. So I went back up the aisle and through the empty lobby, out into the dark and rain outside.

Just when you think things can't get worse, that's when they get worse.

TEA WITH AN ANGEL

Baal was where the map said he would be. When I rang the doorbell, he answered the door with a cup of tea in his hand. The steam made arcane patterns in the air. Baal wore glasses and a cardigan that made him look like a retired professor instead of an angel. Maybe he had been a professor for a time. The angels all had to make a living ever since God had abandoned them to the mortal world.

"I thought you guys would have stopped answering the door by now," I said. "Given what usually happens when I come knocking in the night."

Baal studied me for a moment, then sipped his tea. "Would it have made a difference?" he asked. "Could I simply have fled out the back once you'd found me?"

"Probably not," I said, which was a lie. I wasn't exactly mortal, sure, but that didn't mean I could be in two places at once. There'd been more than one angel who had slipped out the back door on me before. I didn't like to advertise that fact though. It made them think I was soft.

"So," he said, and blew the steam from his tea.

"Yes," I said, keeping an eye on the symbols that danced in the air between us.

"I don't suppose we could talk about this like civilized beings," he said.

"That's a laugh to call yourself civilized after what you did at Gomorrah," I said.

"I was under orders," Baal said, frowning.

"I've heard that one before," I said.

"Very well," he said, "why don't you just tell me what I can give you to make you go away?"

"Not this time," I said. "Not unless you know how to stop a play from killing people."

Baal looked up and down the street, but it was empty of anyone who could save him.

"Which play?" he asked.

"How many plays are there that can kill people?" I asked.

"You'd be surprised," Baal said. He turned and walked down the hallway of his home. "I imagine you're going to come in one way or another," he said over his shoulder.

I took that as an invitation and followed him. I made sure to close the door behind me and lock it. There were three locks. It was almost like he was expecting trouble. Well, one could never be too safe with people like me roaming the streets.

The walls of the hallway were lined with bookshelves that held every sort of book: mass-market paperbacks, encyclopedias and dictionaries, art books, travel guides. There wasn't any order to them that I could tell. The living room Baal led me into was more of the same, only here the books were older tomes, bound in leather and other types of hide. I tried not to let my eyes linger on the titles. That way lay madness.

The couch was covered in stacks of newspapers and magazines, but two chairs were free. Baal motioned for me to sit in one so of course I sat in the other.

"Can I offer you a tea?" Baal asked. "Or perhaps a stronger drink?" He looked at me like he knew what I'd been up to after he'd lost me at Potsdamer Platz. Maybe he did know. The angels are a mysterious bunch. Even I don't really understand how they work. Hell, they're probably mysterious even to each other.

"I'm not here for a drink," I reminded him, and he smiled. See what I mean?

He sat in the other chair and blew steam from his tea again. More arcane symbols danced in the air between us.

"What exactly are those?" I asked.

"They are not unlike the aroma of a tea, in their way," Baal said.

"That is not like an answer, in its own way," I said.

He smiled a little, but just a little. "It's an ancient blend that took considerable effort to acquire," he said. "In fact, it can no longer be found in this world. I could no more describe the symbols to you than I could describe the aroma to a man with no sense of smell. Are you sure I can't interest you in a cup?"

I shook my head. "Thanks, but I've learned my lesson about other-worldly drinks," I said. Although it had taken a few times for the lesson to really sink in. I looked around at the books again. "You work in publishing or a library?" I asked.

"University professor," he said. "Emeritus."

I smiled a little too. At least I still had a gut sense about angels in some ways.

"So," he said again.

"*Hamlet*," I said, cutting to the chase. "It's killing people."

"Is there a new production causing riots?" he asked. "Or perhaps a travelling show with a cast of demons and their minions?"

I winced at the mention of demons. I'd had one too many run-ins with their kind over the years. I shook my head. "I think it's more like some sort of curse with the play itself," I said. "People keep dying from accidents during productions." I didn't mention the faerie or Amelia. Or sweet, sweet Morgana. I didn't want any of the angels to know about my deep, dark secrets. I'd never live it down.

"Perhaps it's the *Macbeth* curse," Baal said. "An old superstition among thespians."

I knew what he was talking about, thanks to centuries of drinking until dawn in various pubs with actors and other characters of ill repute. Anytime something goes wrong in a production of *Macbeth*, actors always lay the blame on the mythical curse. Only it's not mythical, as Baal and I knew.

It was all because of the Witches. Any respectable Shakespeare scholar will tell you the spell the witch characters use around their cauldron in *Macbeth* is a real one—Shakespeare stole it from the actual Witches. And yes, they deserve the capitalization. There are witches and then there are the Witches. They appreciated Will's act of supernatural plagiarism so much that they gave him another spell gratis: the curse.

It's normally a harmless enough thing. Some actor says the name "Macbeth" backstage in a production without thinking and starts the spell running. Soon props are falling apart and actors are breaking legs and candles are igniting curtains. You know, the sort of things that can also be caused by excessive drunkenness, which actors are also known for.

But the faerie show I'd seen had been *Hamlet*, not *Macbeth*.

"Not a bad guess," I said, "but it's the wrong play."

"Not if someone was infected with the curse during a previous production of *Macbeth*," Baal said. "Perhaps they brought it with them to this new play."

The symbols from his tea had made it around the room and now circled his head. I continued to keep an eye on them.

"Curses can infect people?" I asked. That was a useful piece of information, although I wasn't quite sure yet how it was useful.

Baal shrugged. "Magical curses are by their very nature unpredictable," he said. "Sometimes the spell latches on to actors and follows them to other plays. It can even move from player to player. Usually the actors develop a bad reputation and stop getting work, and that's the end of that. But not always."

This is why it's good to sometimes talk to angels rather than just kill them outright. Occasionally, they have something interesting to say. Occasionally.

"So what do you do to get rid of the curse?" I asked. "It doesn't sound like the sort of thing where a prescription can help."

"No, in these cases an intervention is usually necessary," Baal said.

"I'm guessing that means more than throwing salt over your shoulder or running out of the theatre and spinning in a circle three times," I said, thinking about the usual antidotes. Actors loved their silly rituals, even though they rarely seemed to work. Sometimes I think it was the faerie who came up with them, having a little fun at the expense of mortals. They had a long history with the theatre, the faerie did.

"It would definitely require something more dramatic than that," Baal said. "Sometimes it is best to fight witchcraft with things darker than witchcraft."

He eyed the bookshelf beside us, but I held up a hand before he could reach for anything.

"We're not going to even open any of those, let alone read the words in them," I said.

I'd had enough of ancient tomes after one of them had killed the infamous playwright Christopher Marlowe, who had been one of my few friends when he'd been alive. Well, in all honesty, Marlowe was responsible for his own death. But he had a lot of help from a book, if you could even call it that. Most books were just books, but some weren't. Some books were other things entirely.

Baal raised an eyebrow but left it alone.

"Have you tried talking to the Witches?" he asked.

I sighed. "I was hoping to avoid that," I said. "That's why I'm sitting here talking to you."

"There are worse things in the world than the Witches," he said.

"And there are a whole lot of better things in the world too," I said, although I may have been overly optimistic about that.

"Perhaps you should seek out—," Baal said, but I cut him off before he could finish.

"I'm not going to him for help again," I said.

Baal nodded and paid attention to his tea again, and we shared a moment of silence while I thought things over. I ended the moment with another sigh. There was no getting around it. I was going to have to meet with the Witches. This night just kept getting better and better.

"Is there anything else?" Baal asked.

I gave him an apologetic smile. "I'm afraid I need your grace," I said.

He frowned at me. "I thought we had an arrangement," he said.

"What can I say?" I said, shrugging. "I'm a fallen man."

Now it was his turn to sigh. "I expected more of you," he said.

"Everyone does," I said.

"Give me a moment," he said.

"Of course," I said.

He finished the tea and put the cup down on the bookshelf. Then we stopped carrying on like civilized beings.

The arcane symbols from the tea's steam didn't do anything to help him. They were just that: symbols.

DOUBLE, DOUBLE TOIL AND TROUBLE

I left the row house burning behind me and went down the street as the familiar sound of sirens started up in the distance. I was bloodied and beaten, but I had what I'd come for. I felt whole again now that I was full of Baal's grace. How to describe the grace? It's what makes the angels what they are. It's their essence, or maybe the closest thing they have to a soul. It's also what my body uses as power for all the little tricks I've learned over the ages, as well as the ones that just come naturally, like resurrection. When the grace is in me, I think I can almost glimpse God everywhere in the world: in the rays of sunlight coming into a dark room, in the feel of a breeze on my skin, in the scent of the sea air, in those quiet moments where you're drifting to sleep and your mind opens up to everything outside of it. When I've burned through all the grace and I'm empty inside again, I know that God is gone and never coming back.

I was wearing clean pants and a shirt I'd taken from Baal's wardrobe before I started the fire. I had also taken a couple of credit cards from Baal's wallet. I used them to go to the airport and catch a flight to London, but first I used a bit of that new grace to heal all my injuries, so I looked like just another traveller. It wouldn't do to pass through security looking like I'd just killed an angel.

I spent the time in the air staring out the window beside my seat, at the clouds and the sky and all the miracles of creation. I thought about other miracles, like Penelope, my one and only true love. Penelope, who had given off a grace herself thanks to her angel father. Her grace had fed and nurtured me, so I didn't have to hunt the seraphim when I was with her.

I thought of the miracle that was Amelia. A child who never should have been, because I'd been unable to father children during all the ages before I met Penelope. It seemed my divine body and mortal women weren't all that compatible. Which was probably for the best. Who knows what mischief a hundred other versions of me running around in the world might cause?

And then Penelope and Amelia died at Hiroshima and that should have been the end of it. Hiroshima was the end of miracles. Until Morgana gave birth to Amelia.

The first time I had seen my daughter had been when she'd erupted from Morgana's womb in a wave of blood and snakes and black rings on the floor of an abandoned Irish pub the faerie had taken over for their festivities. I don't know how Morgana had managed to reach into the grave to steal Amelia from Penelope's dead womb, but she had. Perhaps she'd done it as an act of simple trickery, as the faerie can be like that.

Or perhaps she'd stolen Amelia as an act of revenge against me for the King Arthur incident. When I first met Morgana, I'd taken her away from a tower in the woods guarded by a troop of men under an enchantment, in order to deliver her to King Arthur. I was trying to become one of the knights of Camelot at the time, and I thought it would earn me some favour with Arthur. As usual, I was woefully misguided. Arthur and Morgana had some sort of history together, but I didn't know the nature of it until he tried to kill her with that strange blade of his. I stopped him by putting my own body in between them to shield her. Perhaps I should have let Arthur kill Morgana and Excalibur drink her blood. Then I wouldn't be in this situation now. But I've never been very good at doing the right thing.

Our relationship was definitely troubled after that. We made up and patched things over, because when you're both immortal or close enough to it, you're going to have to learn to live with each other. And when one of you is a faerie queen, there are definitely going to be drunken nights where you both wind up in the same bed. But there were other incidents over the ages, so we each had plenty of reasons to want to even the score with the other.

But stealing my daughter crossed a line. Morgana had not only stolen Amelia from Penelope, she had stolen her from me. My memories of her now were not what they should have been. When Amelia was born, I should have seen her in Penelope's arms. I should have held her in my own arms. She should have been living and breathing, not stillborn yet somehow still alive. She should never have been taken from the dead by Morgana. This was as far away from a miracle as I was from Heaven.

I'd barely had time to think about Amelia since I'd had that glimpse of her in Morgana's arms in the pub. Dead and unbreathing, but conscious and looking around nevertheless. I'd been too busy battling a group of angels inside a painting in order to free the real Mona Lisa, who was being used as a secret weapon in a war between the seraphim. After that I hadn't even had time to catch my breath before I had to help another angel save the good people of Barcelona from an unnatural peril that had awoken under the Gaudí church at the heart of the city. That one's a long story I don't care to repeat here.

In fact, I'd forced myself not to think about Amelia during all that. Because if I thought about her, I wouldn't have been able to do all those other things. I would have gone to save her instead, and then we'd all have a lot more to worry about than just a curse killing a few fey and faerie. Sometimes you're damned no matter what you do.

I'd returned to the faerie pub after Barcelona for Amelia. But the pub was abandoned once more, nothing left behind but a few bodies of the fey. Morgana and her court had moved on, taking Amelia with them. I had lost my daughter a second time.

But now she had returned. And she was nearly all grown up, even though it had been less than a year since she'd been born. I looked at the patches of land I could see through the clouds. She was down there somewhere. With Morgana and the rest of the faerie court. I had no idea where, but I'd find her. And then I'd take her from Morgana. Even God could not stop me from doing that. And I'd find a way to break the faerie enchantment and make Morgana pay for what she had done.

First, though, I had to stop the curse from killing again. I would not lose Amelia once more.

It was afternoon by the time I walked out the doors of Heathrow airport and into the usual English mist. I took a cab to Kew Gardens and spent the rest of the daylight hours wandering the paths, losing myself amid the flowers and greenhouses. I wanted to keep a low profile, away from any security cameras. That was getting harder by the day in England. I had no doubts the English authorities were still looking for me after my last visit to the country, given the fact I'd broken into the British Museum, resurrected Princess Diana and accidentally turned an

Egyptian mummy into a living god. The Brits tended to frown on things like that. Frown more than usual, anyway.

I spent some time sitting at the edge of a pond, under a cherry blossom tree. I closed my eyes and thought of when Penelope and I had sat under another such tree, on the bank of the Kamo River in Japan during the war years. We'd been in the country looking for angels, because we had reason to believe they'd all sought refuge there for some mysterious reason. But we'd been tricked into thinking that, just part of Judas's plan to lure us to our death.

Penelope had told me she was pregnant under that tree, and the cherry blossoms had showered down around us, like the entire world was celebrating. Weeks later, we took a train to Hiroshima, and the world ended in fire.

I continued on my way through the gardens. I snapped a thorn from a bush and dropped it into my pocket for later, then went back to the front gates at closing time. I hailed another cab and had this one take me to the Globe Theatre—the new one, not the original from Shakespeare's time. Although if anyone could find a way back to the older one, it would probably be a London cabbie.

I bought a ticket with some money I'd lifted here and there from tourists during the day and went inside. I stood in the pit with all the other people who'd bought the cheap tickets. It was raining now, so it wasn't long before I was soaked. It was just like it had been in Shakespeare's time. Strangely, I didn't feel any warm glow of nostalgia.

The play was supposed to be *A Winter's Tale*, but that didn't meet my needs so I changed it. I took my ticket from one pocket and the thorn from Kew out of my other pocket. I jammed the thorn into my finger deep enough to get a good well of blood. Then I wrote the name of the play I wanted over the name on the ticket.

There's more to it than that, of course. There are a few particular words you have to say, in a particular order. But I'm not about to share them with everyone. It wouldn't do to have random people changing a play the instant they get bored. No play would ever finish its run if that were the case.

If you *really* want to know the proper incantation, you can always make a deal with the Witches like I did. But I'd advise against it, unless you've got the same divine blood running in your veins that I have in mine. The Witches charge a high price—one I doubt you could afford.

It was the Witches I was here to see. If they were responsible for the curse that was wreaking havoc with the faerie shows, then they'd know how to lift it. Finding the Witches is a problem for most people. But, as you may have noticed by now, I'm not most people.

So I stood there in the rain for a while, and then the actors came on stage and started the play. It was two women and a man, all wearing business suits. The man carried a briefcase, the women had phones. The stage directions for the play I wanted called for thunder and lightning to accompany the arrival of the witch characters who start the play, and the sky overhead obliged. The whole world's a stage and all that.

"When shall we three meet again?" one of the women asked. "In thunder, lightning or rain?" She wasn't enough of a pro to hide the surprise at the unexpected words that came out of her mouth. They weren't the lines she'd memorized for *A Winter's Tale*, after all. Well, I'd done worse things in my lives, and there were even worse things to come yet.

The man hesitated a few seconds before blurting out the answer to her question. "When the hurlyburly's done, when the battle's lost and won." He half-raised his hand, like he was about to clap it over his mouth.

The other woman was quick on her feet, at least. She raised her eyebrows a little and then gave a shrug, as if she'd decided to roll with it. She said her words like she believed them, like they were the ones she'd been practicing for months.

"That will be ere the set of sun," she said.

Now the people around me started to look at their tickets, wondering what had happened to the play they'd paid their money to see. I put my ticket back in my pocket along with the thorn. I didn't want to just drop those things on the ground and have the Witches find them. The real Witches, not the actors on the stage right now. Who knew what tricks the actual crones could manage with my blood?

"Where the place?" the first woman said, looking at the other actors for help.

"Upon the heath," the man said, looking into the wings for help.

"There to meet with Macbeth," the other woman said. She gave the audience a look that seemed to say, hey, we may as well enjoy the ride.

If you hadn't figured it out yet, I'd summoned the play *Macbeth* up onto the stage. Some people summon demons, I summon plays. I'm not sure what that says about my character. Make of it what you will.

THE DEAD HAMLETS

The first actors exited stage confusion and there was a pause before the next ones entered. But they had to step onto the stage. It was the nature of the spell. So they eventually came on stage right and continued with the play. The show must go on.

Although the show definitely changed as it went on. Each new character that stepped onto the stage wore an older and older period costume, like time was running in reverse in the play. Which it was, in a way. And the set started to fill out, props appearing here and there when you weren't looking. Trees with moss and cobwebs. Swords on a rack. A skull on a stick planted in the ground. Only they weren't props. They were all the real thing.

I waited for the scene I needed and worked on my character while the play manifested itself. I was going to take a starring role in a few minutes, and I wanted the audience to remember me as someone other than I was. I wanted them to remember me as just another man in the crowd. For good measure, I used a bit of Baal's grace to turn some of my blood into wine. A quick way to get drunk, if you have the ability.

And then I noticed the cauldron bubbling away at centre stage, and the Witches clustered around it, stirring their concoction with long, weathered bones. They weren't the same actors as before—now they were three worn women in rags. They were so aged they didn't even look human anymore. If they ever had. These were the real Witches. It was time.

"Round about the cauldron go," one of the Witches said, in a tone that was equal parts weariness and boredom. "In the poison'd entrails throw." She went on with the rest of her speech, but I wasn't listening. I pushed my way through the crowd and climbed up onto the stage. No one tried to stop me. You can generally get away with anything at the theatre, because no one's sure if whatever you're doing is part of the play or not. For instance, when I killed the angel Elijah onstage in Sarajevo during a production of Webster's *The Duchess of Malfi*, I got a standing ovation for it.

"By the pricking of my thumbs," one of the other Witches said, looking across the stage at me. "Something wicked this way comes."

They all turned to look at me and smiled in unison. None of them had any teeth. I don't think they'd ever had any teeth.

"This isn't what I paid to see!" I yelled at them, slurring my words to sound even drunker than I was. It wasn't a lie, not really. "What the hell is this?"

"A deed without a name," the first Witch said.

"A deed without a name," the second Witch agreed.

"Double, double toil and trouble," the third Witch said.

I don't think they have names any more than they have teeth. It doesn't matter. I've long suspected they're the one and the same entity anyway, just split into different bodies. Kind of like the way gorgons are separate beings but all share the same group mind. Maybe it's an ancient monster kind of thing.

I kept playing the part of the drunk and stumbled across the stage to them. "I want a refund!" I shouted, then added in a lower voice, "I also want a favour."

The Witches left the cauldron and circled around me.

"Speak," one of them said.

"Demand," another said.

"We'll answer," the third one said.

I glanced into the wings and saw several of the stagehands talking. I knew I didn't have long before they sent out some of the extras for an improv intervention.

"I want a counterspell for the Macbeth curse," I whispered to one of the Witches. "It's run amok. I need to stop it before someone else gets killed." I didn't tell them who I was worried about getting killed. It's not a good idea to let the Witches know what's really valuable to you. Those are the sorts of things they like to put in their cauldron.

"Seek to know no more," the Witches said, shaking their heads together. "Double, double toil and trouble."

"Tell me," I said. "Or I'll tell the world you've been hiding in this play all these centuries." Now I raised my voice again, so the audience could hear. "Tell me!"

It was the only threat I could use against them, but it was a good one. The Witches had once lived in the real world, until too many people took an interest in them not living anywhere anymore. There's even a hill in Scotland named after the place they met the real Macbeth in his travels— Macbeth's Hillock. It's a farmer's field now. Crops grow very well in that field, thanks to all the blood that's been spilled there over the ages. The Witches didn't have angry mobs chasing them anymore, but there were still other things searching for them. You can't be a Witch—or even a witch—without pissing off someone. And there was no better hiding place for the Witches than in a Shakespeare play. It was better even than fairy tales, because those old legends had some pretty nasty supporting characters that might not like the new neighbours. *Macbeth* was a safe, comfortable home for them, and one they wouldn't want to give up.

The Witches looked at each other without saying anything. I looked into the crowd. Several people were filming the scene with their phones.

"Look at that," I said. "We're going to be online soon."

That made up the Witches' minds. They knew they couldn't allow me to reveal their secret in front of all these witnesses. They pushed me toward the cauldron, striking me hard with their bony hands, harder than old women should be able to hit. Actually, harder than most football players should be able to hit.

"For a charm of powerful trouble," one of the Witches said.

"Fire burn and cauldron bubble," another of the Witches said.

"Don't be shoving me about or we'll be having a proper riot up here!" I yelled at them, back in my drunk character. I played the role well. I'd had my share of practice over the years.

"Like a hell-broth, boil and bubble," the third Witch said and shoved me into the cauldron.

All right, I wasn't expecting that.

I *was* expecting them to give me the counterspell. I *was* expecting them to be unhappy about it and try a little witchery to get even with me—you know, turn me into a small rodent that would be chased by the city's feral cats, or maybe just hit me with a curse that affected my sexual performance for a decade or so. I should have known better. The Witches have always been more Brothers Grimm than Disney. So into the cauldron I went.

It burned pretty much the way you'd expect boiling water and whatever else was in there to burn. I thrashed about, trying to escape, but they pushed me back in with their long bone spoons. I could hear them chanting through my screams.

"Round about the cauldron go!"

"In the cauldron boil and bake!"

"Cool it with a baboon's blood!"

Then I was spilling out of the cauldron and onto the ground as the stagehands suddenly appeared and pushed the Witches out of the way to upend the pot. They screamed as well as the hot metal burned their hands.

I eased their pain with a bit of grace I breathed their way. They were trying to help me, after all. I didn't do anything about my own pain for a moment. I deserved it.

The air was thick with steam from the cauldron, but instead of dissipating it grew thicker, turning into a mist. I took that to mean the Witches were taking the play back to wherever I'd summoned it from.

"Come like shadows, so depart!" the Witches cried from somewhere in that mist, confirming my suspicions.

Fair enough. I had what I'd come for. The counterspell burned in my mind now, even though the Witches hadn't told it to me. In return, they had some new flavours for their soup. Things had worked out well for everyone.

There was more yelling and the sounds of people running into each other and falling over on the stage. I didn't know if they were trying to find me or the Witches. And then came the sounds of the audience shrieking and cursing. The mist must have rolled out to cover them.

I crawled over to the edge of the stage and dropped into the pit. Every inch I moved hurt about as much as you'd expect it to if you'd just been boiled alive. I couldn't see anyone around me because of the mist, so I took a few seconds and a lot of grace to heal myself. I hated to waste the grace, but the skin was already peeling off my body. I shook my head and cursed my own carelessness. The Witches never failed to extract a price somehow.

When I was back to normal, or as close as I come to normal, I joined the rest of the crowd in pushing for the exits and got the hell out of there before the Witches changed their minds and came back to demand a higher price.

It was just like in Shakespeare's time, all right.

SLEEPING AMONG
THE GHOSTS

I expected the mist to lift when I went outside the theatre, but instead it grew thicker. It reminded me of the time I'd cornered Judas at Stonehenge with the help of King Arthur and his knights after that first unfortunate Morgana incident. Judas had summoned a similar mist, which had turned into a dragon that swallowed me. I would have been lost if Arthur hadn't cut me free with Excalibur. I wondered if there was some trick that I was missing but everyone else knew. Maybe all the ancient supernatural beings carried around mist in a bottle just in case they needed a quick escape. If so, I could really use some of that.

Then again, maybe it was just the normal London fog rolling in. It didn't matter. It was a handy way to lose myself so I didn't have to deal with any awkward questions from the other audience members or stage-hands or even police officers.

I went down the pedestrian pathway bordering the Thames as fast as I could without running and drawing attention to myself from the people who materialized out of the mist. I needed another place to hide, and quickly. The scene in the Globe may have drawn unwanted attention.

I found my way to the Tower Bridge, then crossed it and took the Thames pathway on the other side, past the Tower of London. Thankfully, some of the mist, or whatever it was, had blown across the Thames and cloaked this side of the river as well. When I hit a particularly thick patch where no one could see me, I jumped over the side of the pathway and into the river. Even though my skin was healed from the Witches' cauldron, the cool water still felt soothing. I swam down to the bottom and felt around in the mud where the riverbed met the foundation of the embankment. I had to go back to the surface a couple of times for air, but eventually I found what I was looking for. A rusted grille mostly buried in the muck, clogged with plastic bags and strands of rope and the usual underwater detritus. I cleaned everything away from it and then peered into the tunnel behind. It was an old, stone affair, mostly filled with more muck, but there was room for me to pass.

I went to the surface for another breath of air and heard shouting on the pathway above. It could have been just drunks fighting, but it also could have been the authorities looking for me. Or other things looking for me. The angel Abathar had once tried to buy my mercy by revealing the Royal Family had a standing order to dispatch the Black Guard to any reported sightings of me. Which maybe explained the rise in riots and mass murders of late, as the Black Guard cleaned up after themselves and disposed of witnesses. It was time to disappear, just like I'd made Abathar disappear.

I swam back down to the grille, placed my feet on either side, then grabbed the bars and pulled. In ye olden days, when this was a secret entrance, the grille had been bolted on too tight for anyone without grace to move it. But I'd used some grace on it in a past age and nobody had bothered to reattach it again since. Now it was just held in place by mud and time. I managed to pull it far enough back with my mortal muscles that I could slip through and into the tunnel beyond.

It was a short swim to the end of the tunnel and the small stone chamber there. I pulled myself out of the water and up some steps onto a landing, where I spent a few minutes catching my breath. It occurred to me I may have been breathing the same air as the last time I'd come this way. Nobody had probably been down here in centuries. I imagined no one but me even knew about this chamber anymore.

I got up and found the next tunnel in the darkness and followed it, into the maze underneath the Tower of London. It's not a real maze, of course. It's more a random jumble of corridors, forgotten rooms and abandoned dungeons. All of the kings and queens of England liked to add their own touches to the Tower in their times, so they were constantly digging moats and building walls and generally trying to outdo each other. Now all those kings and queens were dead and most of them were gone, and the Tower was just another museum and tourist attraction. Hardly anyone knew about the secrets underneath it. Most of those old queens and kings probably didn't know all the secrets hidden away beneath the Tower.

Which made it a perfect place for me to hide.

It was darker than night down here, so I burned a bit more grace to sharpen my vision. Maybe it was a waste of grace, but I don't like stumbling around in the dark. You never know what you're going to run into. I made my way to another chamber, this one lined with bricks that were older than the British Empire. It was full of forgotten artefacts—suits of armour, ancient cannons, halberds and battle axes. Much of it was half-melted or blackened from flames, so I figured they were things that had been damaged in one of the fires that happened at the Tower from time to time. I was in an old storage room. It seemed as good a place as any to rest.

I searched through the room until I found a wool blanket in a crate in one of the corners. The blanket was wrapped around some bones that had once been a person, so I shook them free. Someone else had obviously thought this would be a good hiding place as well—a hiding place for a body. It looked like they'd been right. I wrapped myself in the blanket and lay down on another crate containing broken swords to keep myself off the cold floor. Then I closed my eyes and tried to sleep.

It was hard, though, on account of the apparitions that kept passing through the room.

The first was the woman in the ragged dress, carrying her head in her hands. She stumbled along, passing through the suits of armour, the pillar supporting the roof, the crate I'd taken the blanket from. Her eyes were open but didn't seem to see anything, at least not anything I could see.

If you didn't have my experience and eyesight, you may not have noticed her at all. Even if you did notice her, you probably wouldn't have recognized her. But I knew her. Anne Boleyn, a queen who had seen better days before she wound up at the Tower. I'd witnessed her doing this routine dozens of times before on previous visits.

I rolled over on my crate to face the wall, but it was no better on that side. A Roman soldier stepped out of the brick and looked around. He wore the armour of a legionnaire, but he was weaponless. He shook his head at whatever he saw and then stepped back into the wall. I'd seen him before too, but only a few times. He was always looking for something, but I didn't know what. He stuck to the lowest and oldest levels of the basement. The Romans had built a fort here once, and they used the blood of sacrificed soldiers in the mortar. But I'd once heard a rumour from a mummified man in a bog that the Romans had just built on even more ancient structures, all with their own violent and dark histories. It was blood and torture all the way down. The Tower was one of those places. Even I didn't know the truth about its history.

I sighed and rolled over again. Anne was gone but she'd been replaced by two boys chasing something I couldn't see through the room. A cat maybe? Or a rat? They kept looking over their shoulders, like they were being chased too. The two princes who were forever lost in the Tower, courtesy of another royal intrigue. It was busy in here tonight. Must have been something in the air.

I didn't bother talking to any of the apparitions. I'd tried that in the past, but they'd always ignored me and just kept on doing whatever it was they were doing. It was always the same thing: Anne wandering with her head, the soldier looking for whatever it was he was looking for, the children chasing something I could never see. And all the others doing their own thing. They weren't like other ghosts. They didn't see the world around them and carry on conversations with the living. They didn't take on real form and bump into walls or pick up swords or do any of the other things ghosts sometimes did. They were trapped in their memories.

Or maybe they were trapped in the memories of the Tower itself. That sometimes happens with important places. They develop a sort of life of their own and the memories of what happened there just won't fade away. Those memories can be so strong that the souls of the people who die there can't escape them and have to relive those memories forever. That's why I tend to avoid places like Auschwitz and Gettysburg, if I can help it.

Well, there were always worse fates than being trapped in the memory of the Tower of London. Just trust me on that.

Besides, the people I saw here meant nothing to me because they were all dead and long gone, and none of them could help me now. I pulled the blanket over my head and settled into my own memories.

TO SLEEP, PERCHANCE TO DREAM

I dreamed of a simpler life. I dreamed I was with Penelope, my dead love, and Amelia, my dead daughter, in a house in the suburbs. It was the same house where I'd once found a demon pretending to be a normal man, raising a family. I'll leave that detail for you to analyze.

The thing about this dream was Penelope and Amelia were alive in it. Amelia was young, maybe five or six. The child I never got to have.

Penelope and I walked Amelia to school in the morning and then made love in our bedroom in the afternoon. I drifted off to sleep after and woke to Penelope standing beside me, dropping cherry blossom petals on my naked body. She had a smile on her face like she knew this was a dream and that our time together was limited. I pulled her back down to me, and we made love again among the petals. That night, I read fairy tales to Amelia in her bed. They were the ones that the Brothers Grimm had lost in the flood that ruined most of their records. Then we slept the sleep of the peaceful and the mortal. In the morning I woke to the smell of bacon and coffee. I opened my eyes as Penelope came into the bedroom with breakfast in bed.

Only it wasn't Penelope holding the tray of food. It was Morgana.

"Wake up, my pet," she said. "There is a mystery to be solved." She looked down at the tray and frowned. "Really? This is what you dream about?" she asked. She shook her head and tossed the tray into a corner. "Humans. You are all so dull and predictable."

I threw myself to my feet and went past her, down the hall to Amelia's room. I opened the door to find her gone. The books I'd read to her were scattered on her torn sheets. The pages that were open were blank now.

"You won't find her there," Morgana said behind me. "You won't find her anywhere."

"Leave her out of this," I said, staring at the empty bed. "She's done you no harm."

"I can't leave her out of this," she said. She walked past me, into Amelia's bedroom. She picked up a brown stuffed bear and smiled at it. Then she plucked out one of its eyes and ate it like a candy. "She is your only reason to live now."

"This is about us, isn't it?" I said. "You're trying to get back at me for all those things I've done to you over the ages."

"I have gotten back at you," she said. "I own even your dreams now." She popped out the bear's other eye and ate it.

"If anything happens to her . . ." I said. I didn't know how to finish it. Amelia was all I had left of Penelope now.

"If anything happens to her, it will be because you have failed as a father," Morgana said. She drew her hand over the bear's empty eye sockets and closed its eyelids. She handed it to me and then walked into Amelia's closet. The door slammed shut behind her. I knew when I'd been dismissed.

I looked down at the bear. Its fur was matted with blood now. When I pushed back its eyelids, the sockets were full of cherry blossom petals.

And you probably thought you had bad dreams.

AN INTERLUDE WITH THE RAVEN MASTER

I woke to find a raven perched on the edge of the crate I was sleeping on. It held a piece of bacon in its beak. When it saw my eyes open, it dropped the bacon beside my head and then waited for a response. Its eyes were white with cataracts.

"I don't suppose you brought coffee too?" I said, sighing. I didn't feel rested at all after that night.

The raven croaked once, very loudly. Enough to make me swipe at it like an alarm clock. It leapt into the air and flew over to the top of an iron maiden leaning against a wall. It made some more noises that I felt inside my skull.

"All right, all right," I said, sitting up. "Tell him I'm on my way."

The raven made a low chuckling sound this time and took flight again, down the same tunnel where the twins had disappeared the last time they'd wandered through.

I ate the piece of bacon and tried to get Morgana out of my head. I hated her for ruining my dream of Penelope and Amelia. But I also longed for her even more than I longed for Penelope. Once again I looked at the ring fused to my finger and thought about how to get rid of it. I had an idea, now that I was back in London, but first things first. I had to eat breakfast.

I got up and combed my fingers through my hair and tried to brush the creases out of my clothes, which were still a little damp from my dip into the Thames the night before. Then I went down the tunnel and up the stairs at its end, to meet the Raven Master.

There have always been ravens at the Tower of London. That probably has something to do with all the bodies that used to pile up around the place. The ravens were wild once upon a time, but then someone somewhen got the idea to domesticate them. I don't know why. Now there are always a few kept on hand for the tourists, their wings clipped so they don't fly away with the others that come to visit from time to time. The lore is they bring good fortune to the empire as long as they remain at the Tower, but I've never known ravens to bring good fortune to anything, not even other ravens. The British can never let go of their traditions, though, even when it leads to heads being chopped off. Actually, chopping off heads is a fine British tradition of its own. So the ravens are here to stay.

I climbed a staircase most people didn't know about inside one of the towers—most staff probably didn't even know about it, for that matter. The secret staircase let me skip the whole tourist experience, which was just fine with me. I'm not really one for lineups and security guards just to look at museum pieces. Not unless I'm on a mission to steal one of those museum pieces, anyway.

The stairs ended in a trapdoor, which was open. I climbed through, into the chamber at the top of the tower. It was a small room lined with open windows and a cupola over my head to protect me from the elements. Not that it mattered today. I could see blue sky and a few wisps of clouds through the windows, although I had to look past the ravens to do so. There were dozens of them, sitting in the window frames or perched on the wooden beams overhead. They were all watching me. As was the Raven Master, who sat on a stool near the trapdoor.

There are the raven masters the tourists see, the ones who wear the fancy costumes, feed the birds and pose for the cameras. Then there is the Raven Master. He wears robes of all black and no one sees him unless he wants them to. But he sees everyone, thanks to the ravens. And he's the only one who truly speaks their language.

There was another stool waiting for me, and a small table covered with scraps of food. More bacon, and some pieces of charred toast, some hard-boiled eggs, a couple of strawberries. All of it bore the marks of birds' beaks, which told me how the meal had got up here. There were no plates or utensils. The Raven Master ate like his flock. He even looked a little like the birds. He was lean, almost skeletal, and had a hooked nose that could have passed for a beak. And he had a way of studying you that was definitely more avian than human. As if he were thinking about plucking out one of your eyes and swallowing it down. His eyes were riddled with cataracts, just like the raven that had woken me.

"I didn't expect to see you back here so soon," he said, his voice as raspy as a raven's. "Not with this lot in charge."

He meant the Royal Family, and that was the other thing that made the Tower such a good hiding spot for me. The Raven Master was its unofficial warden, and he swore no allegiance to anything but the Tower itself. The Royal Family meant no more to him than any of the other royals that had preceded them. His flock was the only thing he cared about besides the Tower. We got along because I'd kept ravens well fed on battlefields around the world for many centuries. I guess they'd spread the good word about me.

"I'm in a bit of a situation," I said. I sat on the stool and grabbed a handful of the bacon and one of the eggs and dug in.

"You wouldn't be here otherwise," he said. He reached down to his side and picked up a thermos and handed it to me. "Tea," he said. "The real thing. Not that swill you drink in your Americas."

"They're not my Americas," I said. I poured myself a cup and drank it down.

A jet passed through the sky outside on its way to Heathrow. The ravens and the Raven Master all cocked their heads to watch it through the windows.

"So, what mischief are you up to?" he asked.

"I have an errand to run in the city," I said, "and then I have to stop a play from killing people."

"People don't have enough reasons to kill each other?" he asked, looking down into the courtyard below, where so many executions had taken place over the years. "Now they're using plays as an excuse?"

I shook my head and forced down some of the burnt toast. "They're not doing it," I said. "It's the play itself. One of those *Macbeth* curses run amok." I didn't see any reason to hide things. Any help I could get would also be help for Amelia.

He just cocked his head in a different direction, as if considering that.

I leaned back against the wall, sated if not full, and sipped some more tea. The raven who'd woken me sat in a window nearby. He looked as ancient as the Raven Master. I looked at him and he looked back at me with those white eyes of his.

"Can he even see anything with all those cataracts?" I asked.

"He sees all the things and places we can't with those eyes," the Raven

Master said. "He brings back the most interesting baubles from wheres and whens that have never been and cannot be."

I decided not to help myself to any more of the bacon. Who knew where it had come from? I looked out over the city instead. The traffic was starting to back up now, and the sidewalks were filling with people. The workday was starting. It was a good time to lose myself in the crowd.

"I should be leaving," I said. "Thanks for the breakfast."

The Raven Master nodded. "You have fed us enough times over the years that you are always welcome to feed with us," he said.

I looked around at all the birds, who were still watching me. "It's a loyal flock you have here," I said.

"Ravens never forget an enemy," the Raven Master said, "and they never forget a friend."

"I hope I stay on their good side then," I said. I went back down the stairway and out into the city of London, where it really wasn't safe for me to be.

DISCUSSING THE MEANING OF LIFE IN THE CREMATORIUM

Now that I was dry and fed well enough for the moment, it was time to take care of a pressing piece of business. I needed to get Morgana's ring off my finger so I could stop dreaming about her and focus on other things. Like saving Amelia. There was only one person I could think of to help me with that.

Scratch that. There was only one *being* I could think of to help me with that.

I went down into the Underground—the transit Underground, that is, not one of London's other undergrounds—and took a train east for a time. Eventually I got off and walked the rest of the way to my destination from the station, enjoying the blue sky and the birds calling to each other and the wind in my hair. It was a good day to be alive. A shame it wouldn't last. It never did.

I made a brief stop to buy a bottle of scotch, then carried on until I reached the City of London Cemetery and Crematorium. I went in through the front gate, no doubt looking like just another mourner on his way to visit a lost wife or child. It was a look I didn't really have to fake. But that's not why I was here, of course.

Once on the grounds I made my way to the crematorium building where all the hard work of getting rid of bodies is done. The first door I tried was unlocked. After all, who's going to break into a crematorium?

It's probably best not to think about that question too much.

Inside the building, I picked up my pace. I'd definitely get noticed as someone who didn't belong if I crossed paths with anyone in here. And I was trying to get rid of a problem with this little trip, not add a new one.

I took the first stairway I found and went down, into the building's basement. It wasn't anything like the pastoral grounds outside now.

Down here it was all stone walls and flickering lights overhead. And the sound of a power saw cutting something down the hall, and through that, the sound of someone singing.

"I remember, I remember, the house where I was born," he sang in a deep, rasping voice I recognized. "The little window where the sun came peeping in at morn."

I followed the voice, past doors marked Caskets and Holding Area 1 and Holding Area 2 and Embalming Supplies and Lost and Found. I tried not to let my mind wander into that last one.

"He never came a wink too soon, nor brought too long a day, but now I often wish that night had borne my breath away."

The door at the end of the hall was open, so I went inside. It was a large chamber with a conveyer belt running through most of the middle of it. The conveyer belt went into the incinerator, where the crematorium went about the business of turning the people back into the dust from whence they'd come. A good method of getting rid of bodies, by the way, if you should ever need to dispose of troublesome evidence. A lot easier than leaving them bundled in blankets in the basement of the Tower. The incinerator wasn't lit right now, which made the room bearable. It could get hellishly hot in here when business was good.

The rest of the room was a jumble of things: wooden caskets piled haphazardly in one corner, a metal table covered in coroner's tools in another—saws and hammers and that sort of thing. An easy chair and a cot near the incinerator, and a small bookshelf jammed with paperbacks. An empty bottle of scotch and a lone glass sat on one of the shelves. It was very homey.

There was a body in a cardboard coffin on the conveyer belt, and another body standing beside it. Except the second one wasn't a body—he just resembled one. His skin bore the pallor of death, as well as more stitches than most autopsy victims. He looked up from the dead man when I entered the room. He held a saw in one hand and the left arm of the corpse, which he'd just torn free, in the other.

"But now, I often wish that night had borne my breath away. . . ." he sang, and then his voice trailed off when he saw me.

"Hello, Frankenstein," I said.

I know what you're going to say. Frankenstein was the name of the scientist, not the creature he created. It's a classic mistake to confuse the two. Well, Frankenstein is what the creature has decided to call himself these days. Who am I to argue with him?

Frankenstein stared at me for several seconds and then dropped both saw and arm to the ground and rushed at me. I stood my ground.

"Cross!" he rumbled and swept me into his arms in his best attempt at a bear hug. He was getting better at this whole human thing. "You are alive!" he said.

"Today, yes," I said. "But I make no promises about tomorrow."

He let go and stepped back, gazing at me. "You drowned in the sea," he said.

I had to think about that one for a moment. There had been so many deaths over the years, and more than one of them had been a drowning.

"With that big ship," he prompted. "The one they turned into a movie."

"Oh, right, the *Titanic*," I said. I'd snuck on board by impersonating a . . . well, it's probably enough to say my plan to rob the first-class cabins didn't end that well. "I floated back to the surface and things turned out all right," I said. Nothing like resurrecting in the middle of the night drifting alone in the ocean, with no land or other people in sight. At least I'd had the stars for company. "How did you hear about that anyway?"

Frankenstein smiled and glanced back at the body. "I have my sources," he said.

"I imagine you do," I said. "You mind if I close the door?"

"My home is your home," he said. He pointed at the chair. "Please, sit."

So I closed the door and sat in his chair and felt the residual warmth of the incinerator behind me. Frankenstein sat on the edge of the bed and smiled at me. I had a feeling it had been a while since he'd had visitors. Of the living kind anyway.

I gave him the bottle of scotch I'd bought and he took it with an even larger smile.

"You have always been very thoughtful," he said.

"I just drink a lot," I said. I looked at the arm and the saw still lying on the floor. "Spare parts?" I asked.

He nodded and held up one of his arms. "This one is wearing out," he said. "I need to replace it. That one has a nice tattoo on it."

I saw that it did. A woman riding a bomb. Well, she could keep him company for a while.

We weren't that different, Frankenstein and me. I needed grace to survive; he needed fresh body parts. We were both freaks of nature. And we were both dreadfully misunderstood.

"So how have you been?" I asked him.

"I have been busy with work," he said. "People never stop dying."

"It's always a growth industry," I said. I looked at the bookshelf. It was mainly philosophy books: Nietzsche, Locke, Hume, the classics. But there were a few other cultures represented: the Tibetan Book of the Dead, some Buddhist sutras, that sort of thing. "Tackling the big questions, are you?" I asked.

"That is Victor's influence," Frankenstein said, smiling that lopsided smile of his. "He is curious about matters of the soul."

"Aren't we all," I said.

He cocked his head, as if listening. "And consciousness," he said. "He wants to know where it begins and where it ends."

I could see how Victor Frankenstein might be preoccupied with such matters. After he had died, his creation now sitting before me had taken the brain from Victor's body and put parts of it into his own head, sewing their brains together. I'd never asked Frankenstein how exactly he'd managed that. Some things are better not known. But he'd managed to keep Victor alive, in memory if nothing else, and the two of them were the same being now. So that was something.

"And what have you learned about consciousness?" I asked.

Frankenstein shook his head at me. "That it is not worth thinking about," he said.

I looked at his books again. "What about where you came from?" I asked. "Do you ever wonder about that?" I'd thought about the question a lot in relation to my own origins.

"Victor made me," Frankenstein said, patiently, as if he were talking to a child.

"Sure, he stitched you up," I said. "But where did the rest of it come from?"

"The rest of what?" Frankenstein said, frowning.

"Your . . ." I struggled to find the right word. ". . . life."

We could have been brothers, Frankenstein and me. We were both strange creations, brought into existence under mysterious circumstances. I'd woken up in a cave in the middle of nowhere, with no idea of who or what I was other than the few memories Christ had left me, he'd woken up on a table in Victor's lab, with who knows what going on in his mind. Both of us monsters.

"Life doesn't come from anywhere," Frankenstein said. "It is just always there."

"Tell that to all the people in the cemetery outside," I said.

"Death is just a different state of life," Frankenstein said. "Victor understood that when he made me."

"You're starting to sound like a mad scientist," I said.

"I was alive before I was who I am now," Frankenstein said. He touched different parts of himself: his arms, his legs, his chest. His head. All taken from different bodies. "When those others died, the life did not leave. It just . . ." Now it was his turn to struggle for words. "Went to sleep," he finally said. "Victor woke it again, only this time in my body."

"How do you know that?" I asked. This was one of the Big Questions, after all.

"I remember it," Frankenstein said. "Don't you?"

Okay, so maybe we weren't so alike after all.

"I'm going to need a drink for this one," I said. I nodded at the scotch. "Do you mind?"

"You are my guest," Frankenstein said, handing the bottle back to me. He really had been working on his manners.

So I poured some scotch into the lone glass and took a long sip, and then another.

"You were saying?" I said.

Frankenstein stared at the dead body on the conveyer belt, a look on his face as if he were remembering something long since forgotten.

"I wasn't me then," he said. "I was the others. Although I wasn't really them either, when I was dead. When we were all dead. We were no one. We just were. And we waited, forgotten in the ground."

"Waited for what?" I asked.

Frankenstein looked back at me. "Why, to be again," he said. "What else?"

"Carry on," I said and took another sip of the scotch. It was too early to be drinking, but if sitting in the basement of a crematorium talking the secrets of life with Frankenstein doesn't call for a drink, I don't know what does.

"I longed to be again," Frankenstein said softly, looking at the incinerator now. "That is what I remember. I was not, but I longed to be.

And then Victor dug me out of the ground in all those pieces and made me be. And now I am someone. And I have other someones for friends." He tapped his head with a finger and smiled at me. "We are alive and life is everywhere and we all are."

I finished the rest of the glass, taking that in. His understanding of life and death was far different than mine, but that didn't mean it was any less valid. It's a big universe and we are all multitudes and all that.

I put the empty glass back down on the shelf. "I'd love to keep talking philosophy and the meaning of life with you," I said, "but I've got a rather pressing problem that I think only you can help me with."

"You need to dispose of more body parts," Frankenstein said, nodding.

"I told you not to bring that up again, but yes," I said. I held up my hand and wiggled my ring finger. "I want you to take this finger."

He stood and came over to take my hand. He looked at my finger like a jeweller appraising a stone. "It's very nice, but the ring is curious," he said.

"It's cursed," I said. "I can't get it off."

He looked at me again without letting go of my hand.

"And the nature of this curse?" he asked.

"Nothing, really," I said, shrugging. "It makes you fall in love with a certain faerie queen."

"Love," Frankenstein said and sighed.

Maybe he wouldn't mind a little undying love to take his mind off his eternal loneliness, but I wouldn't wish the ring on him. I wouldn't wish it on anyone. Well, except for maybe Judas. I daydreamed about that for several seconds, before I suddenly felt jealous about the idea of Judas wearing Morgana's ring.

"Why haven't you removed it yourself?" Frankenstein asked, turning his attention back to the ring.

"I've tried," I said. "I don't have the skill required." That wasn't exactly the truth, of course. I couldn't pull the ring off, no matter how hard I tried. Perhaps I could have cut the finger off and regrown it, but I'd never been able to work up the motivation to do that. I blamed it on the enchantment.

Frankenstein made a sound somewhere between a chuckle and a grunt. Or maybe a groan. "But you think I have the necessary ability."

I nodded at the arm on the floor. "You do have a way with bodies," I said.

He let go of my hand and shuffled over to the table of coroner's tools. He hummed a little to himself while selecting the right tool. Then he came back with a small, circular bone saw.

"I imagine this will hurt a lot," he said, taking my hand in his again.

"Trust me, it can't hurt worse than it already does," I said, although I wasn't entirely convinced of that.

I looked away as he turned on the saw and his grip tightened. I heard the noise of the saw change as it began to cut. But I didn't feel any pain. I did, however, smell smoke.

I dared a look at my hand and saw my plan wasn't working. Frankenstein was trying to cut off the finger at its base, but the ring had shifted up to meet the saw, and the blade was spinning against it without cutting anything. Sparks flew into our clothing.

"It's not bone," Frankenstein remarked. "At least not any bone I've ever seen before."

He slid the saw down my finger and the ring moved to match it, all the way to the fingertip and then back to its original position. It shrank and expanded as needed to fit. Frankenstein turned off the saw and looked at the blade. It was bent and blackened, and little chips were missing from it.

"It appears to be your ring and your ring alone," he said.

I sighed and looked down at my finger, which was unscathed. The ring sat fused with my finger like nothing had happened. I cursed Morgana for the nth time, but the thought of her just filled me with longing and emptiness again. Can you be filled with emptiness? Well, I was.

Frankenstein put the bone saw away and leaned against the bookshelf. He folded his arms across his chest just like a real person would. Yeah, he'd come far.

"Perhaps it is meant to be," he said.

"Nothing is ever meant to be," I said, closing my hand into a fist.

Frankenstein shrugged. "Sometimes we cannot be freed from the things that make us what we are," he said. "It is good to understand that."

"Did you get that from one of your philosophy books?" I asked him.

"No, I learned that from being alive," he said.

I smiled and stood. "Next time I won't come asking favours," I said.

"I am just happy to see you again," Frankenstein said. "You are one of my few friends."

Yeah, some friend. I don't visit for decades and then when I do show up I want a body part cut off and I drink half his scotch. Well, at least I'd never stuck a blade in him, which was more than I could say for some of my friends.

"Tell Victor I said hello," I said, and Frankenstein nodded.

"He says he wishes you well in your quest," Frankenstein said.

I didn't think I'd talked about anything personal other than the ring, but Victor always did see things the rest of us missed. Then again, I'd been on many quests over the ages, even if most of them were misguided. It was probably just a good guess on his part.

We hugged again and then I went back down the hall. Frankenstein's voice carried after me as he returned to his work on the corpse.

"I remember, I remember,
the fir trees dark and high;
I used to think their slender tops
Were close against the sky.
It was a childish ignorance,
But now tis little joy
To know I'm farther off from heaven
Than when I was a boy.
To know I'm farther off from heaven
Than when I was a boy."

Outside, I stood in the parking lot of the crematorium and watched the sky for a moment. As usual, there weren't any answers there. But there were developments.

A raven came gliding over the trees and circled around me. I recognized the whites of his eyes, so I held out my arm and he landed on it. There was a piece of paper in his beak, which I took, because that's what you do when ravens show up with pieces of paper in their beaks.

It was a theatre ticket. *Hamlet*. For a matinee performance in a few hours at the National Theatre.

I looked at the raven.

"I don't know whether to thank you or curse you," I said.

It looked back at me and I expected it to caw or croak or something like that. Instead, it just took wing silently and disappeared back over the trees. A little unnerving, that.

Well, I had some time to kill. There was nothing to do now but drink.

So I found a pub and went about it seriously.

TO BE OR NOT TO BE

When it was time, I went down to the National Theatre, on the bank of the Thames. I was tempted to join all the people who were enjoying the day by wandering the walkway beside the river. In fact, I was tempted to walk right out of London and all its troubles. But I had a dead daughter to save.

I arrived a few minutes after the matinee time on the ticket, so the theatre's lobby was empty. There was only Puck sitting in the box office, wearing a shirt and tie but making no effort to hide the haunch of meat he was chewing on. He waved at me with his free hand.

"We were beginning to think you wouldn't show," he said.

"Did I have a choice?" I asked.

"No, not really," he said. He wiped his lips with his tie.

I went past him and to the usher waiting at the door to the theatre. She was human, I think, but who knows for sure? At least the murmur of the crowd reassured me that I wasn't about to enter another theatre of the dead. I knew I hadn't been brought here just to enjoy the play, though. As the usher took me into the dark and led me to my seat, I sighed and waited for bad things to start. I didn't have to wait long.

"Well, it's about time," said the woman sitting beside me. "What have you been doing?"

I looked at her. Morgana. I couldn't stop myself from touching her arm, breathing in the scent of her. I sighed again and glared down at the ring, which was probably never going to come off. The thought of that filled me with joy and rage at the same time.

"Is the curse afflicting all the productions of *Hamlet* now?" I asked, looking around at the theatre. I couldn't recall reading any bad news about the play in any of the papers, but then theatre didn't really make it into the papers much these days.

"Just the ones we involve ourselves with," Morgana said. "Whatever the problem is, it seems to have started in the glamour."

"That doesn't surprise me at all," I said.

"The show must go on," Morgana said, frowning. "Now." She clapped her hands and, as if on cue, the rest of the audience applauded as well. Probably more faerie or fey. Or just regular people who didn't know what was going on.

A man walked onstage and into the beam of a spotlight. He didn't look like an actor. He wore a simple pair of pants and a cardigan instead of a costume, and he held a clipboard in one hand.

"Ladies and gentlemen, I'm afraid we have a problem with this afternoon's show," he said to the audience. He wiped sweat from his brow and squinted against the light.

"Oh dear, whatever could be wrong?" Morgana murmured, smiling that nasty smile of hers.

I tried to sink down out of sight in my chair. I didn't like the way this was going. But then I never did when the faerie were involved.

"Our lead Hamlet, Malcolm, has had an accident backstage and broken his leg," the man in the spotlight said. "Obviously, he won't be able to perform tonight."

"The curse strikes again," I said to Morgana.

"Not yet," she answered. "Not if dear Malcolm is still alive."

"Unfortunately, our understudy is also out of commission," the man went on. "He's been stricken with food poisoning."

"Actually, too much hummingbird wine," Morgana murmured to me. "He wound up at a pub with Cobweb and the others last night and, well, you know how these things go."

The man sitting on the other side of her laughed and pulled what looked like spider's silk from his sleeve. "He's still sleeping it off," he said and made a quick Jacob's ladder with the silk. "In the glamour." He blew the silk off his hands and it drifted away, coming apart in the air as it went.

Now I definitely didn't like the direction this was heading.

"We have no one who knows the part," the man onstage said. "So it's with great reluctance I announce we have to cancel the show." He wiped his brow again. His sleeve already looked drenched with sweat.

There were groans from all around, but they weren't loud enough to drown out Morgana, who stood and waved her hand at the man.

"Not true," she said. "We have someone who can play the part right here," she said.

"Don't do this," I said. "I'm begging you."

Everyone in the audience turned to look at her, and the man on the stage held up a hand to shield his eyes from the spotlight as he looked our way.

"You have a Hamlet?" he asked.

"No!" I said, but Morgana just waved me down.

"We have a Hamlet who's played the role more times than any of your actors. He knows every line of the play, including the ones that have been lost to the ages." She looked down at me, still smiling. "Tell him."

Now everyone looked at me. So much for hiding in the crowd.

"It's true," I sighed, sitting back up. I decided to embrace events like the actress in the *Macbeth* play had. Like a professional. Plus, I was certain that no matter what I said it wasn't going to change whatever Morgana had planned anyway. "I know the part."

"Put him on the stage and you will have a Hamlet like you have never seen before," Morgana said. Of that I had no doubt.

The man hesitated. "I don't know," he said. "This is . . . irregular."

"It is," I agreed. "Very irregular." I tried to pull Morgana back into her seat, but she resisted me.

"What choice do you have?" she said to the man on the stage, and I recognized the tone to her voice, the charm of it. I was instantly jealous of the other man, to be on the receiving end of that.

He was oblivious to me now. He just smiled and nodded at Morgana. "Of course," he said. "The show must go on."

"Indeed it must," Morgana said and pushed me toward the stage.

I went because of course I would do anything for her. How could I not? And I went because, well, what would you have done? It's not like there were other options waving from the audience. But I couldn't help but frown at the other man as he climbed down off the stage and went to sit with Morgana. I found myself hoping she didn't turn him into a fey, because I didn't want to see him with her again, and then I shook my head to clear such thoughts. I tried to tug the ring off my finger once more, but it was stuck on there as solidly as usual.

A couple of stagehands dressed in black met me at the stage and pulled me into the wing.

"You're sure you know all the lines?" the man asked as the woman pulled a tunic over my head.

"Oh sure, I've seen this play thousands of times," I said.

He paused in buckling a belt around my waist. "Seen it or acted in it?" he asked.

"Both," I said. Which was probably true. When you've been alive as long as I have, who can remember every moment?

The woman dusted my face with some makeup. "We don't have time to walk you through all the staging," she said, "so just try to follow the other actors' cues as best as you can."

"I don't see as I have any other choice," I said.

She frowned and shook her head, no doubt at the insanity of the situation. But that's theatre for you. Then the lights went down and actors pushed past me to get on the stage and it was show business like usual. I stood off to the side and tried to remember the lines of the play, but all I could think about was Morgana sitting out there in the audience, watching me. I adjusted my costume again to make sure I looked my best as the other actors went on with the play. I ran my hand through my hair one way and then another. I tried to remember when I'd last brushed my teeth. I cursed Morgana's name to all the hells, and then I checked my clothes again.

And then one of the stagehands was pushing me forward and it was my turn onstage. I walked out with Claudius and Gertrude and Laertes and all the others. I tried to hide in the crowd, which was difficult given that everyone in the audience was staring at me. No doubt waiting to see how badly I was going to mangle the part. I thought even the spotlights were shifting to me. I started to sweat.

And then I realized there was a pause in the conversation and all the other actors were glancing at me. It was time for my first line. I delivered it from memory, without even having to think about it.

"A little more than kin, and less than kind," I said in an aside to the audience, and they applauded my ability to speak.

And so we were off.

What can I tell you about that performance? The rest of the play was adequate. The other actors were true professionals, no doubt trained in the best schools in all of England. It was *Hamlet* at the National Theatre, after all, even if it was a matinee. They did what they could with an amateur in the lead role and carried on. And I did what I could, mainly by lifting bits from other Hamlets I'd seen. I spoke the lines with the confident rhythm of Burbage. I carried myself with the weariness of Betterton. I delivered my soliloquies with the quiet brooding of Olivier. It wasn't pretty but it was passable. And I think the audience was too bewildered by my schizophrenic performance to really judge me, which is just as well. Or maybe they'd been enchanted by Morgana to clap whenever I spoke. Either way.

It all went well enough until my first scene with Ophelia.

It was in the third act, during my soliloquy on the nature of existence and other such trivialities.

I walked out from stage right and delivered the lines to the audience. "To be, or not to be; that is the question." I tried to say the lines much in the same way Keats had said them to me when we were in that villa in Rome, dying together. It turned out we had both sides of the question covered.

Anyway, I came out saying my lines and then stopped when I saw Ophelia waiting for me on the other side of the stage. It was Amelia, of course. She had enough makeup on to almost make her look alive. Almost.

The rest of the lines went out of my head, so she jumped in.

"Good my lord," she said, "how does your honour for this many a day?"

"Well," I said. "Well, well."

There were a number of lines I missed in there, about dreaming and dying and sleeping the everlasting sleep, but no one seemed to notice their absence. Or if they did, maybe they passed them off to artistic license.

Amelia crossed the stage to me and took my hands in hers. They were cold to the touch but that didn't matter. It was the first time I had ever held my daughter. She squeezed my hands and I squeezed them back. It was all I could do but I wanted to do so much more.

"My lord, I have remembrances of yours that I have longed to redeliver," she said in a voice barely above a whisper, as if her words were meant only for me and not the audience. "I pray you, now receive them."

"No, not I," I said, the words spilling out of me over the words I wanted to say to her. "I never gave you aught."

I looked at Morgana in the audience as I said the next lines. My longing for her was as strong as ever, but my longing to kill her for putting Amelia in the play with me, for putting her in the role of the one I had to reject, it was running a close second. A very close second. Morgana nodded at me like she knew my every thought.

"I did love you once," I heard myself say.

"Indeed, my lord, you made me believe so," Amelia said.

"You should not have believed me," I said. "For virtue cannot so inoculate our old stock but we shall relish of it. I loved you not." The words I spoke made me want to cry out in protest, but I couldn't do that to the audience or the play. I had to stay true to my character, no matter how much it pained me. Now Amelia pulled away from me and we were separated again.

"I was the more deceived," she said, and I could see in her eyes the same pain I felt.

"I could accuse me of such things that it were better my mother had not borne me," I said. "I am very proud, revengeful, ambitious, with more offences at my beck than I have thoughts to put them in, imagination to give them shape, or time to act them in. What should such fellows as I do, crawling between earth and heaven?"

Yeah, it was almost like Shakespeare knew me.

And with each word I spoke, I stepped back against my will, away from my daughter, until I stood at the edge of the stage and it was time for my exit.

"Be all my sins remembered," I breathed and then moved into the shadows, where I leaned against a wall and tried not to let anyone see my face.

Luckily, that was my only part on stage with Amelia. The rest of her lines with me were divided up among the other actors. I suspected Morgana's meddling. Sweet, beautiful Morgana. I stood in the wings while Amelia was onstage, and while I was onstage I looked at her in the wings. She hugged herself as she watched me. I wanted to talk to her—talk to her for real, not just deliver scripted lines—but I didn't know what to say.

I was so distracted I didn't notice the curse until it was upon me.

It was the end of the play, my duel with Laertes, who didn't much care for Hamlet on account of Hamlet skewering his father, Polonius. The stagehands who had dressed me explained the director's script called for Laertes and me to stab each other with our rapiers, and for Claudius and Gertrude to drink from the same poisoned cup, which was filled with cheap scotch to make them grimace. They started to explain how the scene was supposed to reflect the dual nature of existence, but I just nodded and told them I got it. I wanted this performance over with so I could go back to Morgana. I mean, talk to Amelia. I wanted it over so I could get the hell out of there.

I went onstage and sneered a bit at Claudius, then argued with Laertes and moved things along to the duel. From the moment our rapiers touched I knew that's where the curse lay. Mine rang hollow with the fake collapsing blade, but his had the solid sound of a true blade instead of the other stage sword it was supposed to be. I quickly hissed out the words of the counterspell, but not too loudly. I didn't want anyone else to hear them. And I'm not going to let you in on them either. That kind of knowledge can be dangerous, and we can't have every actor in an amateur theatre production muttering Witches' spells because they think their show is afflicted with some enchantment. Magic has a life of its own sometimes, as the curse was ample evidence of.

Laertes lunged forward, as the script called for him to do. And I lunged at him, as was my role. Our rapiers passed each other's guard. I smiled at Morgana in the audience. I wanted to show her I had found the curse and dispelled it. I wanted her to approve of me. I wanted her to love me like I loved her.

The blade of my rapier collapsed back into itself when the point hit Laertes' chest. His blade bit into my chest and kept going, piercing my heart and continuing on through me. Laertes' eyes widened as I cried out, and the audience gasped as one. Except for Morgana. I heard her sigh in exasperation, and I felt a fresh pain in my chest at having let her down.

I'd been wrong. I'd been wrong about everything. The Witches' counterspell didn't work, which meant it wasn't the Macbeth curse. Either that or the Witches had tricked me. That was a possibility, granted, but I couldn't see them doing that when their safety was at stake. Besides, they'd already given me their punishment.

"O, I die," I heard myself say. I looked around until I caught sight of Amelia standing to the side, her hand over her mouth, as if to smother a scream. I dropped my rapier and reached out to her. Then I collapsed to the wooden floorboards of the stage, and into a mess of my own blood.

And then, of course, I died.

'DO YOU KNOW ME, MY LORD?'

I woke lying on a mess of ancient books.

There were a few things strange about this. First, I woke on a mess of ancient books and not the wooden floorboards of the stage. I had so much grace in my system from Baal that I should have resurrected before anyone had a chance to move me from the theatre. Yet somehow I'd moved or been moved to wherever I was now.

The second strange thing was that I woke, not resurrected. Instead of the sudden and violent surge of life into me that usually accompanies a resurrection, I gradually came to, like out of a dream.

The third strange thing was some of the books were burning. I leapt to my feet to get away from the books blazing around me. That's when I noticed the next strange thing.

The rapier was still stuck through my chest, although it didn't hurt any more than as if I'd been hit with a prop sword. I looked over my shoulder and saw the point sticking out behind me, through the shirt. The blade was covered in my blood, and it was still wet. I couldn't have been dead for that long.

I decided it was time to figure out where I was, so I looked around. And things got stranger still.

I was in a library of some sort. I thought it was a library, anyway. The walls were lined with books. In fact, the walls were made of books. They rose up all around me, thousands of them stacked upon one another, forming their own shelves. Leather volumes and texts bound in other sorts of hide. They were jammed together in no order I could tell: some were spine out, others were face out, while others still were upside down. The covers and spines were damaged or outright destroyed on most, but I could make out a few names on some of the others. *A Botanist's Guide*

*to the Aether. The Collected Works of Fairlisle, an Angel of the Seventh Rank.
A Most Memorable Account of a Pope's Exorcism. The Goblin Index, Third
Edition.* And so on.

They formed the floor, too, spreading out everywhere underfoot.
And the ceiling: they hung in a sagging, interlocked jumble that looked
as if it should have collapsed already but somehow hadn't. Books were
burning here and there in the midst of all this, but their flames didn't
seem to be spreading to the adjoining books. Perhaps because many of
them were dripping wet with water, or covered in mud or mould. There
were even tables and chairs made of books. On one of the tables sat an
inkpot turned on its side, as well as a white quill and sheaf of papers. The
quill and papers were the only things in the library not made of books.
Besides me, that was.

"Well, well, well," I said to no one in particular.

But it turned out there was someone. When I spoke, a section of
books in the floor near me exploded outward as a hand thrust through
them. Then a second hand punched through the books, followed by a
head. I watched as a man climbed out from underneath the floor. He'd
been lying in what looked like a grave of books, but my words seemed to
have woken him. He stood and turned to me, and I recognized him.

It was Polonius. The same Polonius who'd been skewered on the stage
in Berlin. Just like I'd been skewered on a stage in London. He wore
the same costume as when he'd been killed, the same bloody stains on
it, although he was lacking a blade through his body. I remembered he
had slid off it and to the floor when he'd been stabbed, giving Puck and
Morgana the opportunity to defile his body a bit more with the prop
turned weapon. His face was pale and tears ran down his cheeks.

"I thought you were dead," I said by way of greeting. At least, that's what
I tried to say. Different words came out of my mouth instead, unbidden.

"What may this mean?" I asked. "Why is this? Wherefore? What should
we do?" I recognized the words. They were from one of Hamlet's speeches.

The words weren't the only thing that came out of my mouth. A mist
came out as well when I spoke, forming the shapes of letters that faded
in and out of one another. The letters hung together like words before
drifting apart, but they were no words I recognized. It was as if they
were in some strange language that I didn't know, and I thought I had
learned them all over the ages.

I looked around again at the room made of books and wondered if this was some sort of faerie hoax. Or maybe a dream. Because those were the only things that made sense to me.

"Do you know me, my lord?" Polonius said, stepping closer to me. He didn't seem to notice the rapier sticking through me, or at least thought it polite to not mention it. More mist came out of his mouth when he spoke and formed words in the air to match his speech. They were as equally strange and foreign as mine. It was like Baal's tea symbols all over again.

"You're the fey who played Polonius," I said. Or rather, failed to say once more. Instead, I continued on with Hamlet's words.

"Ay, poor ghost," I said.

I had no control of my speech. It was as if something was forcing me to say the words it wanted. As if I were possessed.

"That's very true, my lord," Polonius said. More lines from the play. It seemed we were both being forced to speak them against our will. It was like the spell I'd used to summon the Witches, where the actors had been forced to say lines from *Macbeth*. Had someone cast a spell on us? Even if they had, it still didn't explain our strange surroundings.

I noticed now that the burning books still hadn't spread their flames any. This place should have gone up like a bonfire, no matter the condition of the other books. But the fires didn't seem to be consuming the books at all. They looked no more burned than when I had first woken here.

Polonius grabbed a book from the table with the inkpot and quill then and thrust it into my hands. It was an ancient folio, like the kind that Shakespeare and the others of his time had used to publish their works. The kind of book that hadn't been in circulation for hundreds of years.

"Read on this book!" Polonius cried. I looked down at the cover, but it was blank and so faded as to almost have no colour at all.

"Words, words, words," I said.

A wind blew through the room at that moment, and the flames on the burning books flickered.

"I will most humbly take my leave of you," Polonius sighed.

Then everything grew dim, like a slow fadeout during a play.

"O, I am slain!" Polonius cried.

And then the room went black and I resurrected.

ENCORE

I sat up on the stage in the National Theatre and tried to parry Laertes' rapier. But I was holding the book Polonius had given me instead of my rapier. And Laertes' blade was still buried in my chest. It was back to hurting like hell now.

There were gasps from the audience, and a couple of screams, and the actors and stagehands gathered around me stumbled back. I caught a glimpse of Amelia watching from the wings, but her face didn't reveal any of what she was thinking now, not even surprise. Like father like daughter, I guess.

"Don't move," Laertes said, crouching beside me. "We've called an ambulance." I was somewhat relieved to see that no mist came from his mouth when he spoke.

"You need to stay on script," I told him. "Good actors don't break character, no matter what happens." I pushed myself to my feet and stood there swaying for a moment, still dizzy from the resurrection and the emptiness inside me because of all the grace it had cost. I stumbled a few steps toward Morgana, who was out of her seat and coming up the aisle now, the director following her like a faithful dog.

I slid the book into one of my pockets to keep it safe. Then I pulled the rapier out of my chest in a smooth, well-practiced motion because I'd had lots of chances to do that over the years. Luckily, the grace I had left did its job and kept me alive before the move killed me again. It hurt worse than hell, but I was used to that sort of pain by now. Half the audience applauded, the other half shook their heads and started for the doors, as if they thought this was some sort of experimental theatre production. Well, I'd seen worse.

"It doesn't look like your little trick worked," Morgana said, stopping at the edge of the stage.

"No," I agreed. I handed the bloody rapier to Laertes. "Don't stab me with that again," I told him. He stared at me and then the blade in his hands. He was going to be ruined for this play now.

"Do you have any other ideas?" Morgana asked. "Maybe one that could actually take care of our problem?"

Against my will, I fell to my knees to be close to her. Or maybe it was the aftereffects of being killed and all.

"Not really," I admitted. I reached for her hand to kiss it, but she pulled it away from me.

"You had best come up with a new plan then, my pet," Morgana said. "Before we put on our next show."

And then smoke bombs went off all around the theatre, and the faerie began to disappear back into the glamour. Cheap and showy but effective. I got up off my knees and looked into the wings again. Amelia mouthed something to me which I can't repeat to you now, and then she was gone in thunder and lightning too. There was no one there now but the stagehands and a few bewildered actors. I doubled over from the new emptiness inside me at Morgana's absence and tried to vomit, but there wasn't even that in me.

The paramedics came in through one of the theatre doors then, fighting against the crowd, so I ran in the opposite direction, grabbing my street clothes as I went past the stagehands and confused actors, toward the emergency exit door in one of the walls. I couldn't be too careful with people in uniform in England. Maybe the paramedics were really paramedics but maybe they weren't. For all I knew, they could be scouts for the Black Guard. Either way, I didn't need help. Not for my wound anyway.

I found myself in an alley behind the theatre, the sounds of the fire alarm I'd set off when I'd taken the emergency exit ringing in my ears. I stepped behind an overflowing dumpster and changed out of my Hamlet costume. Then I took a moment to examine more closely the book Polonius had given me.

There were no markings on the front or back. It was wet with blood, but I wasn't sure if it was my blood or Polonius's. Or maybe someone else's. I had no idea how it had come back with me from wherever it had been I'd visited when I was dead. Every day is an adventure, whether you want it to be or not.

THE DEAD HAMLETS

I figured the book had to be a clue of some sort for solving the mystery. Why else would Polonius have given it to me in that strange library? But when I opened it, I discovered the pages inside were blank too. I looked at the night sky and sighed.

It turned out I needed help after all—help figuring out what was going on. And I knew just who could provide that kind of assistance to me.

The problem was he'd been dead for centuries.

ALICE'S ADVENTURES IN THE BRITISH LIBRARY

So I needed to perform a resurrection, and I needed to do it fast. But I barely had any grace left after resurrecting myself. I was really going to have to stop getting myself killed. It was just too much trouble.

Luckily, I had some grace hidden away in secret storage spots for just this kind of emergency. The complicating factor was I didn't know exactly *where* it was stored. I'd had Alice take the memories away from me so I wouldn't waste the stuff while I was high or drunk. I've never really been the type to resist temptation.

So, first things being first, I had to find Alice.

I went back down the pathway by the Thames. I checked Big Ben as I walked and discovered the afternoon was nearly gone. The place I needed to be was going to close soon, so I picked up my pace.

I went down into the Underground at Waterloo Station and took the subway over to King's Cross. A few minutes later I was in the British Library. God bless England and its transit system—but not the Queen or any of the other Royals, if it's all the same to you.

If you're new to my circle of my friends, you may not know Alice. You may want to keep it that way. Alice is a little unpredictable. When you do find her, she could be marching down the aisle of a library at the front of a line of mannequins made with stitched-together body parts, singing "Ring Around the Rosy." Or she could be sipping a cup of tea on the back of a giant caterpillar munching its way through the shelves. Or she could be browsing a collection of books that had mirrors for covers, which you didn't want to look too closely at because once the mirrors had your reflection they didn't want to let it go.

Luckily for most people, Alice isn't the easiest person to find. You can only manage it in libraries, by going through all the mis-shelved books until you discover the one that summons her. Which meant the British Library wasn't the ideal choice for finding her. There were too many books to go through, especially when I didn't have much time. And most of them were sealed off from the public, so it wasn't like I could get at them anyway.

Thankfully, though, the British librarians are like the British museum curators and can't resist showing off their prized treasures. There was an exhibit in one of the galleries, and I went in and began to browse the books secured safely in their glass cases. None of these books were in their proper places, which happened to be the special collections department, so I figured they could all be classified as mis-shelved. Luckily for me, Alice agreed.

Even I have to admit the British Library has an impressive collection. I moved through the crowd, which wasn't what it should have been given the works on hand, and studied a crumbling manuscript of *Beowulf*. The info on the case said it was the only surviving copy, but I knew better than that. Moving on, I read a page of Dickens' *Nicholas Nickleby* in another case, complete with corrections from the author, and tried to decipher the handwriting on a page of Virginia Woolf's *Mrs. Dalloway*. I found what I was looking for near the case holding an illustrated copy of Chaucer's *Canterbury Tales*. It was hand-written and the illustrations hand drawn. The paper was probably even hand-made. But I didn't have time to appreciate the craftsmanship because I bumped into Alice, who was looking down at a book in another case. She was wearing a Victorian-style dress—authentic, not stage wardrobe—and twirling a parasol. So my shortcut to her had worked. Beats going through every shelf of ancient tomes in the library.

Alice frowned at the book in the case. "This is all wrong," she said. "It didn't happen like that at all."

I looked at the book. There was an illustration of a woman talking to a rabbit, and another hand-written story. The placard on the case said *Alice's Adventures Under Ground*.

"I know it's been too long since we've talked and all that," I said, "but I'm in kind of a hurry. It's a life-or-death kind of thing."

Now Alice twirled her parasol the other way. A number of beetles fell out of it and scurried underneath the cases. "Which is it?" she asked, not seeming to notice them.

"What do you mean?" I said.

"Which is it?" Alice asked again. "Life or death? It can't be both."

Frankenstein may have argued with her on that point, but I didn't want to get into another philosophy discussion. "I'm trying to keep it life," I told her.

"Good," she said. "That's so much more fun than death. Or maybe a different kind of fun. I don't know which."

"Alice, I need to know where I hid my emergency grace," I said, trying to press on to the things that mattered. After all, life and death always sorted themselves out, didn't they?

Alice closed the parasol and then opened it again in my face. I flinched, expecting a shower of beetles, but there was only the smell of absinthe.

"I'm not allowed to tell you," she said. "You made me promise. Didn't you?"

I gently pushed down the parasol with my hand until I could see her again. "If I recall correctly, I had you take the memory of where I'd hid it until I really needed it again. Now I really need it again."

"That's right!" she said and threw the parasol to the side, into a group of people clustered around the display case for Blake's "The Tyger." "I remember now. And I remember you told me when I gave you the memory back I could take another memory in its place." She clapped her hands in excitement.

I didn't remember that, but she could have been telling the truth. How was I to know at this point?

"Fine, just make it quick," I said. "I need to get going." The people at the Blake case were eyeing us now. I sensed a call to security was forthcoming.

"Done," she said. And just like that I remembered. I remembered where the grace was. Such an obvious hiding place. And then I cried out a little when I realized what Alice had taken from me. The words Amelia had mouthed to me at the National Theatre before she disappeared.

"Why that?" I asked. "Why did you have to take that?"

"Because it's a good memory, silly," Alice said. "Why else?"

I braced myself on the display case. Alice frowned at me like she didn't understand. "But it's what you wanted," she said. "Isn't it?"

I took a deep breath and tried to tell myself what was gone was gone. I studied the drawing of Alice and the rabbit in the display case. She looked so innocent there. I thought about what she'd said when she appeared, that the book was wrong. I thought about how she always knew things like that about books.

"What do you know about *Hamlet*?" I asked.

She rolled her eyes all the way back, until only the whites were showing. "He's such a complainer," she said.

"I mean the play, not the prince," I said.

"Oh." She bit her lower lip and drew blood. "Which version?" she asked.

"It doesn't matter," I said. "I just need to know if it's cursed. Or something." I didn't really know how to explain my encounter with the dead Polonius, wherever it had been.

"Of course it matters," Alice said, pouting, her eyes still all white. "Every book matters."

"Alice," I sighed.

"Well, some of the versions are haunted," Alice said. "Although I don't know about the ones in the Forgotten Library."

"What's the Forgotten Library?" I asked.

"It's the place you went when you met Polonius," she said. "The dead Polonius, not the live one. Because you can't be both. That's why you were dead when you were there."

"How did you know where I went?" I asked. I didn't remember seeing Alice there, but that didn't mean anything. She had a strange relationship with libraries.

"I read it in a book once," she said. She twirled her hair with one finger, and I saw there were some worms hidden away in her locks.

"What book was that?" I asked. If there was a guide to my life, I wouldn't mind reading it myself.

"It was one of those books that doesn't have an ending," Alice said, twirling the worms around her finger now. "And no one knows who wrote it." Her eyes turned black. "And I don't want to talk about it because I really don't like some of the things that happen in that book."

I knew from experience with Alice that I was never going to get anywhere on that subject, so I let it go.

"Tell me more about the Forgotten Library then," I said.

"It's a library of all the books that used to be but aren't anymore," she said. One of the worms wiggled into one ear and then out the other, back into her hair. She didn't seem to notice. "It's where books go when they're not books anymore."

"Can you take me there now?" I asked. Maybe if I could go back to that library I could figure out what was going on.

But Alice shook her head. A couple of dice fell from her hair and she caught them with one hand.

"Oh, I was wondering where those were," she said and ate them.

"The library," I reminded her.

"I can't take you there because it doesn't exist," she said. "A library that has all the books that aren't obviously can't be. I can only take you to libraries that are."

"So where is the Forgotten Library then?" I asked, wondering how I'd managed to visit the place, if only briefly.

"You can only find it in other places that don't exist," Alice said. "At least that's what Shakespeare told me when he came back from it."

"Will visited the Forgotten Library?" I said.

"Maybe he wasn't real either," she said, nodding. Then she paused in mid-nod, as an idea struck her. "But then who would have written his plays?" she whispered.

"This is all very interesting," I sighed, "but it's not helping me with my problem. Let's get back to *Hamlet*. So it's haunted. Like a ghost kind of haunting?"

Alice giggled. "Are there any other kinds of haunting?" she asked.

"I'm not really sure," I said. I thought things over. I supposed a ghost could be the source of the faerie's problems. But usually there are more signs of ghosts, like spectral figures wandering around in the dark and complaining about the cold, that sort of thing. Still, it wouldn't be the first time Morgana hadn't told me everything.

"Haunted," I said again. The more I thought about it, the more it made sense. Could it have been a ghost that possessed me and made me speak those words in that strange library? Could a ghost even possess someone? I'd never seen it happen, but that didn't mean it was impossible. Besides, I'd seen impossible things happen before.

"Very haunted," Alice said, nodding. Her eye sockets were empty now.

"All right, let's skip to the obvious," I said. "Who's the ghost haunting it?"

"The Hamlet ghost, of course," Alice said. "Why would any other ghost want to haunt *Hamlet*?"

I looked around the room to see if anyone was paying attention to us. Everyone was paying attention to us. That usually happened when Alice was around. I had a feeling we would soon be out of time. "I've got an idea," I said. "Why don't you tell me everything you know about the ghost?"

Alice nodded at the book in the case. "Everything I know about the ghost is in the play," she said.

I looked down at the manuscript of *Alice's Adventures Under Ground*. Only it wasn't *Alice's Adventures Under Ground* anymore. Its pages were blank now. Empty. Even the drawings were gone. And the paper looked older, like it was withering away. In fact, it was. It started to crumble before my eyes.

"There's nothing there," I pointed out. I tried not to think about what Alice had just done to a national treasure.

"That's why it's a ghost," Alice said, shaking her head at me like I just didn't get it. "If it was still something, it wouldn't be a ghost, would it? It would be in a case."

I didn't know what to say to that, but I didn't have to come up with anything. A man in a shirt and tie brought the parasol back over to Alice with a frown on his face.

"I believe you dropped this," he said.

"No, I threw it at you," Alice said, smiling in delight. "But thank you." She took the parasol back from him and curtseyed.

The man stepped back at the sight of her empty eye sockets, his mouth hanging open. Then he looked into the display case, his eyes no doubt drawn by the whirlwind of dust that had suddenly sprung up where the manuscript had been.

"Vandals!" he cried. "Terrorists!" He staggered away from us like we were going to turn him to dust next.

We didn't have much time now, so I took out the book Polonius had given me. "What can you tell me about this?" I asked.

Alice stared at it but didn't reach for it, which was unusual because she loved books. Especially mysterious books, and I thought this was a very mysterious book indeed.

"What is that?" she asked.

"It's a book that I took from the Forgotten Library," I said. I looked down at it. "Isn't it?"

"I only know the books that are," Alice said, "and that isn't."

"What is it then if it's not a book?" I asked.

"It's not anything at all," Alice said. "Can't you see that?"

I realized that I wasn't going to get anything else useful out of Alice, so it was time to say goodbye. More than a few people in the crowd around us were talking on their phones. The security guards and then the police would be here soon. I didn't want to stick around to find out what came after the police.

"It's always a pleasure," I said and leaned in to kiss Alice on her cheek. I saw the antennae of some insect or another wave out of her mouth for a second.

"No, it's not," she said with another giggle, and I had to admit she was right.

"Until next time," I said, and then I left the gallery and the library and went confused into that good night.

DANCE OF THE DEAD

I took a taxi to Heathrow, where I lifted a couple of wallets from weary travellers whose trips were about to take a turn for the worse. I used the credit card in one to buy a new shirt and pants. I put my old clothes in the store's bag and threw the bag in a garbage can. I tried to stay away from the airport's cameras and their face recognition software. By now the Royals had no doubt been alerted to my presence in the country by the incident at the library, if the trick with the Witches hadn't already tipped them off. I didn't want to make it easy for the Black Guard to find me. One encounter with them in a lifetime was enough. In fact, one in several lifetimes was enough.

I used the credit card from the other stolen wallet to buy a ticket on the next flight to Paris. I tried to sleep on the plane but couldn't. Would you have been able to sleep after being killed, then waking to find yourself in some strange library with a dead man, and then resurrecting with a book that somehow isn't a book, all the while racing against the clock to stop your dead daughter from being murdered again by a mysterious ghost of some sort or another?

I didn't think so.

We landed in Paris in that time between the late hours of the night and the early hours of the morning. I took a taxi to a street near the Montparnasse cemetery. The taxi driver looked at me in the rear view mirror a couple of times but didn't say anything. I imagine he thought I was just another fare with a fetish for graveyards. If he only knew. I wanted to visit the dead, all right, but not that particular group of dead.

I had him drop me off at a random point on the street and I waited until he drove away. Then I went down the sidewalk, to the entrance of the catacombs. The entrance is in a simple stone building that used to be one of the city's gates. I remember going through that gate on a rainy night a few lifetimes ago. On important business, no doubt, although I can't remember that part of it. I just remember being wet and cold. The gate was a ticket booth now, and the catacombs were a tourist destination. The way things always went.

I expected the door to be locked, and I was prepared to pick the lock or kick the door down, but it was open despite the time. There was even a woman at the ticket booth.

"You are here for the event?" she asked in English. I guess I didn't look French to her. It was probably the lack of a cigarette or wine bottle in my hand that gave me away.

"The event is exactly why I'm here," I said, having no idea what she meant. The catacombs were supposed to be closed right now. But one had to be flexible when travelling in France. The French make their own hours, as many a tourist has discovered the hard way.

She handed me a ticket and I handed her some money, and down the stairs I went, into the darkness under the city. At the bottom of the stairs I passed through a stone archway that marked the beginning of the ossuary. There were words carved in the stone. *Arrête, c'est ici l'empire de la Mort*. Stop, this is the empire of Death. Indeed.

On the other side of the archway, the bones began. The walls were lined with them, and they filled the ancient chambers. Hell, they *were* the walls and ancient chambers. Tens of thousands of the dead, and that's just in the catacombs that are open to the public.

And the public were down here too, even though they shouldn't have been. There were people crowding the already crowded tunnels, standing around with drinks in their hands and shouting over the music that was playing somewhere farther along. I would have thought it some sort of Walpurgisnacht if I hadn't bought a ticket to get in. So I figured it was just a regular sort of party among the dead. I guess the revellers didn't realize they'd be down here soon enough.

All these people complicated things a little, but not enough to change my plan. Such as it was. I went through the catacombs, looking at the locked gates that led to the side tunnels, the ones where the public wasn't supposed to go, until I found the one I remembered, thanks to Alice restoring my memory. It was a simple enough lock to pick—I could do it with the contents of my stolen wallets—but I didn't exactly want to show off my skills in front of all these people. So it was time for some acting.

I leaned against the gate and pretended to vomit a little, then spat a bit on the ground. It had the desired effect. The people around me swore and moved away, down the tunnel in either direction. No one wants to be near a sick man in an underground sepulchre. I continued to pretend to puke and used my newfound privacy to open the lock. I took a quick look around to make sure no one was watching me at the moment, then slipped through the gate, closing it behind me.

I went around a bend in this new tunnel empty of partiers, and then I was in a simple chamber. There were more skulls and bones piled against the walls here, but these ones were covered in dust. No one had been here in years, maybe even decades.

Maybe not even since I'd put them all here.

They weren't the bones of ancient Parisians, like all the others in the catacombs. They were the remains of forgotten saints I'd bought or stolen from specialized collectors and stored here in a rare fit of forward thinking back around the early part of the last century. I'd had a feeling I'd need them one day, and that day was today.

There were no markings on any of the bones, nothing to distinguish them from each other or to identify who they'd once been. So I just grabbed the nearest skull and set to work sucking the grace from it.

The thing about saints is they are actually people who have been touched by God, or at least one of the angels. But as far as I can tell, it's all random. They're given grace and then left alone, to wander the world trying to earn their gift or at least wonder what it meant, until the grace runs out and they're just like everyone else again. Why them? I don't have any answers. I doubt even the angels have any answers.

And most saints die the same deaths as the rest of us: anonymous, unloved, having lived lives that didn't matter and didn't change anything. Just because you have a gift doesn't mean you know what to do with it. Or that the world will let you do anything with it.

That's what I tried to tell myself, anyway, as I hunkered down in the underground chamber and sucked the grace out of the bones like some sort of animal, until there was nothing left in any of them and I wept at what I had become.

When I was done, I wiped the tears from my face and slapped myself a bit, as I had so many times before. I forced my feelings back down into the catacombs inside me and returned to the party. I pushed my way through the crowd until I found another forgotten tunnel barred by a locked door. This time I didn't bother with picking the lock. I used some of the saints' grace to open the door and then lock it again behind me, so none of the revellers could follow and get lost in these true catacombs.

I took the new tunnel into the darkness. The music and laughter faded behind me until I was alone again. Well, alone except for all the anonymous dead. So I guess we're never truly alone, are we?

I climbed some stairs up to a stone slab that I shoved aside enough to squeeze through the opening. I exited the catacombs into the Montparnasse cemetery. I sat there for a moment, breathing the cool night air and staring up at the starless sky overhead. I felt like I had when I'd first crawled out of Christ's burial cave all those ages ago. Alive. I wished I could go back to that time and erase all the memories in between. But if I couldn't redeem my past, maybe I could at least redeem my future by saving Amelia.

I pushed the slab back in place so it looked just like another grave again rather than a secret entrance. I won't reveal exactly which grave it is, but it's near Samuel Beckett's final resting place if you're really interested in that sort of thing.

While I worked I became aware of the sounds of people in a nearby part of the cemetery. I moved between the gravestones until I had a better view. Two of them, a man and a woman. Lying with each other on top of one of the graves. Maybe they were part of the group partying in the catacombs, maybe they'd just met here for a romantic night out. There was a bottle of wine on the grave beside them, after all.

I went on my way, careful not to disturb them. We all have our own ways to find grace in life.

ELSINORE

I returned to the airport, where I convinced a currency exchange machine to give me some money in return for some pieces of newspaper. And all it cost me was a little of that new grace I had. I caught the next flight to Copenhagen, using a round-trip ticket. I wasn't planning on flying back to Paris, but I wanted to throw off anyone who might be tracking me.

I rented a car at the Copenhagen airport and drove into a mist that looked as if it could be hiding the Witches. But it was just another day in Denmark. Less than an hour later, I parked the car outside the castle Elsinore. That wasn't its real name, of course. These days it was officially known as Kronborg castle, on the shore of the Oresund sound between Denmark and Sweden. It was a grand affair, surrounded by a moat and fortifications and even the bustling city of Helsingør. But once upon a time there had been another castle in its place, and before that another castle, and so on. It was one of those places.

At one time in its history it had been known as the castle Elsinore, and it had been a very strange place indeed then, populated by people and things who have long since moved on. Word of the strange happenings in its court reached across the lands and even the seas, all the way to England, where the name Elsinore found its way into a certain play. I needed to find out if anything else had made its way into Shakespeare's *Hamlet* from the castle.

I wandered from the parking lot to the castle along with all the other tourists, buying a ticket at the admissions booth with my stolen credit card. I paused on the bridge to take in the moat and pretend to marvel at the walls and towers. They looked like they were in better shape now than they had been back in the days when the castle was occupied by soldiers and royalty instead of tourists and retail workers. I noted the security cameras I could see and tried to guess the locations of the ones I couldn't see. I knew it was just a matter of time before one of them caught me, but I wanted to delay that as long as possible.

There was a group of people forming inside the courtyard of the castle. A man dressed in an overly theatrical and not at all historical doublet and pants stood near a sign advertising a *Hamlet* tour of the castle. The man held a fake skull in one hand, showing it off to the people in the crowd, who couldn't take enough photos. It was just another tourism board attempt to cash in on the popularity of *Hamlet*, but I walked away from there as fast as I could. I was afraid the man was going to start acting out the play and I'd wind up dead again before I'd found out anything useful. If there was anything useful at all to find here.

I wandered through the rooms of the castle, just another lost tourist. I made my way from the great hall, with its beautifully tiled floor and walls lined with paintings no doubt stolen from some other castle, to the chapel and its ornately carved pews. I lingered a while in the royal bedrooms, eyeing the beds and wardrobes and even more paintings for any signs of something supernatural. There was nothing. It was just another museum. In fact, it was even more mundane than most of the museums I knew. Nothing had come to life during my visit, after all.

But I wasn't done yet.

I went down into the tunnels below the castle. In their time, they'd been a mix of dungeons for the prisoners and sleeping quarters for the soldiers. There wasn't much of a difference between the two back in the day. Fewer people wandered about down here, perhaps because of the cramped quarters, or the chill, or the dim lights recessed in the walls, or all of those combined. And that suited me just fine. I tapped the lights as I went, burning them out with little sparks of grace and leaving darkness behind me. I wanted to be alone down here, and no tourists were going to explore pitch-black catacombs that went who knew where.

I found a statue in one corner of the underground chambers. A Danish warrior seated on a throne, slumbering away. He was ready for action, though. A sword rested on his lap and a shield leaned against his throne. He even wore a helmet while he slept, as if ready to spring into battle the second he awoke.

The official lore was he was a king who went by the name of Holger Danske, and he was resting here in the basement of the castle until

Denmark needed him again. As was usually the case, the real story was a little different.

The myths had gotten the name right, at least. But that was about it. He wasn't a king, and he wasn't waiting here to protect Denmark from some future threat. He'd been one of Arthur's knights, but he'd been long gone by the time I encountered that ragtag bunch. He'd been seduced by Morgana at some point earlier and had become just another one of the fey. I'd seen him in her court a few times during my dalliances with her, drinking his way into forgetfulness as fast as he could, just like the others. She'd left him sleeping here after she'd grown tired of playing with him, and he'd gradually turned to stone over the ages. It was one of those faerie things.

I stepped close and breathed grace into his face and then moved back and waited. It took some time for him to stir, but eventually he did. He blinked his eyes a few times and then lifted his head. He looked around the room until his gaze fell upon me.

"Has Morgana finally forgiven me then?" he asked, and his voice was like rocks grinding together.

I didn't know what he had done to offend Morgana and I didn't care. All I cared about was the fact that he thought Morgana even remembered him. I knew he couldn't love her as much as I possibly loved her, so why would she even bother herself with him? I shook my head to clear it of such thoughts.

"She may yet forgive you if you can reveal the secrets of Elsinore," I said.

"Elsinore," Holger said. "I know the word and yet. . . ."

"It's the castle where we are now," I said. "It was one of the castles, anyway."

"I was in Morgana's court," he said, slowly looking around. "It was a place like no other. . . ."

"It's certainly that," I said. "But now it faces a danger like no other. A curse of some sort that is connected to the play *Hamlet*. I need to know if it's also connected to Elsinore. The real Elsinore."

"I will fight for Morgana," Holger said, reaching for the sword in his lap with the speed you'd expect of a statue. "I will fight for my love, the greatest queen of all."

"Save it for Denmark," I said, gritting my teeth. I had half a mind to challenge him to a duel for her love, the curse be damned. "Just tell me any strange things you might have noticed in the centuries you've been here. Like, say, a haunting."

Holger fell silent for a time, and I wondered if he'd fallen asleep once more. Then he sighed. It was a sound like a landslide.

"There is nothing haunting this place but loneliness," he said. "I am alone here with my memories. My sleep is without dreams. If there was anything else here that was in any way connected to Morgana, I would seek it out. I would know it like I once knew her."

I felt for him in that moment, because I understood. I knew as well as he did what it was like to be in the thrall of Morgana.

"I'm sorry," I said, because there was nothing else I could say.

He looked back up from his sword, at me again. "You think you are the chosen one," he said. "You think you are worthy of her love."

"I'm not really worthy of anyone's love," I said, which was more or less the truth. But what I would give to be Morgana's chosen one. . . .

"Maybe you will save her court from this curse you speak of," Holger said, "and maybe you won't. If you don't, someone else who loves her will. And one day she will tire of you like she tired of me. She will hide you away like she hid me. And then you will slumber for all eternity. For there is no escape from the faerie queen. She has never allowed such a thing and will never allow it."

"I am not like you or any of the others," I said.

"Not yet, perhaps," Holger said. "But given eternity, a man cannot help but fail."

"I've already covered that more times than I can count," I said. And then, because I didn't want to hear him talk about Morgana any more, I laid my hand on his shoulder and took the grace back out of him. His head slumped slowly down again and his eyes closed as he fell silent once more. It didn't make me feel any better.

I went back up to the castle proper and retraced my steps until I was in the courtyard again. The man in the theatre garb with the skull was gone, but there were just as many sightseers wandering around as before. It would have been easy to lose myself in the crowd, but I didn't try to hide. Instead, I found one of the cameras I'd spotted before and walked directly in front of its field of view. I didn't try to hide my face. I wanted to be seen.

I thought there was a good chance that someone else had figured out I was interested in *Hamlet* by now. Between the Witches and my death onstage at the National Theatre, there were enough clues for those whose business it was to keep an eye out for such things and understand what they meant. A shrewd servant of the Royals might think the castle would be a good place to watch for me. I wanted them to know they were right. I wanted them to send the Black Guard after me in the castle here. I wanted them to discover my return flight to Paris and send the Black Guard there. I wanted them to send the Black Guard anywhere but where I was heading next.

I was going back to England.

If I was to understand what was afflicting *Hamlet*, who better to ask than the author?

I was going to resurrect William Shakespeare.

A HISTORY LESSON

Of course, it's never that easy. Not for me, anyway.

A dark fog poured through the front gates of Elsinore as I approached them, and the blue sky overhead darkened to night in the space of a few seconds. If that wasn't enough of a sign that this was no longer a normal day, lightning split the air.

For a few seconds, I wondered if the Black Guard had found me. They worked fast, but this would have been moving quick even for them. And it was rather public for the Black Guard. They didn't like to show themselves unless they had to because they didn't like to leave witnesses. That usually meant a lot of cleaning up after themselves whenever they travelled anywhere. I knew the Royals truly hated me, but did they hate me enough to slaughter every tourist and staffer at Elsinore today?

I looked around to see how the others were reacting to the sudden shift in weather. The Danes were a hardy bunch, but this was a lot even for them. I didn't see anyone else at all. The courtyard of the castle was empty of everyone except for me and the fog, which was spreading around the walls of the place now. Everyone else had vanished.

That's when I realized what had happened. They hadn't vanished. I was the one who'd disappeared.

I was in the glamour.

As if to confirm my suspicion, Morgana emerged out of the darkness in front of me, wearing a flowing black dress and leading a mob of the faerie and fey. It looked like most of her court. A dozen or so of the fey were dressed in uniforms from different ages and different military branches. A couple of men wore muddy garb I knew all too well from the trenches of the first world war, a few more wore dress uniforms from different ages of the English navy, one man was dressed in torn desert camo from Afghanistan or Iraq, while another wore the gear of what looked like the flight deck crew of a modern aircraft carrier. They all had one thing in common: they carried bared swords in their hands.

Behind them came the rest of the fey, and many of them were dressed in other costumes. A few wore the helmets of knights, while others rode about on sticks with stuffed horses' heads. Several of them carried a large, four-poster bed on their shoulders, with veils hanging from the posts.

There were other strange things, but there are always strange things when you're dealing with the faerie. I didn't pay any attention to them. Instead, I scanned the crowd for Amelia.

I saw her standing in a dress made of cherry blossom petals with a battle axe made of cardboard on her shoulder. I had enough time to see that she looked unharmed, at least as unharmed as someone already dead can look. Then I couldn't help but look back at Morgana.

"Hello, pet," she said.

Her words stung me. Perhaps they would have stung me to my very soul if I still had ownership of it. "Pet." Not "my pet." I was just like any other pet to her. She cared so little about me that she didn't even bother mentioning ownership of me. I was nothing. I wanted to find out what I had done wrong, so I could become her pet again. And then I wanted to slit my own wrists for even thinking such a thing.

"What is it now?" I sighed.

Morgana just smiled as she looked around the castle courtyard. The rest of the faerie and fey spread out to form a circle around me, although they gave me plenty of room. I caught sight of Puck grinning at me from within a knight's helmet with the visor up. The helmet was in the shape of a snake's head.

"I thought I would check in and see how things were proceeding with your little quest," Morgana said, as if my daughter's fate meant nothing to her. And maybe it didn't.

"You could have just called me," I said. "They have these things called phones now. Much easier than taking your whole court on an expedition around the glamour."

"I've always preferred face-to-face encounters," Morgana said, moving around me in a circle. Whichever way I turned to look at her, she wasn't there. Instead, she was suddenly behind me. "You can't tell someone's real character until you see them break in person," she said.

I stopped trying to keep an eye on her and studied the fey with the swords instead. "Is that why you're here?" I asked. "Are you going to break me even further?"

"Now, why would I want to do that?" Morgana whispered in my ear.

"I don't know," I said. "Why don't you tell me? The things you've been doing lately, they're extreme even by your standards. And I didn't even think you had standards."

"I thought you might say something like that," she said. "That's why I brought along my court for this little scene."

"Not another *Hamlet* show," I pleaded. "Not yet." I wasn't ready to save anyone yet. Not Morgana, not Amelia and certainly not myself.

"Oh, it's not *Hamlet* this time," Morgana said. And now she was suddenly lying in the bed the fey were carrying. She pulled one of them into the bed with her, an old man with a long beard who wore the battered armour of a knight. He began to weep, until she ran a hand over his eyes and he fell asleep beside her. I wanted to kill him for being so close to her. For taking the place where I should have been.

"Do you not recognize the scene, pet?" she asked.

For a moment, I didn't know what she was talking about. And then I did.

"It is the moment we met," I said. Her in bed with a slumbering knight, surrounded by an armed guard under an enchantment. "When you were a prisoner of Meleagant." And I was tasked by King Arthur to free her from the enchanted tower in the English countryside if I was to join his merry knights of Camelot.

"Do not forget I am queen of the faerie," Morgana said. "I was not a prisoner."

"And this is not Meleagant's castle," I said.

She shrugged as she looked around the glamour version of Elsinore again. If only the tourists could see us now.

"One mortal castle is the same as another," she said. "It's just bricks and mud, mortar and blood."

"Why are you doing this?" I said.

"I am reminding you of our history together," she said and nodded at Puck. He threw me a sword I had no choice but to catch, and then the fey in the uniforms rushed me.

I slaughtered them just like I had slaughtered Meleagant's men all those centuries ago. The circumstances weren't that different, after all.

Meleagant's soldiers had been under a spell to guard his tower in the woods near where I'd found Arthur and his ragtag band of knights. They didn't put up much of a fight because they couldn't. It was as if they were half asleep, or in a daze. I'd thought Meleagant had been the one who had enchanted them, but I didn't realize until later that Morgana had been responsible. These fey were no different. They stumbled toward me like they didn't know what they were doing. They struck clumsy blows at me that I easily deflected or dodged. They left openings in their guards that I couldn't help but take advantage of. One by one they dropped, all with a look of relief on their faces as I finally freed them from Morgana.

Then I was surrounded by bodies without a wound on me. Puck moved among them, checking their pockets for valuables and giggling to himself. There was no one between Morgana and me. No one except the man in knight's armour slumbering in the bed beside her.

I looked at Amelia and she looked back at me without expression. I wanted to apologize for what she'd just seen. I wanted to apologize for what her father was. But then Morgana spoke my name and drew my attention back to her.

"Cross, do you recall what happened next?" she asked. "Do you remember how you saved me from the evil clutches of the dark knight Meleagant?" And then she took one of the sleeping man's hands and laid it on her breast.

The rage swelled up inside me and I couldn't help myself. I lunged forward and drove my bloody blade through Meleagant's chest. I mean the poor fey cast in the unfortunate role of Meleagant. I even threw some grace into the blade to make sure it pierced the sleeping man's armour.

He gasped and opened his eyes as I rammed the blade through his heart. He looked up at me and I couldn't look away from him.

"I'm sorry," I said, although I wasn't. The rage and jealousy from Morgana's enchantment were still upon me.

"Don't be," he whispered, and then the life faded from his eyes.

"I see it's coming back to you now," Morgana said.

"Damn you," I said to her and dropped the sword to the ground. "Damn you to all the hells."

"You are the one who is damned, pet," she said.

She ran a finger down her dress and her nail slit the fabric. It fell away, leaving her naked.

"Not in front of Amelia," I said, but I was already falling into the bed with her, pushing the body of the dead fey aside. I could not look at my daughter.

But I didn't have to, as the veils on the bed posts fell around us, blocking the others from view.

"Oh, I will not share this with anyone else," Morgana said. "This is our moment and our moment alone." And the world outside the veils darkened, and I had a feeling that if I looked out there I wouldn't see a world at all.

"Now what have you done?" I asked. I couldn't stop myself from running my bloody hands along Morgana's naked body.

"We are in a glamour within the glamour," Morgana said. "What happens here, only we will know it."

"There's another glamour inside the glamour?" I asked. I shook my head. "I don't understand any of this."

"The glamour is what I make it," Morgana said, and then she pulled me down to her.

It went more or less like the time we'd shared in the real Meleagant's bed. The dead fey watched us with sightless eyes just as the dead knight had centuries ago. By the time we were done, we were all covered in blood: Meleagant's, mine, and Morgana's.

I collapsed in between the two of them, gasping for breath. I stared at the veils drifting overhead, with nothing beyond them.

Morgana ran a finger idly down my leg, drawing more blood in the process with her nails as sharp as a knife.

"That first time, do you remember it?" she asked.

"How could I forget?" I said.

"I thought at last I'd found a mortal worthy of me," she said. "One who would slaughter the entire world if I asked for it."

"I would," I said. "I will."

"And do you remember what happened then?" she asked.

I did. I pulled my pants back on, because I had a feeling our pleasant time here was done.

"Arthur," the corpse beside me said. Only when I looked at it, it wasn't the dead fey anymore. Now it was Puck lying in the bloody bed beside us. He grinned at me and wiggled his eyebrows like he knew what we had been up to. I wondered how long he had been there.

"Arthur," Morgana agreed. "You tried to capture me just like so many other mortals had over the ages. And you took me and threw me at Arthur's feet. Like I was some fey and not the queen of the faerie."

She stood and stepped off the bed, pulling down the veils as she went. Now we were back in the regular glamour, surrounded by the faerie and fey again.

"And do you remember what Arthur would have done to me?" Morgana asked. She surveyed her court with her back to me, but I could hear the smile in her voice. I went to pull my shirt back on before I dared look at Amelia, but then Puck was throwing himself past me, swinging a blade at Morgana.

I moved reflexively, dropping the shirt and snatching up the sword. I met Puck's blade with my own. I caught it mere inches from Morgana's back. Just as I had when I'd delivered Morgana to Arthur and he'd tried to kill her with Excalibur. Puck grinned at me and then Morgana turned around and I saw she was indeed smiling. She didn't seem surprised at all by his attack. I would never understand life in the faerie court.

"Arthur would have slain me when you gave me to him," Morgana said.

"I guess it's a good thing I was there then," I said. I shoved Puck back and he fell to the ground, rolling in a backward somersault and then springing to his feet again with a laugh.

"Yes, you saved me when no others would have," Morgana said.

"I've got a long history of making the wrong choices," I said.

Morgana stepped closer to me and ran a hand down my cheek. I felt the trickle of fresh blood follow her fingertips.

"The question is whether you were acting of your own free will," she said. "Or were you already under my spell then?"

I didn't answer her because I didn't have an answer for that.

She slipped past me and walked back toward the gates, hidden in the churning fog. Her court followed along after her, the fey picking up the weapons and the dead as they went.

"You wonder why I am treating you in the fashion I have?" Morgana said over her shoulder. "How could you even ask?"

"Where are you going now?" I said. I stared after Amelia, whose back was to me.

"We are going where we are going," Morgana said. "And we will arrive there when we arrive there." She turned and looked back at me once more. "What of you, pet? What will you do now?"

"I'm going to find out the secret of *Hamlet* even if it kills me again," I said. "Who better to ask about it than the author?"

Morgana raised her eyebrows. "You're going to raise Will? Even I would not dare such a feat. His grave is well guarded, as I'm sure you well know."

I shrugged and gave her my best devil-may-care look. "Sometimes the greatest risks have the greatest rewards," I said.

"And you don't know what else to do," she said.

"There is that, too," I said, nodding.

She shook her head. "It was a pleasure playing with you when I could," she said. "Farewell, pet."

Then they were gone, exiting the way they'd came. The fog flowed back out after them, like a tide retreating out to sea.

And just like that I was standing in the courtyard of the castle amid the tourists once more. Several of them stopped and stared at me, standing there shirtless and bloodied, with a wet blade in my hand. The only sign the faerie had ever been there was the dark patches on the ground where the bodies had fallen.

Some of the tourists applauded the sight of me, like I was just another performer who had somehow snuck up on them, while others took photos. I glared up at the cameras on the walls. If anyone had missed me before, they wouldn't now.

"Show's over," I said. I threw the sword to the ground and pulled my shirt on again. Then I went back out through the gates of Elsinore before something worse than the faerie came through those gates.

ENTER THE GRAVEDIGGERS

I flew back into Heathrow, disguised as just another businessman on his way to a meeting. The sleight was just an illusion and wouldn't hold up to any serious scrutiny, but it would be enough to fool the security cameras and bored airport guards. I rented a car and told the agent I had business in Brighton. Then I drove to Stratford-upon-Avon, the final resting place of William Shakespeare.

I adjusted the sleight to change appearances again as I went, so now I just looked like another pensioner on vacation. Once I reached my destination, I left the car in a lot near the river and walked along the Avon for a bit, taking in the trees and swans and tour boats and all the other postcard perfect sights. My wandering eventually led me to the Holy Trinity church, where Will was buried along with his family. I joined the people wandering the grounds, taking photos of the grave markers that surrounded the church, before I went inside. I wanted to make sure I hadn't been followed from Elsinore or been recognized since my arrival back in England.

I caught sight of a tall figure dressed in black pants and a black coat with the hood up walking past the church grounds. It wasn't the sort of weather to be dressed like that, so it rang some alarms in my head. But whoever it was kept on walking and that was the end of that. The Black Guard didn't erupt from the doors of the church, and the dead didn't rise from their graves. There was nothing to worry about. Not yet, anyway.

In fact, the only people who seemed to notice me at all were an elderly Irish couple who asked me to take a picture of them in front of the church with their camera. I made sure to frame it in a way that didn't include any grave markers. They'd be getting their share of those soon enough.

When I was confident I looked like just another sightseer, I joined the lineup to go inside the church. I managed to squeeze in between two groups of middle-aged travellers, and both thought I belonged with the other group. I didn't even have to pay when we went through the doors and into the church.

The inside of the church looked much like other churches of a similar vintage. There were the pews and the stone arches and the stained glass windows featuring various saints and angels. If you've seen one church, you've seen a thousand churches. The only remarkable thing about it was the grave markers of Will and his family in the chancery, flat stones set into the floor in the fashion of the time. That was what everyone was here to see, of course. I kept on using the tour groups as a cover and moved through the area. I shuffled past the grave markers and read the words inscribed on Will's grave.

Good friend, for Jesus' sake forebeare
To digg the dust enclosed heare;
Bleste be the man that spares thes stones,
And curst be he that moves my bones.

I supposed it was a threat of some sort, but I wasn't worried. I was no stranger to curses.

I finished my scouting mission without seeing anything untoward. Which meant nothing, of course. It wouldn't be much of a security system if I could see it. I left the church and walked the river some more, until I found myself at a pub, which seemed as good a place as any to kill a few hours. I remembered how my current troubles had begun with a trip to the pub, and this time I kept my hands to myself. When night fell and it came time to pay for my drinks, I sent some grace into the outlets in the wall and blew the circuit breakers. The power went out in the pub. By the time the lights came back up, I'd already left the place and was halfway back to the church.

There were fewer people walking along the banks of the river now, which was a good thing. Unless of course they were agents of the Royals in disguise, which would be a very bad thing indeed. But I was committed. There was nothing to do but follow through on my course of action.

It was easy enough to enter the grounds of the church. I simply hopped over the stone wall surrounding the place, which barely came to my waist. The wall wasn't really meant to keep people out, though. After all, who would want to break into a church in the middle of the night?

THE DEAD HAMLETS

A mist cloaked the gravestones as I walked through the grounds toward the church. I didn't take that to be a good sign, as there hadn't been a mist on the other side of the stone wall. As it turned out, I was right for once.

A light grew out of the mist near the church. Or rather, it was the opposite of light. It was a small black glow, darker than the night. It came toward me, bobbing up and down in the air around head level. It moved about the speed of a walking man, which made sense when the man walked out of the shadows to stand before me.

No, not a man. Not even close.

He had the body of a man, granted, but his skin was as black as a starless sky. He had the head of a jackal and it was equally as dark. I could barely make out his eyes studying me. He wore only a simple cloth on his waist and carried a staff in his hands. The staff was made of what looked like charred bone. It ended with an ankh on the top, and the ankh was made entirely of that strange black light.

"Hello, Anubis," I said. "It's been a while."

Anubis. Once the Egyptian god of the dead. Now a faithful if not willing servant of the Royals, along with the rest of the Black Guard.

He said nothing in return. His nostrils flared, perhaps savouring my scent. His eyes gave away nothing. His pointed ears twitched a little.

"Where are the rest of the Black Guard?" I asked. "Don't tell me my little trick in Elsinore actually managed to lure them all away from England?"

Anubis still didn't say anything, but he never had been the talkative type. He walked in a slow circle around me and I let him have the moment. Why not? There was only one way this was going to end, after all.

He came to a stop in front of me again, and I saw more of that black light flickering across his skin. Tracing hieroglyphs that covered every inch of him, black upon black, like hidden tattoos. Then he lowered the staff and touched the strange ankh to the ground. The earth withered where the black light touched it, and lines of dead grass streaked away from us, deeper into the graveyard.

Then I heard sounds I knew too well. The noise of something or several somethings digging out of the earth. I knew the sounds because I'd made them myself enough times over the ages, when I'd woken buried under the ground. That was no comfort to me in this particular graveyard, though. Especially as I hadn't brought any weapons with me.

I glanced around and saw the shapes rising from the graves surrounding me. I didn't have to inspect them closely to see it was the dead pulling themselves from the earth. They looked like the dead tended to look after being left to rot for a time: they were mostly bone, but scraps of leathery flesh clung to them here and there, along with the disintegrating rags of clothing. There was even some clods of dirt in eye sockets and rib cages thrown in for good measure.

"I don't imagine you raised Will for me as well, did you?" I asked, but Anubis just lifted the staff from the ground. That seemed to be the signal for the dead to take action, because they began to shuffle toward me then. It was hard to estimate their number because of the mist, but I put it at fifty or sixty. That I could see, anyway. Things were about to get interesting.

And then they got even more interesting. Another figure came out of the night, this time behind me. The figure in the black coat I'd glimpsed earlier in the day. He came the same way I'd come, tracing my steps through the graveyard. When one of the living dead turned to face him, he lashed out with a knife in his hand. The head fell from the dead body and rolled behind a grave marker. The newcomer pushed the body out of his way and kept coming. He pulled back the hood as he walked, so I could see his face.

Frankenstein.

"This is a pleasant surprise," I said.

"Victor said that maybe you needed help," he said. He gazed around the graveyard. "Victor is never wrong."

Behind him, the headless body turned in our direction. So it was going to take more than that to kill them. I wasn't surprised.

"And how did Victor know I'd come here?" I asked.

"We asked a few questions of the dead after your visit," Frankenstein said, grinning a crooked smile. "We learned a little of your troubles. Victor says there are few places you could go to find the answers you seek."

The dead—they were always talking. That's why you had to be careful what you told them.

"Next time I'm just going to ask Victor what I should do," I said. I turned back to Anubis. "Now you're in trouble," I said. "Why don't you let me do what I came here for and I won't tell the Royals what happened. It'll be our little secret."

Anubis looked at Frankenstein like he was trying to figure out what he was. Which was a waste of time. Frankenstein was Frankenstein, and that was all you needed to know about that.

"I don't suppose you brought any more weapons?" I asked Frankenstein.

He smiled at me and opened his coat wide with both hands. The insides were lined with the tools from his room in the crematorium: scalpels and long knives and bone saws and picks and other things that don't bear discussion in polite company.

I reached over and took a hatchet that looked as if it would be at home on a medieval battlefield. The solid weight of it felt reassuring in my hand—as reassuring as something can feel when surrounded by the risen dead while facing Anubis in a graveyard, anyway.

"All right," I said, "let's get on with it. If you're not going to give me Shakespeare, we'll just have to take him."

That should have been the moment I attacked, but instead it was the cue for the dead to rush us. The circle of them collapsed in on us in a silent, shambling charge. There was none of the moaning and snarling you see in the movies. There was utter silence on the part of the dead. I guess they'd become good at being silent after all that time spent in the grave.

Frankenstein drew another long knife from his coat and then threw himself into the midst of them, both blades flashing. A skull dropped to the ground, along with the bony arm from a different one of the walking dead. It didn't matter. They kept coming, as if they'd suffered no more than flesh wounds. That was the problem with fighting the dead. It was hard to kill them even more.

I turned and kicked the first one that Frankenstein had beheaded, straight in the rib cage. Bones shattered under my foot and the thing fell back amid the graves. The cracked ribs gave me some heart. The dead weren't too supernatural then, if they could still break and be chopped apart.

I spun back to Anubis in time to turn his staff aside from my stomach with the hatchet. He thrust the staff like a spear, even though the end was just that glowing ankh. I suspected it had more uses than raising the dead.

I hacked at the staff but my hatchet merely bounced off of the bone without leaving a mark. That's the way things go when you fight gods. Anubis spun the staff in his hands and struck at me several times, from several different directions. I burned some grace to give me the speed of an angel and dodged one blow, ducked under another, blocked one aimed at my head and then another at my feet, then danced backwards to avoid a diagonal slash across my body.

"Every time we meet this is what happens," I said. "I really think we need to re-evaluate our relationship."

Anubis didn't press the attack. Instead, he stepped back to check on how his minions were doing. It would have been a good moment for me to strike, but it could have been a trap. Plus, I was curious about how things were going myself. So I stepped back and did the same, in time to see Frankenstein chop both arms off one of the dead in a double strike.

A half dozen or so dead surrounded him in various pieces. There was no obvious way to kill them, seeing as they were lacking organs or any other vital spots, so Frankenstein had settled for dismembering them. If there was anyone who was an expert at dismemberment, it was Frankenstein. He knew exactly where to strike and with how much force. I almost felt sorry for the dead, except that I didn't think there was actually anybody home in any of those bodies.

I expanded my vision a little to check them out and saw nothing but the corpses. Normally, if I look hard enough I can see some sign of the souls trapped in the dead. But there was nothing in these dead.

No, that wasn't quite true. There was something. That strange black light again. It flickered through the dead, running inside their bones. Anubis hadn't raised the dead so much as he had animated them. I guess that particular ability was one of the perks of being a one-time god of the dead.

Anubis sprang into the air, striking down at my head with that staff. I dodged to the side and hacked at where I thought he'd be landing, but the blade cut through nothing. Anubis had twisted mid-leap and landed behind Frankenstein now. Unnatural agility was another benefit of being a former god. He rammed the staff into Frankenstein's back before I could shout a warning, and the glowing ankh slid right into Frankenstein and disappeared.

The black glow expanded, spreading from Frankenstein's back and racing up and down the length of his body. For a second, I worried that Anubis's sneak attack would de-animate Frankenstein, the opposite of what he had done to the dead. Or even worse, it would place Frankenstein under Anubis's control, just like the rest of the dead. Frankenstein was one of the few people in the world who I really didn't want to fight.

Neither of those things came to pass, though. Instead, Frankenstein just turned and grinned at Anubis. "Silly dog," he said. "I will take your bones." And the black glow faded away from his skin.

It seemed Victor had known a few secrets about the dead himself when he created his creature.

Anubis flicked the staff at Frankenstein, but it wasn't another attack. It was a command. The dead rushed at Frankenstein then, swarming him like, well, like the walking dead in a graveyard.

Anubis took a few steps back toward the church and waved the staff at me, too. A line of the dead maybe a dozen strong broke off from attacking Frankenstein and put themselves in between Anubis and me. And between the church and me.

Anubis kept falling back, toward the church now. I was surprised he didn't want to stay and fight. He was one of the Black Guard, after all. Even without all the dead at his side he would probably have the edge on Frankenstein and me. Then I realized what he was probably up to, and I cursed.

"He is going to secure Will from us," I said.

"Victor says you must follow him now," Frankenstein said, his blades flashing. "I will take care of this lot." Then he disappeared from sight under a wave of the dead.

I didn't have much choice. If Anubis could prevent me from raising Will and questioning him, I'd really have nothing to go on.

There was only the small problem of the dead in between me and the church.

I sighed and waded into them with the hatchet. When in a graveyard with the walking dead, it's probably best to act like Frankenstein.

If I were a normal mortal, they probably could have stopped me with sheer numbers. A few of them could have held me down while they did whatever horrible things Anubis wanted them to do to me. Given what I knew of Egyptian burial practices, I probably didn't want to find out what that was.

I used some more of the saints' grace and moved among them like a deadly whirlwind. I struck off arms and legs with the hatchet. I spared their heads, though. Not because I felt some sense of misguided sympathy for them, but because I knew it wouldn't slow them down any. Arms and legs, on the other hand. . . .

I leapt over the last of the dismembered bodies, the hands still clutching at me, and ran for the church. Anubis had already disappeared inside the front doors. Who knew what he was doing inside there?

I glanced Frankenstein's way as I ran. I couldn't see him under the seething mass of the dead, but I caught a flash of those blades still at work. And there did seem to be more body parts scattered about, so I figured he was still in fighting form. And if he wasn't, I'd have to deal with that later.

Anubis had gone in through the doors, which meant I'd have to find another way in. The front doors of the church were almost certainly a trap. So I threw myself into the air and at one of the stained glass windows running down the side of the church. The man on the window looked like some saint or another. Maybe it was even one of the ones whose grace I'd fed on in the Paris catacombs.

I crashed through him, glass shards slicing my arms and legs and teasing a few curses out of me. I fell down into the pews on the other side of the window, which deserved a few more curses. None of my latest injuries felt fatal, though, so I stood up and brushed slivers of colourful glass from me and looked around.

I was in the middle of the pews. The one I'd landed on was cracked but had otherwise held up admirably well. The doors were open at the end of the church, and I'd been right about the trap. Four lines of black light surrounded the door frame, hanging in the air and forming a square that I would have run through if I'd followed Anubis. I didn't know what would have happened then, but I was pretty sure I didn't want to find out.

I looked the other way and saw Anubis. He was standing by the stained glass windows at the back of the chancery that stretched from floor to ceiling. He was holding a coffin in his hands instead of his staff. The staff stood on the ground beside him, perfectly balanced. As I watched, Anubis threw the coffin into one of the windows, the one that depicted Christ on the cross looking down at a faithful follower. Like there had been any friends there that day.

The window didn't break from the impact of the coffin. Instead, the coffin disappeared into the window. The glass rippled a little, as if it were water, but that was it. It kept on rippling even after the coffin was gone, which made it unlike the other windows surrounding it.

I also saw where the coffin had come from. Shakespeare's grave. Anubis had ripped up the grave stones of Will and his family. They were empty now. There was only one coffin left, at Anubis's feet.

"If you won't come back and fight me like a man, then how about you fight me like a god?" I yelled at him, appealing to any sense of nostalgia Anubis might have. Which was admittedly a long shot, as the gods of the dead didn't tend to be the sentimental types.

I knew what was happening. Anubis was under orders to keep Will's body safe. Maybe he could have taken me and Frankenstein, with or without his army of the dead. But why chance it? If we somehow managed to win, then Shakespeare would be lost. So he was playing it safe and making some kind of escape. Exactly what kind of escape, I didn't know. But I still had a shot at stopping it.

Anubis ignored me and picked up the other coffin. He shoved it through the window the same way he had the first one, and then that coffin was gone, too. Now Anubis grabbed his staff again and looked at me as I came down the aisle at him.

"Have it your way," I said. "We'll see which one of us is the better man thing today, and then I'll just climb into that window and drag those coffins right back out here." I wasn't exactly sure how to do that, of course, but if Anubis had found a way into that window then there had to be a way out.

But Anubis wasn't interested in fighting. He threw himself through the same window. The colours in the glass all turned black for a second, then faded back to their normal state. The rippling subsided.

I ran up the aisle, but I was too late. By the time I reached the window, it looked like all the others around it. As if there was nothing mysterious about it at all. I reached out and touched the glass but my hand didn't go through it. The window felt like regular stained glass.

I looked back into the graves but they were empty. I grabbed a handful of dirt from the side of Will's grave and tossed it up at the window where Anubis had disappeared. It struck the window and fell back to the floor of the chancery. There was a stain on Christ's side now, though. The mark of my failure.

I took a few steps back, then ran at the wall and threw myself at the window after Anubis and the coffins. I crashed through to the outside, falling back into the cemetery surrounding the church in a shower of glass.

The window was just a window again. Whatever door it had been for Anubis, he had closed it behind him after he went through.

I really hated the Black Guard.

I went back to help Frankenstein but found he was doing just fine. The dead surrounded him in pieces, still writhing and reaching for him and snapping their teeth and so forth. But they were more or less harmless to us now. He'd taken off his shredded coat and was leaning against a grave marker, stitching his left arm back on with a nasty looking needle and some thread as thick as a small rope. It looked like one of the dead had chewed off his arm, right above the tattoo of the woman riding a bomb, but he didn't appear to be in any pain. He was even whistling a little tune.

"I need to bring you along with me more often," I said. "I sure could have used you a couple of times in the past."

Frankenstein looked up from his arm, smiling. The smile faded when he saw I was empty handed.

"Where is Shakespeare?" he asked.

"Anubis got away with the body," I said.

"Then we will follow until we catch him," Frankenstein said, standing. He put his coat back on and slipped the needle and thread into a pocket.

"I have no idea where he's gone," I said. "And we need to leave now. The rest of the Black Guard are probably already en route."

"We have failed then?" Frankenstein asked.

I looked around the cemetery but didn't say anything. I couldn't admit it.

"You should let me stitch your wounds," Frankenstein said, eyeing my cuts from the glass.

I just shook my head. What was the point? I'd heal on my own. But nothing would heal Amelia when she died again. Nothing would heal the pain I felt at letting down Morgana once more.

"Let's get out of here," I said, making for the stone wall surrounding the place.

"I will stay and hide these away," Frankenstein said, gazing at all the twitching body parts surrounding him. "Perhaps there will be something useful among them."

I stopped and stared at him for a moment, then at the remains of the dead.

"We haven't failed yet," I said. "You've given me an idea."

"You think these dead hold some secret you can use?" Frankenstein asked.

"Not these dead," I said. "There is another. Although I don't know if he'll talk to me or not."

"What did you do?" Frankenstein asked.

I shrugged. "I kind of killed him and then hid him away," I said. "But it wasn't really my fault." That's what I told myself anyway.

Frankenstein did that thing with his head, where he cocked it and looked like he was listening to someone.

"Marlowe," he said.

"Marlowe," I said, nodding.

"I wish you luck then," Frankenstein said. He bent down and began to gather up the fallen limbs in his arms, like so much firewood.

"Thanks," I said. "I'll need it."

And with that, I left the grave of Shakespeare behind, hopefully for the last time.

O FAUSTUS, LAY THAT DAMNED BOOK ASIDE

If you live as long as I do, things eventually come full circle. Most likely several times. Here I was trying to raise Christopher Marlowe from the dead when it wasn't that long ago I'd helped to bury him. And, in a way, helped get him killed. Although I think Marlowe himself deserves the lion's share of the blame for his death.

The official story about Marlowe getting killed in a tavern brawl is more fantasy than fact, as is usually the case with such things. But the people telling that story had good reason to make up a tale. The real story is simply too dangerous to reveal, not only for the person telling it, but also for the listener.

So make sure all of your doors are locked and your loved ones safe before you learn the truth of how Christopher Marlowe died.

It began with a knock on my door in the middle of the night. A knock like that was best left unanswered in the London of the 1500s, but curiosity has always won out over common sense for me. I rose from my bed, where I was reading the diary of a particularly deranged angel I had killed in Sweden the previous winter, and I opened the door wide to let in whatever was on the other side.

It was Marlowe, looking wet and miserable from the rain. And bloodied.

"Did you wander down the wrong alley again, or did a lover's husband find you out this time?" I asked, stepping aside to let him in.

Marlowe didn't come in, though. He remained on my doorstep, staring at me like I actually was the Second Coming.

"I have a horse for you," he said. "Bring a weapon. Bring all the weapons you have. By the grace of God, they will be enough."

"What have you done this time?" I sighed.

Marlowe swallowed and looked away, into the night. "I have unleashed Hell upon London," he said.

Like I said, curiosity always gets the better of me, so I grabbed a few of my favourite blades and went out into the night after him. I still had the grace of that angel inside me, and I was feeling rather cocky. I didn't have to change into street clothes because I slept in my street clothes in those days. A knock on the door in the middle of the night wasn't an unknown thing to me in the London of Marlowe's time.

He said nothing to me as we mounted up, and we rode too fast through the deserted streets to carry on any sort of conversation. Strike that—the streets weren't entirely deserted. Soldiers ran here and there, their weapons ready, and horsemen patrolled with bare blades, searching for someone or something. A few of them reined in their horses when they saw us ride past and studied us with hard eyes, but continued on their way when they saw Marlowe. I knew whatever he had done, it was worse than usual.

He took me to his theatre. It was a small place, a mere quarter of the size of Shakespeare's Globe. I won't mention its name here, because it was erased from history after that night. And for good reason.

The area was surrounded by more soldiers: men in the uniform of the royal guard. They lowered their weapons a little when they saw Marlowe, but only a little. He was a servant of the Royals by this time, and there were rumours he had sworn some sort of blood pact of loyalty to them in exchange for . . . well, no one knew. As for me, I wasn't on the outs with the Royals back then, although that would change by the end of the night.

And there was another man there, standing off to the side and watching the theatre. He wore a simple black doublet and stained hose. He looked like he'd been drinking all night, but it was more likely he'd been reading, for he carried a battered folio under one arm and a black quill in his other hand.

Out of all the men running around that night, he looked the least threatening. But he was the most dangerous of us all, for he was William Shakespeare. And he held no ordinary folio and quill. The Black Quill, for that was its name, was rumoured to be from the wing of a long-forgotten angel, whom even the other angels refuse to talk about. As for the folio, I didn't know its true history, although I did know that men had fought and died over its possession.

"Surely you didn't invite him?" I asked Marlowe as we dismounted. Will and Marlowe would hardly call themselves friends, despite the fact they were both playwrights. They were sworn rivals, after all, when it came to the stage and their other lesser known activities.

"He is the last person I would invite to anything, even my funeral," Marlowe muttered. "But Will always knows when something like this has happened."

"And when are you going to tell me exactly what's happened?" I asked.

"Inside," Marlowe said, nodding at the theatre. We strode for the entrance, going past Will without saying anything or even acknowledging his presence.

"How many times have I told you not to disturb things best left unimagined?" Will said, falling in with us. It wasn't like we could have stopped him if we'd so desired. Not as long as he had that damned quill, anyway.

"This is not the time or the place," Marlowe said.

"I cannot imagine a more suiting time or place to point out your own folly," Will said as we entered Marlowe's theatre.

Once inside, I saw that Marlowe had been right. He had unleashed Hell.

The theatre was full of bodies. Or rather, it was full of body parts. Arms, legs, heads and other bits lay all over the ground where most of the audience would have stood. More of the same draped the balconies of the box seats. There were a few bodies that were more or less intact, if you didn't count slashed throats or gnawed-off faces. But they were in the minority. I tried to estimate the number of the dead, but it was impossible given their condition.

"A full house?" I asked Marlowe. He nodded and I winced.

"A first reading of my new play for a special audience," he said. His lips were as thin as razors.

I knew the play he spoke of. *Doctor Faustus*, the tale of a man who sells his soul to the devil for forbidden knowledge. It was a subject Marlowe knew all too well, for when he wasn't a playwright he was a demon hunter for the Royals. He was a real jack of all trades. But now it looked as if his two worlds had collided.

"A fine play," Will said, looking around at the scene. "I followed its progress as you crafted it." Marlowe shot him a look, but Will went on as if he hadn't noticed. "It deserved a better showing than this," he said.

He looked unmoved by the grisly sights. Most bookish men would have fainted or soiled themselves in some fashion or another by now. But Will had seen his share of bodies before. We all had.

I walked through the pit of the theatre, stepping over pieces of what had once been people. I didn't bother trying to keep my boots clear of the blood. That would have been impossible. I looked for some sign of a demon hiding among the dead, but I didn't see any trace of its presence beyond the obvious signs to be found in the dismembered bodies.

"What happened?" I asked. "Something didn't like the subject of your new play and tried to warn you off?" I glanced at Will.

"Oh, it wasn't me," he said. "I was rather looking forward to this play, even if I wasn't invited to the premiere."

"Just as well," I said. "Or you may have wound up like the others."

"Now you mock me," Will said. "I am no mere player at the mercy of some greater author's whims. You, if anyone, should know that."

"I don't think whatever did this is your typical author," I said. And then I saw it. The book on the stage. I let out a long sigh and looked back at Marlowe.

"And that's not your typical book," I said. "Tell me you didn't use that in the play." But I already knew the truth. And Marlowe said nothing rather than lie to me.

I went up to the stage and looked at the book lying amid the blood and gore. It was stained so much I couldn't see the title carved into the hide cover. Which was just as well. It was a book best not named, which was why all who knew it called it simply The Nameless Book. It was an appropriate enough description, given the horrors it contained had no names either, at least none spoken in the languages of the mortal and the sane. There were others like it—the Necronomicon is a popular one with those who have a death wish—but they were all mere shadows of The Nameless Book. It was the book to end all books.

I tore my eyes away from The Nameless Book before it could capture me and I turned back to Marlowe.

"Why?" I asked him. "Why in the name of all the heavens that once were would you use such a thing?"

Marlowe stared at the book on the stage. "Research," he said.

"Research," I repeated. I looked around the theatre turned abattoir. "Research."

"I wanted the play to speak the truth," he said. "So I put the truth into the play."

I closed my eyes but it didn't do any good. I could still smell the blood in the air. The air *was* blood.

"The actor wasn't actually supposed to read from the book," Marlowe said. "It was just meant to be a prop to be held and shown to the audience. For authenticity. But then James must have decided to improv a little." Marlowe shook his head. "He only read for a few seconds. But that was enough to release a demon."

And that few seconds was enough to end the world, at least for the people in the theatre.

"'Tis more likely the book acted through him and forced the poor soul to read from it," Will said, stepping up to my side and gazing at the book. I noted that he had tightened his grip on his quill. So there were some things that made even William Shakespeare uneasy. That was good to know.

"Some truths are better left unknown," Will added, and I reluctantly agreed with him, although I didn't give him the satisfaction of saying so.

"Surely that is a jest coming from you," Marlowe said. "As if I don't know the things you have done for your plays."

"I have never had a premiere quite like this," Will said, gazing about the theatre again.

"I was looking forward to seeing your play," I said to Marlowe, "but I think it should be retired to an early grave now. The fewer people who ever hear of *Doctor Faustus* after this, the better." Okay, so I'm not right about everything.

I scanned the balconies surrounding the pit. It was more bodies and body parts up there.

"Where is the demon now?" I asked, already knowing the answer.

"It escaped in the madness," Marlowe said. "That is why I came for you. You have a talent for tracking them."

"What better to fight madness with than more madness?" Will said. To be fair, he had a point.

My eyes caught on one of the box seats. Specifically, my eyes caught on one of the bodies there.

"Is that . . . ?" I asked, and Marlowe nodded.

I sighed. "The Royals are going to have you drawn and quartered for killing one of their own," I said. "And that's just the beginning."

"I didn't kill him," Marlowe said, glancing up at the box and then away. "The demon did."

"Let me know how that explanation works out for you," I said.

"We are wasting breath while the demon makes good its escape," Will said.

"We have patrols searching the streets," Marlowe said. "But they have turned up nothing."

And they probably wouldn't turn up anything either, I thought. Demons were hard ones to find when they wanted to stay out of sight. They could possess the body of anyone and hide in it as long as they wanted. Thankfully, their nature usually got the better of them and they eventually went on a killing spree. That wasn't good for the people around them, of course, but it made them easier to find.

I turned to the theatre exit. "Let's join the search then," I said. "Before the creature makes it out one of the city gates." It would be lost forever then.

"What of the theatre?" Marlowe asked, gazing around at the sorry audience for his play.

"Burn it," Will said, so softly I almost didn't hear the words. "Your theatre days are over."

Marlowe looked at me and I nodded. "You must make it seem like a fire," I said. "It's the only way to account for all these deaths. No one else must learn of the book."

Marlowe looked stricken, as if I had just delivered him a grievous wound. I suppose I had, in a way.

"It is my life," Marlowe whispered.

I shook my head. "I'm sorry, my friend," I said, "but your life is over. It ended the moment he died." I nodded at the body up in the box seat. "The best you can hope for now is a clean and honourable death."

Marlowe took a moment and then nodded. "I will hide the book," he said. "So no others wreak the same havoc I have."

He started for the stage, but I stopped him with a hand.

"Burn it too," I said. "If there is anything here that deserves the flame, it is that book."

"I cannot," Marlowe breathed, not looking away from the book. "The secrets it contains. . . ."

"Those secrets must be lost," I said. "Or we are all lost."

Will had the good grace to say nothing, although I knew he agreed with me.

I stood there, keeping Marlowe away from the stage, until he nodded. He took a torch from one of the holders on the wall, and touched it to a banner hanging from a box seat. The cloth took the flame immediately, and Marlowe moved on to the next one. Will walked back outside. I waited until the walls of the theatre were fully ablaze before I made my own way out.

"Once it is burned to the ground, the ashes should be scattered so no one can ever find the book again," I said to Will.

"I have already given the orders," he said, watching the flames start to rise above the theatre's roof.

I got back on the horse and rode off into the night. I had no idea where to look for the demon, but I had to look for it. The sort of thing that would slaughter a theatre full of people wasn't what you left to wander the city alone at night. I had no idea what to do when I found it. Demons are all different. When hunting them, I find it best to take one step at a time.

I rode aimlessly through the streets, until the flames of the theatre lit up the night sky behind me. I stopped and turned the horse around so I could watch the place burn for a moment. That fire would be but a taste of things to come if we didn't find the demon.

And then I cursed and dug my boots into the horse's side as I realized where the demon was hiding.

I rode at full speed and dismounted in front of the theatre without even coming to a complete stop. Marlowe and Will stood outside with a handful of guards, watching the building burn.

"Come with me!" I said and ran for the theatre entrance.

"Cross! What do you seek inside?" Marlowe cried after me. "I left the book there as you commanded."

"The demon!" I yelled. "It hides in the flames!"

And with that I charged into the burning theatre.

The inside of the theatre was completely ablaze now. It wasn't the sort of place any mortal could survive for long. But as you well know, I'm not a mortal. As for Will and Marlowe, they had their own tricks they'd picked up over the years.

We ran into the middle of the audience and looked around. The stage hadn't quite caught yet—only a few parts of it here and there were on fire. The book sat untouched. As if waiting for someone to pick it up.

I looked around at the bodies. Where would the demon be . . . ? Ah. There.

I looked up at the box containing the dead Royal. It was engulfed in flames, the bodies burning like torches. Nothing could possibly live there. Nothing but a demon.

"I know you're in there," I said, coughing from all the smoke. "Why don't you come out and get this over with?"

For several seconds, nothing happened. Then a low, rasping chuckle rose above the sound of the flames and the dead Royal sat up in his seat, still blazing.

"I was beginning to think nobody would find me," the demon said. "And what a shame that would have been."

"I should have known," Marlowe said, shaking his head. Maybe he should have, but I was willing to give him a pass given the circumstances and all.

"Come out of that body if you know what's good for you," I said to the demon. That was actually more advice than a threat. The Royals wouldn't approve of one of their own being possessed, alive or dead.

"I don't think so," the demon said. "I rather like this body. It has many secrets and I haven't finished uncovering them all yet."

"It's been my experience that you won't want to learn all the secrets of a Royal," Will said. He opened his folio and poised the Black Quill above it, ready for action.

"Silence, scribe, or I will make your soul scream for all eternity," the demon said. He must have been in The Nameless Book a long time if he didn't know of Will or recognize the Black Quill.

It could have been worse, I reflected. It was only a demon and not one of the truly unspeakable horrors of The Nameless Book. It was the equivalent of a footnote in that tome. Still, if it was bound in the book, that meant it was trouble. It could be more than enough for the three of us to handle.

It was like the demon read my mind.

"I think I'll be going now," it said. "And I'll be taking that book with me."

"I don't think so," I said and showed it my blades. Marlowe stepped up to my side with his own blade and a grim expression on his face. Will just licked the end of his quill.

The demon laughed—not exactly the sort of response you want when you menace something with a weapon.

"Steel can't hurt me any more than tooth and claw can," the demon said. "And you will never know the secret of what can harm me."

"I'll warn you now then that we have our own secrets," I said. I hoped the demon didn't know me. And if it did, and it proved too much for the three of us to handle, well, I'd just shove one of the others at it and make my escape. Better to live to fight another day than get torn to shreds by a demon and resurrect who knows where, I always say.

The demon smiled at that. "There is nothing I love better than secrets," it said. It drew the Royal's sword, and fresh flames ran down the length of the blade, only these flames were as black as Will's quill. Then it threw itself off the balcony at us, still burning, and brought that blade down over its head in a sweeping strike.

I dodged to one side and Marlowe the other. I threw up my blade to parry and Marlowe went for the kill, thrusting his blade up and into the demon's chin. The point of his blade ripped through the top of the Royal's skull, and the body collapsed down upon Marlowe, making him stagger back under its weight.

It all happened in the blink of an eye, but not so quickly that I didn't notice the Royal's body sagging lifelessly before Marlowe had even struck. The demon had already left the body by the time Marlowe's blade kissed flesh.

I threw my blade out in a blind parry behind Marlowe's back. I'd encountered a demon or two before in my life, and I had an idea how they thought. It turned out to be the right idea, as one of the corpses littering the ground suddenly threw itself up at Marlowe as the demon possessed it, striking at Marlowe's back with a knife. My blade caught the knife before it could catch Marlowe, and then that body was falling, too, slumping to Marlowe's feet.

"Ware!" Marlowe cried, shoving the body of the flaming Royal off his blade and at me. I sidestepped it and the dead Royal fell into another corpse rising from the ground, also armed with a knife. Everyone carried a knife or something longer in those days.

The newest corpse to rise stumbled over the Royal and fell to the ground, and then a ring of the dead rose around us, one body after the other. A man missing one of his arms stood, then started to slump back down almost immediately as I batted his punch away. At the same time, a headless man sprang to his feet, and Marlowe barely deflected his rapier. Then the headless man fell, too, at the same time as a man who had been disembowelled jumped up and lashed us with a strand of entrails. I kicked him away, and a man who'd been flayed threw himself at Marlowe, who sank a knife into his face with his spare hand. And on it went, one corpse after another rising and striking at us, then falling back down a second later. The demon was flying between the dead as fast as the blink of an eye, possessing each one for only a second or two before it moved on to the next.

This went on for several seconds, bodies rising and falling all around us, and then it started anew as the demon came full circle, animating the blazing Royal for a wild punch that grazed my head, then jumping back into the one-armed corpse for another punch that actually caught Marlowe a glancing blow, then back into the headless man for a rapier thrust that I narrowly managed to deflect away from my stomach. The demon moved so quickly between the bodies that when it left them they didn't even have time to fall to the ground before the demon was back, possessing them for another attack. We were surrounded by a dozen or so corpses dancing like deadly marionettes on strings, striking at us over and over.

"It's only a matter of time until he catches us," I said, sliding away from an eyeless man's knife thrust and then ducking under another punch to my head from the disembowelled man.

"You must think like a demon!" Will said from the edge of the scene, outside our macabre little circle.

And then the body of a man with gaping holes where his organs should have been leapt from the ground in front of Will, hands reaching for Will's throat.

"I don't think so," Will said, scribbling quickly in the folio with the Black Quill. The corpse tripped over someone's head and fell at Will's feet. Will took a step back, out of arm's reach.

"You do not know who you are crossing," he said.

"No, but I would know," the demon snarled, pushing the body up to its feet. And then the body fell back to its knees as the demon left it.

It did not return to the circle, though, as the corpses around us continued to fall and none rose up to attack again. It took me a second to figure out where the demon had gone. That is, where it had attempted to go.

Will kept on scratching in that folio with his damned quill, and then the body before him that the demon had last left suddenly flew backward, as if something had smashed into it. Or been smashed into it. It rose once more, shaking its head like it was trying to clear it.

"The Black Quill has already written my end," Will said to the demon, his face expressionless. "You cannot possess me because you do not figure anywhere in that tale."

Marlowe strode past me, toward the demon. "Do not hesitate to kill me if you must," he said, and I knew what he meant. This demon was stronger and faster than any I had seen. Marlowe had enough experience to fend off a lesser creature, but perhaps not this one.

But this demon suddenly vanished, disappearing back into the dead. The corpse it was inhabiting fell back to the ground, empty of any animating force, but no others rose around us. I turned in a slow circle, as Marlowe stepped back to me, scanning the theatre himself.

"Beware now," Will said. "Think not like a mortal, but think like a hellspawn instead."

"If I was a hellspawn, I'd be trying to get away from us," I muttered, eyeing the dead.

Then Marlowe sprang my way. "Behind you!" he cried, and I spun around.

It was the wrong move, I realized, even as I was doing it.

Think like a demon, Will had said. And this demon was clearly dangerous and had been around much longer than any of us.

There was no demon behind me.

The demon was in Marlowe.

And then something gripped me and spun me about. Another force that took control of my body and turned me before I could turn myself. I thrust with my blade, and I caught Marlowe in the chest with it, even as his blade scored my side. Better that than my back, which he'd been targeting. The look on his face was a mingled expression of surprise and relief, as he fought the demon for control.

"There is no happy end," Will said, scribbling away. "Not for any of us."

Then the demon was back in the body of the Royal again, only this time it stayed there. It grinned a fiery grin at me as I caught Marlowe in my arms and slid my blade out of him as gently as I could.

"I don't know what you lot are," the demon said, "but you are closer to my kind than you are to mortals."

"Words always did get me into trouble," Marlowe said to me. He tried to laugh, but he choked on his own blood.

I didn't have to look at the wound to know it was fatal. Will would have written nothing less with the quill when he had me turn and strike Marlowe. I'm not sure the Black Quill would have let him write something that didn't end in death.

"I will raise you," I said.

"Save your grace," he said. "Dispatch the demon back to whence it came."

The demon raised its hands as if receiving a blessing.

"The book is the only prison that can hold me," it said. "But it would take the secret powers of a dozen angels to force me back into that particular hell."

I didn't have the power or secrets of a dozen angels. But I did have the grace of one angel, give or take. And I had my own secrets.

I lunged at the demon then and rammed my blade through the body it was possessing. I used a little of the grace to move fast enough it couldn't leap into another body before I caught this one with my blade, but only a little. I was saving the rest.

The demon didn't try to switch bodies again. Instead, it just grinned even wider at me. "Your grief has made you deaf with bloodlust," it said. "I already told you your weapons cannot harm me."

"I'm not trying to harm you," I said. "I'm trying to do something far worse."

And then I threw all my grace down that blade into the demon.

It would have been satisfying if it had shrieked or convulsed or exploded or something like that. Instead, it just looked confused.

"What have you done?" it asked.

"I have bound you," I said, and the demon's eyes widened as it understood.

The truth was I didn't know how to bind a demon back then, although I've learned a few tricks since. Standing there in Marlowe's burning theatre, I didn't know how to force the demon back into The Nameless Book. But the grace. I understood grace and I knew what to do with it.

I kicked open the cover of The Nameless Book and looked away before I could read any of the words there. And then I took hold of that grace I'd put into the demon and forced it down into The Nameless Book.

The demon howled and lashed out with a burning hand suddenly turned into talons, but I dodged it. The demon's realization of its fate was too late anyway, as the grace pulled it and the body it occupied into the book like I had thrown it into a void. Maybe I had in a way. I kicked the book shut again, and now there was no sign of the demon or the Royal's body. They were gone, bound into The Nameless Book together along with the grace of the angel I'd killed so long ago. I kicked The Nameless Book again, this time into the flames, and then I turned back to Marlowe.

He lay on the ground, staring at The Nameless Book as it burned. His doublet was a bloodstained mess now, and his chin crimson with his own mortality.

"It was the only possible ending to this sorry tale," Will said, but I ignored him. I lifted Marlowe in my arms and carried him from the burning theatre, as sections of the balcony began to collapse all around us.

I took him outside and laid him on the ground. I cradled his head on my lap and his lifeblood ran out over my hands as the royal guard looked on. Will came and stood at our side but said nothing. He slipped the folio and Black Quill back into his pockets.

"You should throw those damned artefacts into the flames as well," I told him. "They are as dangerous as the book."

"I have need of them yet," he said. "And I have found a safe place to keep them when I am gone."

I knew it would not be so easy, because it is never so easy with things such as that. But I also knew there was nothing I could say to change Will's mind. We fell into silence and watched Marlowe's theatre burn to the ground.

"Oh, Mephistopheles," Marlowe sighed at one point.

And when the flames died away, so did Marlowe.

I helped bury him on a rainy day in a graveyard I won't name now because it doesn't matter anymore. The funeral party was only five other men and me. They were all important types in their day, but they've been lost to history too. It happens to everyone. Maybe it will even happen to me one day. There's always hope.

We lowered the coffin into the grave with ropes that burned our hands. We didn't refrain from cursing the pain or the day, because after all it was

Marlowe we were laying to rest. There was no one else watching us, unless you counted the stone skulls adorning the gates to the graveyard. Who knows—the times being what they were, maybe the skulls were watching.

When we'd put the coffin in its resting place, we took turns filling in the grave with shovelfuls of wet earth. This was back before the days of bulldozers and such. We've come a long way when it comes to burying the dead. And making the dead. When we buried someone back then, we did it the old-fashioned way, with blood, sweat and tears.

When we were done, there was nothing to mark the grave but the freshly turned dirt. There was no gravestone, no marker to designate the final resting place of Christopher Marlowe, one of the finest playwrights and bravest demon hunters to have walked the earth.

We left the grave unmarked because we wanted to maintain the guise of secrecy, like we were trying to hide Marlowe's final resting place from his countless enemies. But we all knew they'd find him eventually. Those were just the kind of enemies he made. That's why the thing we put in the coffin wasn't Marlowe. In fact, it bore no more resemblance to him than the story about his death in that tavern brawl.

We all stood around the grave and observed a moment of silence. None of us prayed, because we were beyond that now. Then the bell in the church tower began to chime, telling us it was time we were on our way.

When I looked up, I saw Will standing at the edge of the graveyard, dressed in mourning clothes. I didn't know where he had come from. There was no horse or carriage. We looked at each other but said nothing.

I turned to the man beside me and offered him my hand. "Keep him safe and secret," I said, and he said the same to me. I went around the circle, repeating the same thing with every one of them. One for each of Marlowe's body parts. His arms, his legs, his torso. And me with his head. I don't know why, but I'm always the one who gets the head for safekeeping.

"Keep him safe and secret."

I made my way out of the graveyard to Will. He looked at the bag in my hand, then back at me.

"Wherever your travels take you next, may it be far away from England," he said. "The Royals have not taken kindly to what you did to one of their own."

"You mean throwing that body into the book?" I said. "I don't see as I had any choice."

"You had no more choice than any other man," Will said. "But the Royals have never been one to forgive or forget. Flee while you are still able."

I knew his words were honest, and I nodded my thanks. "Until next time then," I said.

"There will be no next time," he said. He looked at the bag again. "Keep him safe and secret," he said.

Those of us who buried Marlowe rode out of the graveyard and away from there in separate directions, each of us knowing only where we were taking our own burden for hiding. It would be a devilish enemy indeed that would be able to find all the parts of Marlowe and unite them to claim his soul. Which meant that there was a fair chance it would happen anyway. But we did what we could to protect him, for we were his friends of a sort. As much as any of us could lay claim to friendships, anyway.

And now everyone was dead but me. I planned to change that, though. Soon everyone would be dead but me—and Marlowe.

ALAS, POOR MARLOWE!
I KNEW HIM

I parked in the lot of a place called The Garrick Inn, which some call the oldest building in Stratford-Upon-Avon because it dates back to the 1400s. I guess that claim is true enough if you're only counting the places that mortals like to frequent.

I walked down the street to the Royal Shakespeare Company theatre. I made a brief stop at a store to buy a bottle of wine I tucked under my coat. I was lucky enough to arrive at the theatre at the same time a busload of Americans were lining up for a tour. I slipped into the back of the pack, paid my admission and went inside with them. This was one of those times I definitely didn't want to stand out from the crowd.

I didn't know where all the different pieces of Marlowe were hidden these days. They'd probably been moved around numerous times since they'd been spirited away from that cemetery all those centuries ago. I'd certainly moved Marlowe's head enough times over the years, although it was just a skull now. The last place I'd left it had been here, in the theatre. Marlowe loved the stage too much to be able to quit it, even in death, so I'd done what I could to oblige him.

A tour guide led our group into the theatre and started to go into the history of the place. The people around me ignored her as they took photos of the refurbished seats and empty stage. The theatre reminded me of Morgana, which reminded me of how much I missed her, which made me want to burn the building down. Which wouldn't have been the first time someone had torched this place. Look up the official history if you're curious, but I swear innocence on all charges.

Eventually the guide got tired of telling us about all the famous actors who had once graced the theatre with their presence—it's a long list, after all. She took us backstage, to show us how the magic was made.

That was when I left the group. She led them down one hall to show them the wardrobe room, and I went down another hall, to the props room.

The door was locked, but I think I've made it clear by now that's not a problem for me. I slipped inside and closed the door behind me. It was a small room, barely the size of a London apartment. It wasn't meant to store all the props for the theatre—there was a larger warehouse space a short drive away for that. This room was just for props that were being used in current productions. And a few items that never left the theatre. Like the only prop really necessary for *Hamlet*: Yorick's skull.

I searched the room until I found the skull on a shelf at the back, under a pile of moth-eaten cloaks that looked as if they dated back to some 1960s production. The skull was yellowed and cracked in several places. No doubt from being dropped in performances or after-show parties. If people only knew who they were really holding. But if they did, someone would have stolen it by now, and then where would I be?

I brought the skull to my lips and breathed some grace into it, and called Marlowe back. Then I sat down on a fake wooden throne in a corner and waited for him to arrive.

It didn't take long. There was nothing that outwardly changed about the skull, but I had a distinct feeling it was gazing at me now with those empty sockets. I've developed a sense for this sort of thing.

"Welcome back, my friend," I said.

He chuckled. The sound of a skull chuckling isn't something I can really describe, so I'll have to leave it to your imagination.

"Cross," he greeted me in that voice that only skulls can make. See above. "I don't know what surprises me more: that I live again or that you still walk the earth."

"There have been times when we've shared the grave," I said. "I'm just a little more resilient than you."

"Well now," he said. "That remains to be seen, does it not?"

"You may have a point there," I said.

"At any rate," he said. "It is good to see you again. Have you come to raise me?" He bumped around a bit on the shelf, as if looking for the rest of his body.

"I'm afraid not," I said. "I've no idea where the other parts of you are." In fact, I had no idea if the other parts of him still even existed. The world was a hard place sometimes, especially to the dead.

Marlowe sighed. It was a sound that . . . well, you'd have to be there to understand.

"You know I'd raise you if I could," I said. "I figure I probably owe you that much for killing you in the first place."

"Tis nothing I wouldn't have done to myself given more time," Marlowe said. "Besides, I know it wasn't you. It was that damnable Will."

"True enough," I said, happy to shift the blame. "I've long harboured the suspicion he was just trying to eliminate a competitor. You were always my favourite playwright."

"Don't lie to the dead," Marlowe said. "It's a terrible sin."

"All right," I said and laughed. "You were my favourite next to Webster."

"Worthy enough company, I suppose," Marlowe said. "At least you didn't say Beckett."

"What the hell do you know about Beckett?" I asked. Marlowe had been dead for hundreds of years before Samuel Beckett even thought about writing *Waiting for Godot* and his other plays.

"Enough to know he relied too much on things not said and not enough on saying things properly," he said. "Hardly the stuff of poetry."

"I don't know how to break this to you," I said, "but the 20th century killed poetry."

"Why, this is hell then," Marlowe said.

I pulled the wine out from under my jacket and opened it.

"Think'st thou that I, who saw the face of God, and tasted the eternal joys of Heaven, am not tormented with ten thousand hells?" I said.

Marlowe was silent for a moment, then chuckled again. "All right," he said. "Let's have some of that."

I poured a bit of the bottle over the skull, and the wine seeped into all the cracks. None of it made it to the shelf.

"Oh, that is fine," Marlowe said, which reminded me of how bad the wine had been back in the day. I took a swig from the bottle myself. Well, I'd definitely had worse.

"If you are not here on my behalf, then I take it you are here on yours," Marlowe said.

"Close enough," I said.

"It must be a strange artefact of knowledge you seek then," he said, "to risk raising me from my slumber."

I wasn't sure what he meant by "risk" but I decided not to question him on it. The dead had their own way of seeing the world. And talking about it.

"I need to learn more about whatever it is that's haunting *Hamlet*," I said.

"If I recall correctly, it's the ghost of his father," Marlowe said. "Hardly an original idea."

"I mean what's haunting the play, not the man," I said. And I told him everything I knew, leaving out the parts about Amelia. Sometimes, when talking to the dead, it's best to keep some secrets. But I did bring out the book, because I still needed someone to explain it to me.

"What is that?" Marlowe asked. So it appeared I would have to keep looking.

"I was hoping you'd know," I said. "Polonius gave it to me. When I was dead. And he was dead. In the Forgotten Library."

"The Forgotten Library!" Marlowe exclaimed. "How did you manage to travel there?"

"First I had to get killed," I said. "And the rest is a bit of a mystery to me. You know of the place?"

"Will told me of it in one of our rare moments of rapport," Marlowe said. "It sounded both wondrous and terrifying."

I nodded. "That sounds about right," I said.

"I pressed him to take me there, or at least grant me the secret of how to find it," Marlowe went on. "But he said it was a place best left unvisited by those who valued their soul."

"For once I'm inclined to agree with him," I said, thinking about my encounter with Polonius there.

"What wonders does the book contain then?" Marlowe asked. "It must be grand indeed for the dead man to force it upon you."

I opened the book and showed him the blank pages.

"Well, the dead can be mad sometimes," Marlowe said.

"Believe me, I know," I said. I put the book back in my pocket. "Whatever it is, though, I suspect it's somehow connected to the haunting."

Marlowe didn't say anything for a moment. Then he said, "More wine, if you please."

So I poured half the bottle over him. I wasn't sure if you could get a skull drunk or not, but I figured I didn't have anything to lose by trying.

"What's in this for me?" he asked after he'd soaked for a suitable time.

I settled back in the throne and now it was my turn to savour the drink.

"What would you have?" I asked.

"Life and limb," he said.

"I just told you I have no idea where your limbs are," I reminded him.

"Life then," he said. "Let it not be said I make unrealistic demands."

"You have life," I pointed out.

"I have life on your terms," he countered. "By your grace. And if anyone knows how quickly grace granted can be lost, it is I."

"Fair enough," I said. "Name your terms then."

"A simple favour," he said.

"I've learned there is no such thing when the dead are involved," I said.

"An errand, really," he said.

"Even worse," I sighed.

"I'd like you to travel to London and visit the abbey," he said.

"Which abbey?" I asked.

"Westminster, of course," he said. "What other abbey would there be worth visiting?"

I sighed again, because it was the sort of situation that called for more than one sigh.

"Go on," I said, so he did.

"Find Spenser's tomb," he said, "and open it."

"Edmund Spenser?" I asked. "Author of *The Faerie Queene*?"

"Indeed," Marlowe said. "I'm glad some semblance of literacy remains with you."

"You know what I miss?" I said. "The good old days when quests involved simple things like slaying dragons."

"Be careful what you wish for," Marlowe said. "Bring me what you find in the tomb, and I will give you the answers you seek."

"Why do I suspect your answers will bring more riddles?" I asked him.

"Oh, I have no doubt of that," Marlowe said. "But that is your concern, not mine."

I nodded and pushed myself up out of the fake throne. "Don't go anywhere," I said. "I'll be back soon."

"Sooner, later, I'll be here," Marlowe said. It would have been a good moment for him to chuckle again, but he didn't.

I poured the rest of the wine over his skull then exited the scene.

THE STUFF OF LIFE

So, back to London I went. I pushed the rental car as fast as I could and I hit the city's outskirts in under an hour. I remember when the trip would have been an overnight one and involved sleeping in a stable. I don't know if they were better times or worse times, but they were certainly simpler.

I wasn't about to try driving in the city core—some tasks are too much, even for me—so I left the car in a parking lot and took the train the rest of the way in. It was late afternoon by the time I found myself on the steps of Westminster Abbey, in a lineup of more American tourists. They seemed to be everywhere these days. But that was all right. I had a plan for them.

We all went inside and the Americans immediately brought out their cameras, which brought the abbey staff over to lecture them about photography not being allowed. Americans never really understood that. I used the distraction to move through the nave and directly to Poets' Corner without anyone noticing I wasn't gawking at the marvellous aged stone and sculptures on the walls. I'd gawked at them plenty of times before, when I'd stood in this very space for the weddings of kings and queens. And their funerals. Like I said, back in simpler times.

Poets' Corner is the part of the abbey that has all the memorial statues and busts and plaques and such of dead poets, with the poets' remains hidden away behind the walls and under the floorboards, so to speak. I sometimes joke that no one else wanted them, so the abbey took them, but the truth is the abbey is the best equipped to deal with them. Many poets of the past have been magicians with more than words.

I went straight to Spenser's memorial in one of the walls and tried not to laugh at the inscription.

THE DEAD HAMLETS

Heare Lyes (Expecting the Second Comminge of our Saviovr Christ Jesus) the body of Edmond Spencer the prince of poets in his tyme, etc.

Sorry, Edmund, but not this tyme.

The memorial wasn't Spenser's grave. Nobody knew exactly which of the graves in Poets' Corner was his. The bodies in the abbey are all a bit mixed up. Most people think it's because the abbey staff weren't exactly keen on record keeping in the old days. But the fact is the locations of the bodies were kept deliberately confusing. It's a good way to prevent them from being stolen by grave robbers and things best not mentioned in religious places. And some of the graves just contain dirt because the people that were supposed to be buried in them had ideas of their own when it came to the everlasting slumber.

The truth is Spenser wasn't in any of the graves in Westminster Abbey. I was one of the few people left who knew his burial site, and once again the last one living. Not because I'd been there when he'd been laid to rest—I was on the outs with the Royals by then. But because sometimes it's good to trade favours for that kind of information. Case in point.

So, here I was at Edmund Spenser's tomb. Now I needed a distraction.

Thank you, American tourists.

I breathed a few words in their direction and waited. It only took a minute. One second they were arguing with the priests about their God-given right to take photographs, the next they were shrieking in tongues and ripping their clothing from their bodies. A parlour trick, really, but better than setting the place on fire.

The people wandering the nearby parts of the abbey rushed back to the nave to see what was happening, as did the priests stationed here and there throughout the place, more guards than spiritual advisers. Now I was alone in Poets' Corner, for a few seconds at least. But a few seconds was all I needed. I touched Spenser's memorial and let the grace flow through my fingertips. The memorial separated from the wall with a crack, the sound barely audible over the shrieking and wailing from the nave. I pulled the stone out farther, until I could see the dark hole in the wall behind it. I slid through the hole, into the burial chamber hidden in the wall behind the memorial.

Given that it was a tomb, I was expecting bones, and maybe some clothing and ritual remains. A bible, a cross, that sort of thing. But there was nothing. The chamber was empty.

Well, not exactly empty. There was a scrap of parchment on the ground with writing on it. I picked it up and studied it. I recognized the handwriting, as I'd seen it enough back in the day. Shakespeare's. It was a sonnet.

Not marble, nor the gilded monuments
Of princes, shall outlive this powerful rhyme;
But you shall shine more bright in these contents
Than unswept stone, besmear'd with sluttish time.
When wasteful war shall statues overturn,
And broils root out the work of masonry,
Nor Mars his sword nor war's quick fire shall burn
The living record of your memory.
'Gainst death and all oblivious enmity
Shall you pace forth; your praise shall still find room,
Even in the eyes of all posterity
That wear this world out to the ending doom.
So, till the judgment that yourself arise,
You live in this, and dwell in lovers' eyes.

I rolled up it carefully but the paper wasn't as brittle as I expected. It was as if it had been put there yesterday. I tucked it into one of my pockets and took another look around, but that was it. Even I had to admit it was anticlimactic. I shrugged and stepped back into the abbey.

I headed away from the commotion in the nave, toward the gift shop and the exit. The charm I'd worked on the tourists would wear off in another minute or so, and then everyone would try to figure out what happened. Some of them would believe it was a divine seizure, and that's the story the media would run with. How could they not? There'd be no proof, though, so the story would die in a few days, and the tourists would be free to make what they would of their memories.

But I knew the church officials wouldn't let it go at that. They'd look for other explanations, for signs of an attack. And when they noticed the memorial had been moved, exposing the secret tomb behind it, they'd start checking their security cameras. Which meant it was only a matter of time before the Black Guard would be hot on my trail. And this time it wouldn't be just Anubis I'd have to deal with.

I couldn't get back to Marlowe quick enough.

It was evening by the time I returned to the theatre in

Stratford-Upon-Avon. The tour groups were gone and now the lineup was an audience waiting to get in for a production of *Twelfth Night*. I breathed a sigh of relief that it wasn't *Hamlet*. I just had to find a way back into the prop room without attracting attention.

It was simple enough. Theatres aren't exactly the places you imagine when you think high security. I bought a ticket and went inside and mingled in the lobby along with everyone else. When one of the ushers stepped away from her post to direct someone to the washroom, I slipped through the door behind her and into the auditorium, which was still empty at this point in the evening. I went down the aisle, hopped up onto the stage and carried on into the wings. There were actors and stagehands getting ready for the show back there, but they only glanced at me before going about their business. I grabbed a clipboard off a table and moved through them. If you look like you belong, you don't even need to cast a sleight to appear invisible.

I made it out of the backstage area and into the hallways beyond. There were more people running around back here, wearing headsets and harried expressions. I held up the clipboard like a ward and they went past me like I was just another extra in their drama. Perfect.

I slipped into the props room and locked the door behind me. I found Marlowe's skull sitting on the throne now. I didn't bother asking how he'd got there. Like I said earlier, he'd learned a few tricks in his time. I took out the parchment and showed it to him.

"If you'd wanted a sonnet, I could have recited you one from memory," I told him.

"I didn't want any sonnet," he said. "I wanted that one." I swear he leaned toward it.

"I was expecting something else," I said. "Magic bones, maybe, or a forgotten gift from the faerie to Spenser." I looked down at the poem. "But this?"

"Give it to me," Marlowe said. "Make haste now."

I eyed him sitting there on the throne. "How exactly should I give it to you?" I asked.

"Must I still spell everything out for you?" he said. "Place it in my mouth."

I shrugged but did as he asked. I set the parchment in his jaw and waited to see what happened.

It wasn't what I expected.

As soon as I put the poem in Marlowe's mouth, the ink started flowing on the paper. The lines dissolved and moved into each other, then across the parchment. When the ink reached the edge of the sheet it kept going, flowing into Marlowe's skull.

"That's the stuff of life," he said.

Then the ink was all gone and only the parchment was left. The paper crumbled into dust and was gone.

"What, perchance, was that?" I asked.

"Some of Will's original ink," Marlowe said. "It grants immortality to that which it touches, which is why so many of his plays have survived this long instead of being lost to the ages. I stole the poem from him and left it with a friend to hide away for me in case a day like this ever happened."

"You always were a rogue," I said.

"I am but true to my nature," he said. "Alas, I don't know where Will kept his supply of ink, or where it came from in the first place. Believe me when I tell you I did my best to discover his secrets."

"This is well and good," I said, "but what does it have to do with the *Hamlet* haunting?"

"Nothing at all," Marlowe said with a laugh. "I just wanted a second wind for myself in case you decided to withdraw your grace from me. And now I have it, thanks to the ink."

I picked him up. "I don't imagine you will enjoy your life so much if you are in pieces on the floor," I said.

"The ghost you seek isn't Shakespeare's," Marlowe said. "It is far older than that."

I put him back on the throne and leaned against the shelf that, until recently, had been his resting place. "You have my attention," I said.

"Yes, I thought I might," he said. "You know, of course, that Will was carefree in borrowing material for his plays."

I nodded. Everyone knew that the great Shakespeare had lifted from other works to flesh out his own. All the writers did it back then. It was before the age of copyright and lawsuits. Well, copyright anyway.

"There was an earlier version of *Hamlet* written by another," Marlowe said. "Lost to time and this world, until Will stumbled across its grave in the Forgotten Library. He took the words from that play and made them his own. But he left the original to rot in obscurity."

"He stole *Hamlet*," I said. I could scarcely believe it. Then again, it was Will we were talking about.

"He copied the text there in the Forgotten Library," Marlowe said. "He used that special ink of his to ensure his play would live on. But it granted life to more than *Hamlet*. Will told me he felt a presence there in the library and he fled in great haste."

"He brought the ghost to life," I said, understanding.

"There you have it," Marlowe said. "When he wrote *Hamlet* in that place with his special ink, he meant to give it eternal life. And so he did. But he also gave life to the ghost from that other text."

"And now it haunts Will's *Hamlet*," I said.

"Tis a tale fit for a play," Marlowe said.

Things were beginning to make sense. It wasn't the first time I'd encountered a haunted work of art, after all. Although it was the first time I could remember a ghost from one work haunting another work. Well, there were no rules for things like this, at least not any rules I knew about.

"A terrible waste of that ink," Marlowe sighed. "For all the world knows, it may have been the last of Will's supply."

"I think he left it behind in the Forgotten Library," I said. "There's an inkpot still sitting there."

"Do not taunt me so!" Marlowe cried.

"Keep it down," I said. "I don't want anyone walking in on this particular conversation."

"You tell the truth, then?" he said.

"I think so," I said. "But I can't really vouch for my sanity at the moment. You know what dying can do to a person."

"And what of Will's quill?" Marlowe said. "Was it there, too?"

I shook my head. "There was a quill, but it was white," I said. "He must have taken the Black Quill to the grave with him."

Marlowe fell silent, as if thinking things over. That made two of us. I had some answers, but not enough.

"Why the faerie?" I wondered. "Why does it haunt them?"

"Who knows the minds of ghosts?" Marlowe said after a moment. "Perhaps the glamour is nearer the Forgotten Library than our own world. It is a somewhat impossible place, after all. Perhaps the faerie unwittingly made a blood sacrifice that summoned it to their realm during one of their shows. It wouldn't be the first time some poor fey has given his life for the art."

"Now the faerie have brought the ghost to our world," I said, thinking of the National Theatre production.

"And there are many more *Hamlets* to haunt here," Marlowe said.

"How do I stop it?" I asked. I tried not to think about what would happen if the hauntings spread throughout the mortal world.

"That's where I can't be as helpful," Marlowe said. "Ghosts were never my specialty."

"Tell me more about this other play then," I said. If I could learn its name, or even its author, then I would have something to go on when it came to dealing with the ghost.

"I've told you everything that Will let slip over wine," he said. "The rest you'll have to get from him, I'm afraid."

"Even though you've been in the grave some time now, I'm sure you know that's not possible," I said.

"It's not a venture I'd care to undertake," Marlowe admitted. "But there it is."

I studied him but it's hard to tell from a skull's facial expression whether or not it's being truthful. I was going to have to believe him. I didn't see any reason why he would lie to me or hold anything back. Which didn't mean he wasn't lying or holding something back, of course.

"Have you thought about talking to . . . ?" he began, but I cut him off with a shake of my head.

"I'm not that desperate," I said. "Not yet."

"I understand," he said, and I knew he did.

I needed to leave this place and get on with things. I laid my hand on him, ready to take back the grace if he didn't need it. "Just so I'm clear, Shakespeare's ink is enough to give you life?" I asked.

"It's truly a wondrous thing," he said. "Now I know how you must feel upon your communion with the angels."

"You have no idea how I feel," I told him. I decided to let him keep the grace. After all, I needed a new reserve now that I'd drained the saints.

"No," he said. "Nor do you know how I feel."

I nodded. He had a point there. "Until next time," I said.

"Good fortune," he said. "You'll definitely need it."

I left him there on the throne and went back out into the night. The stars overhead mocked me, but no more than usual.

ANOTHER GHOST, ANOTHER DEAD HAMLET

All right, I'd finally figured out the *what*. Now I just had to understand the *why*. Why was the ghost haunting *Hamlet*? What did it want, or what did it have to gain?

I had an idea how to find out. I was going to talk to another ghost.

I filled the rental car's gas tank with petrol and I topped myself up with coffee. Then I headed back to London. I was starting to feel like a delivery driver.

I didn't really want to return to the city because that's where the Royals would start their search for me. I would have much rather preferred a quiet exit from the country—maybe a boat to Ireland and a flight back to the continent from there, to escape the security and the wardens at Heathrow and Gatwick. But the only ghost I knew how to find these days lived in London. Well, dwelled in London. Or whatever it is that ghosts do.

I abandoned the car on a side street near Hampstead Heath. If I were looking for me and had a nation's security service at my disposal, I'd have someone check recent stolen credit cards to see if anyone had used them for renting cars. Then I'd start looking for those cars. So farewell, stolen car. I took the Tube into the city. It was too late to buy a hat or anything that disguised my appearance from the security cameras. I was just going to have to take the risk. It was a short ride anyway. By the time it would have taken anyone to respond to an alarm in a security office somewhere, I was already walking out into the street at the Covent Garden station and losing myself in the nighttime crowd.

Still, I walked quickly to my destination, which happened to be another theatre. I was spending more time in theatres in the past few days than I had in the past few years.

But this one was special. The Drury Lane theatre. Known around the world for its ghosts. Many theatres claim to be haunted, because it seems to be good for ticket sales. For some reason, many people appear to be intrigued or even titillated by the idea of a dead person dropping a light on the head of an actor or, better yet, the person sitting next to them. But most ghost stories are just that: stories. The ghosts in Drury Lane, however, are real.

Thankfully, this theatre was even easier to break into than the last one. By the time I arrived at the front doors, they were locked, the ticket booth empty. The last show of the night was finished and the audience had gone home. Perfect.

I used the stolen credit card in my stolen wallet for the only thing it was probably good for now: to open doors. I hunched over the door like I was fumbling with my keys. A couple of seconds and I was inside the lobby. I locked the door behind me again. It wouldn't do for just anyone to wander in.

I went straight to one of the auditorium doors and listened at it for a moment. There were voices, and the sounds of things being moved around onstage. The stagehands cleaning up after the performance. I sat on a bench in the lobby and thought about my plan while I waited. So far my plan consisted of reminding myself to come up with a plan sometime soon.

When the voices faded away, no doubt heading for the back exit and a nearby pub, I went through the door and into the auditorium. It was empty and dark, the only illumination a single spotlight trained on the stage, which was also empty. I made my way down an aisle and hopped up onto the stage. I didn't stand in the light though. That's not the place to look for a ghost.

The best place to look for a ghost is in the shadows, where it's a little easier to see them. Most ghosts are like that. I think it has something to do with their age, or how much energy they're willing to expend to appear visible. If they use up too much, they get tired and just drift away entirely for a while. Most don't bother putting any effort into being seen at all. It generally just causes problems when they are visible anyway.

You've probably seen a ghost once or twice in your life. A blur at the edge of your vision, or a glimpse of a person who wasn't there when you looked again. You likely passed it off to a trick of the light. If you train your eyes properly, you can learn to see them, but that would take most people longer than their entire lives.

You can also see them easier if you've ever been dead and brought back to life. Just trust me on that one. Or if you're a cat. For some reason, cats have no problem seeing ghosts. Hey, I don't understand the rules, let alone make them.

So I stood there and waited, and eventually I spotted the ghost I wanted standing up in the flies, the walkways high over the stage where the curtains and scrims and ropes and all that are stored, out of sight. The ghost was dressed in a grey dress jacket, cloak, and an old-fashioned tricorne hat. He smiled when he saw me looking at him and mouthed a few words of greeting.

This is the other problem with ghosts. You generally can't hear them when they're spectral, which is how they are most of the time. Ghosts can take on corporeal form and carry on conversations, like a certain art dealer I'd once known, but they generally don't like to, because it expends all their energy and they spend the next few years drifting in and out of existence. And ghosts don't like fading out any more than the living.

But that doesn't mean you can't communicate with ghosts at all. You just have to be more creative. After all, they're creative with the living. This ghost, for instance, liked to shift the lights to the best spots on stage for actors to deliver their lines. Actors, being what they are, always go to the lights. I guess the ghost knew the right places from watching lifetimes of performances.

I went over into the wings and checked the stagehands' station until I found a folding knife hidden under a wine-stained copy of a script. A knife is one of the essential tools backstage, used for everything from cutting ropes that get tangled in set pieces to encouraging drunken actors to go onstage for their parts.

And for communicating with ghosts.

I went back out into the spotlight and unfolded the knife. The ghost watched with interest. I sliced open the palm of my left hand and let a good amount of blood drip onto the stage. Then I bent down and dipped my finger into it like an inkwell and wrote a few words on the wooden floor.

I hope you've been well.

That got his attention. He climbed over the side of the walkway and shimmied down the proscenium arch. He probably could have just floated down, but I guess old habits die hard, even for ghosts. He landed in silence. He adjusted his jacket and coat, then walked over to my side and studied the words. He smiled. He bent down to write his own words with my blood.

I have been, he wrote, *and that is well enough.*

I nodded and squeezed out some more blood.

A question, I wrote. *Why are you here?*

He raised his eyebrows, then shrugged before answering. *Where else would I be?*

"In the grave?" I suggested, not bothering to write the words now that we were in conversation.

The ghost studied the empty seats in the audience for a moment, then stained his fingers in more of my blood.

All the world's a stage, he wrote, *and the stage is my world.*

I considered his words while he licked the blood from his fingers. I cut my hand again to make more ink for him.

"Are you trapped here?" I asked.

He chuckled silently. *No more than you,* he wrote. *No more than any actor.*

"So you can leave?" I asked.

Where would I go? he wrote. *I have been here since the first theatre was built on this site. I will be here until the last one burns down.*

"Who were you before?" I asked.

The same as I am now, he said.

"Then why do you haunt the theatre?" I asked.

He was quick in his answer. *I haunt nothing,* he wrote. *The show goes on. I play my role.*

"You're not seeking vengeance for your death?" I wrote. I didn't know why else a ghost would haunt something if it had a choice in the matter.

He looked around at the stage before answering.

As long as I have my role, I am no more dead than you, he wrote.

I rubbed my face and stared at my blood. I had a feeling his answer changed the way I needed to think about things. I just wasn't sure how yet.

He bent down and wrote some more.

What of you? he asked. *What part do you play?*

I shook my head. "I'm still not sure about that," I said.

THE DEAD HAMLETS

To know your role, you must first know the play, he wrote.

I thought that over. He was right, in his own spectral, mysterious way. I was trying to stop the *Hamlet* ghost from killing Amelia when I didn't know anything about the ghost because I *couldn't* know anything about it. Not when I was little more than an audience member, watching and waiting to see what happened next. I had to learn more about the ghost, and the only way I could do that was by understanding the play it was from. I had to go back to the Forgotten Library and find the play Will had ransacked.

"Do you know *Hamlet?*" I asked.

The ghost chuckled in silence again.

I know every play that has ever been staged, he wrote. *And many that have not.*

I nodded and straightened up. I looked out into the empty audience and took a deep breath. Then I started into the play.

"Where wilt thou lead me?" I asked. "Speak; I'll go no further."

The ghost studied me for several seconds, then smiled.

"Mark me," he said, and now I could hear him for the first time. I guess the play was still the thing with him.

"I will," I said.

He moved down the stage, closer to the empty seats. He turned to face the audience that wasn't there.

"My hour is almost come," he said. "When I to sulphurous and tormenting flames must render up myself." His voice was deeper and richer than I had expected. He spoke the lines like they were meant to be spoken.

"Alas, poor ghost," I said. I looked around the stage but nothing happened. No one came to investigate the sounds of our performance. No other ghost showed up to watch.

"Pity me not, but lend thy serious hearing to what I shall unfold," the ghost said.

"Speak," I said, the lines coming naturally to me now, like I was recalling an old conversation I'd actually had. "I am bound to hear."

"So art thou to revenge when thou shalt hear," the ghost said.

"What?" I asked. I wondered if I needed to overact a little and throw in some big gestures. Maybe I should swoon a little. Hamlet was a bit of the swooning type, after all.

Now the ghost turned back to me.

"I am thy father's spirit," he said. He seemed to be enjoying himself. Well, I guess he didn't have the opportunity to exchange too many lines with the other actors that usually walked this stage. "Doomed for a certain term to walk the night," he went on. "And for the day confined to fast in fires, til the foul crimes done in my days of nature are burnt and purged away. But that I am forbid to tell the secrets of my prison house, I could a tale unfold whose lightest word would harrow up thy soul, freeze thy young blood, make thy two eyes, like stars, start from their spheres, thy knotted and combined locks to part, and each particular hair to stand on end. Like quills upon the fretful porpentine."

I did like that bit. It's stood up well over the ages. Except for the part about the porpentine.

"But this eternal blazon must not be to ears of flesh and blood," he went on. "List, list, O, list! If thou didst ever thy dear father love—"

"O God," I said, trying for wryness but hitting world weariness instead.

"Revenge his foul and most unnatural murder," the ghost finished.

"Murder," I said, and thought that would be a good line for the *Hamlet* ghost to strike on.

And that's when the spotlight fell from the darkness and killed me.

IF WORDS BE MADE OF BREATH, AND BREATH OF LIFE

I awoke on the books again. I was lying face down on an ancient tome with the words *An Encyclopedia of Madness* emblazoned on the cover. I sat up quickly and looked around. I was back in that same room in the Forgotten Library. I didn't see Polonius, though. I didn't see anyone else.

I was almost relieved to be dead. I hadn't been sure if my little trick would work if I wasn't with the faerie when I launched into *Hamlet*. But I suspected that even if the Macbeth curse wasn't to blame for the deaths, the ghost might operate in the same way as the curse, following actors from production to production and haunting them. Maybe the ghost was like the Tower's ravens and never forgot a face.

I looked at the table with the ink pot and loose papers amid the scattered books. I wondered if one of those books was the play I needed to find. I took a step toward the table, and that's when the dead woman erupted from the wall.

She smashed through the books and came stumbling toward me. I saw another body behind her, slumped in an alcove that had been hidden by the books. Polonius. He looked as dead as ever. The alcove was made of more books. I was beginning to suspect the Forgotten Library was nothing but books all the way.

"No more," the woman said, mist issuing forth from her mouth and forming more of those strange words. She stopped opposite me, and that's when I saw she wasn't a woman at all. Or even human, for that matter. It was Peaseblossom, one of the faerie, who stood opposite me. He was wearing the same dress as he had been back in the theatre in Berlin, when he'd been among the dead in the audience. His skin still bore the sickly colour of someone who had been poisoned, so I knew how the ghost had claimed him.

"What are you doing here?" I asked him. Or rather, tried to ask him. But once again the words that came out of my mouth were not the words I intended to say. Instead, I said, "How is it with you, lady?" And I knew the scene.

Peaseblossom smiled at me. Let me assure you that a dead faerie smiling at you in an impossible library is not comforting.

"Alas, how is it with you," Peaseblossom said, stepping toward me, "that you do bend your eye on vacancy and with the incorporal air do hold discourse?"

Once again, I wasn't exactly sure what was going on. But I did know the lines we were speaking. It was the scene from *Hamlet* right after Hamlet has slain the servant Polonius in Queen Gertrude's closet. The same scene Morgana, Puck, and the poor fey had played in Berlin to start this sorry tale. I took Peaseblossom to be playing the part of Gertrude here, while I was cast in the role of Hamlet. And there was poor Polonius in the wall behind her, playing his part.

"I will bestow him, and will answer well the death I gave him," I heard myself say. Which made no sense at all, as I hadn't killed Polonius. Puck had. My line only made sense if I were Hamlet. Which I wasn't. Except something was making me play the part of Hamlet here in the Forgotten Library. It had to be the ghost.

But then there was the fact that Peaseblossom appeared to be possessed, too. Was there more than one ghost? This was wondrously strange indeed.

"If words be made of breath, and breath of life, I have no life to breathe," Peaseblossom said to me.

And then I felt that cold wind again, and everything went dim. Peaseblossom lunged forward, trying to wrap his arms around me. Instead, they went through me, as spectral as a ghost, and then he was gone and Polonius was gone and all the books were gone.

Blackout.

THE SHOW MUST GO ON

I resurrected, lurching upright again on the Drury Lane stage and throwing myself to the side to avoid the spotlight that had already killed me and now lay broken on the floorboards.

Someday I'd get used to this whole death and resurrection thing. Someday.

I dry heaved a little and then caught my breath and looked around. The theatre was still dark, the audience still empty. I'd resurrected quickly, although it had cost me a lot of grace. I'd have to find another angel soon. Or another reserve of grace.

Then I caught the flicker in the corner of my eye and I turned to look at it. The ghost, still standing there.

"The play's the thing," he said.

And then he was gone too, fading away back into nothing.

I wondered why he'd waited around for me to come back to tell me that. I doubted he'd been just continuing to act out the play while I lay dead at his feet—although that wasn't an impossibility, I guess. But I had a feeling he was trying to give me a message with that parting line. If only I knew what it meant. I got to my feet and briefly considered cleaning up the broken spotlight and the blood on the stage. I decided to leave it though. The spotlight had wiped out the record of my conversation with the ghost, so now it just looked like the scene of an accident. Let the stagehands find it in the morning and add to the legend of the theatre ghost.

I left the theatre and found it was still night outside, which meant not that much time had passed. I lost myself in the surrounding streets, stopping only long enough to buy a couple slices of pizza from a late-night shop that obviously catered to drunks. I say obviously not because of the clientele but because of the quality of the food. I ate the slices anyway, but they did little to stop the hunger inside me. The longing for grace was a special kind of emptiness.

I replayed the latest scene from the Forgotten Library in my head as I ate. I still didn't know where it was, or why I woke up there when I died. It clearly wasn't of this realm though. It was more like the play the actors at the Globe had found themselves in when I'd summoned the Witches, where they'd been forced to say the lines of the *Macbeth* play. I'd been forced to utter the lines from *Hamlet* the same way. I was just as confused as the actors had been.

What was clear was I'd been possessed twice now, likely by the ghost Marlowe had told me about. Or maybe ghosts, given that I hadn't been the only one possessed each time I'd visited the library. I had a feeling that I would have been trapped in the library along with Peaseblossom and Polonius if I hadn't resurrected, pulling me back to my body. So which part of me had been in the library with the others then? My soul? The parts of my consciousness that continued to exist after I died? It was a mystery fit for Frankenstein.

I knew I couldn't leave Amelia to that fate.

I tossed the empty pizza plate into the garbage and walked away from the shop before I lingered long enough that someone might remember me later. I continued to think things over as I went. I'd succeeded in returning to the Forgotten Library, but I hadn't been able to get the information I needed. I wasn't sure how much I could learn about the other play if the ghost kept possessing me every time I visited that library. And I was running out of time. Amelia was running out of time.

I sighed. I knew who I had to turn to for answers next. And as I'd made clear to Baal and Marlowe, I really didn't want to see him again. But I was out of options.

I found my way to Kensington Gardens to hide out the night. It's one of the safer spots to seek refuge in London if you're on the run from the authorities. They tend to leave it alone on account of it reverting to faerie rule after the sun sets. One of those clauses in the treaty between the faerie and the Royals. The faerie didn't make much use of the gardens these days, but you never knew when they felt like making mischief. I imagined the Royals figured better safe than sorry when it came to policing the place.

I made my way along the Serpentine until I reached the statue of

Peter Pan, tucked into a forested glade by the water. The official lore is that J.M. Barrie had the statue created to entertain the children who played in the area at the time he lived. I could tell you the true story, about how it's not really a statue and wasn't created by anyone human, but why ruin such a happy tale?

I crawled into the shrubs at the edge of the clearing and tried to quiet my thoughts enough to sleep. I didn't quite manage that, but I did manage to rest for a while, until the sky began to lighten and Peter began to play his pipes, and all the faerie and animals frozen in the base of the statue joined in with their own calls and songs.

I sighed and sat up, brushing the twigs out of my hair. I wished I had a coffee. I wished I had a bed. I wished I had the life of a regular person who wasn't awoken from his slumber by a twisted, whistling Peter Pan statue come to life.

Peter turned his head to look at me. "That was a clever piece of improv, playing that scene with the ghost."

The voice was the sort of voice you'd expect from a set of bronze lips, but I knew who it was instantly from the longing that welled up inside me, pushing even the hunger for grace aside.

Morgana.

"You were there?" I asked. I felt ashamed for not noticing her presence in the theatre, and then I felt angry at myself for my shame.

Morgana smiled and the rest of the creatures on the statue kept up their cacophony. I wondered if they were faerie or fey or just an effect created by Morgana.

"The ring you wear has many uses," she said. "Keeping you bound to me is just one of them, but it is by no means the most amusing one."

Not for the first time, I regretted my poor decision-making that had led me to falling into her power again.

"And what have you learned from your latest venture into the theatre world?" Morgana asked.

"I've got good news and bad news," I said.

"It is always the way with you," she said.

"The good news is I figured out what's haunting your plays," I said and told her about the ghost that Will had brought to life.

She cocked her head to study me. Well, Peter's head. Now everything fell silent. That was a small relief, but I suspected it wouldn't last.

"The bad news is I don't know how to stop it," I said. "Not yet. Give me more time."

"I have to admit I expected more of you," Morgana said. "I expected you to have solved our little mystery by now. You are a disappointment. As always." And her words stung me worse than any blade.

"Well, I did find out about the ghost," I said. "That seems pretty significant to me."

"Admiring its significance is not the same as stopping it," Morgana said.

"I'm only human," I said, which was stretching things a bit. "I can only manage one thing at a time."

"Well, that's a pity," Morgana said. "Because we're almost ready to perform our new show. It would have been best for all concerned to have this matter settled before we raise the curtain on it."

The rest of the creatures on the statue looked back and forth between us.

I stood up and stepped closer to the statue. "I say again, leave her out of this," I said.

"Cross, my love," Morgana said, and the word "love" felt like it cut me to the bone. "The show must go on."

"Amelia isn't just another one of your fey to be casually sacrificed on a whim," I said. "If she dies before I can figure out how to make this ghost leave you alone, I'll have no reason to help you anymore. I'd sooner let you keep ownership of my soul for the rest of eternity and watch the ghost destroy your kingdom." I meant every word, even though her spell made me want to fall to my knees and beg for forgiveness.

"Perhaps that is what will happen," Morgana said. "And perhaps I could prevent it by doing what you say. But I must admit to a certain curiosity, and Amelia is the key to satisfying my interest."

"Curiosity about what?" I asked.

"About the nature of the drama we find ourselves in," Morgana said, smiling that wicked smile of hers, which looked downright eerie on the face of a Peter Pan statue. "Will it be a comedy? Or a tragedy? Only the fate of Amelia can decide it."

I cursed her then, and I cursed a few other people and gods who had nothing to do with this particular set of events. I even cursed myself a little, because why not?

Then one of the faerie at the base of the statue turned her head to look at me.

"Father," she said, and I knew as sure as Peter Pan was Morgana that this faerie was Amelia.

And I didn't know what to say to her.

"Do not fear for me, Father," she said. "For I do not fear death. I cannot fear what I am."

And that put an end to my threats and cursing. How could I not try to save her after that? I could not let my daughter utter such words without at least trying to show her what it was to live.

"We will see you again very soon, Cross," Morgana said, and her voice seemed almost sad now. Perhaps it was just the bronze speaking. "I suggest you stop wasting time sleeping in the bushes like Puck and use your time instead to put an end to this haunting. Someday, you will have all eternity to sleep."

If only.

And then they were gone and the statue was just the statue again, and a white swan went past on the Serpentine—which could have been a sign or could have just been a white swan. The sun made an appearance behind the trees and the breeze ran its fingers through my hair and it was time to go to work again.

THE LOST PLAY

Maybe if I had more time I could have figured out how to stop the ghost on my own. But I didn't have more time. If I didn't do something soon, Amelia was going to wind up trapped with the others in the Forgotten Library. Then I'd only get to see her again in those fleeting moments when I was dead after being killed on stage. It wasn't exactly the ideal father-daughter relationship.

It was another of those moments when I needed help. But none of the usual suspects were going to do now. I needed specialized help.

I needed the Scholar.

I left the park and joined the crowd surging into the nearest Tube station for the morning commuter rush. I made my way around London's underground maze until eventually I was sitting on a train heading out of the city, toward Oxford.

The Scholar had been in Oxford for centuries. Before that he'd been in the Sorbonne, and before that in the Vatican library, long before it ever became the Vatican. I don't know where he was from originally any more than I knew his real name, but it wouldn't have surprised me to learn he'd been in the great library of Alexandria before that had been destroyed. He was a bit of a snob about the libraries he chose to frequent.

Case in point: I found him in the Queens College Library at Oxford, tucked away in the wooden stacks, hunched over some ancient tome he'd pulled from one of the shelves. The air around him was thick with dust but it wasn't from any of the books. The air around him was always thick with dust. That was just his nature.

He was shaking his head at the book and muttering to himself as I approached.

"If this is what passes for research these days, we're all doomed," he said. He ran a hand down a page and the ink flowed from the page and into his skin, travelling up his arm. I watched letters swirl across his eyes, and when I looked back at the page it was blank.

I placed the tome in his hand around the fifteenth century, only slightly older than the ornate wooden shelves around us. I decided not to say anything about the Scholar's views on modernity. He could get a little cranky at times.

He frowned at me as I approached. Which was really his way of saying hello. He didn't like to be bothered. Being bothered got in the way of reading books. And, apparently, consuming them.

"What is it you seek this time?" he muttered. "More scraps of useless trivia about the lost treasure ship of Columbus?"

"If I'd found it, I could have changed history," I said.

He snorted and put the book down on a shelf, then took off his glasses to polish them on his dusty shirt. They were the sort of spectacles no one had worn in hundreds of years. As far as I could tell, he was just moving the smudges around on them.

"Yes, you would have been able to buy more expensive spirits with which to waste away your life," he said.

All right, he may have had a point there.

The Scholar sighed and shook his head at the selections on the shelves. "This may as well be the children's section of a public library," he said. He scowled at a passing student, who quickened his pace to get away from us.

"What do you know about *Hamlet?*" I asked.

"Dreadfully misguided," the Scholar said. He put his glasses back on and blinked at me like I had just appeared there. "Wasting all that time with plotting and vengeance when he could have been reading more books. That's why he died, you know. If only he'd read more, his fate would have turned out differently." He picked up the book again and shook his head at it.

I should point out the Scholar wasn't trying to be funny. He owes his immortality to reading. I don't know how it works exactly, but as long as he keeps reading and learning things from books, he stays alive. Maybe it has something to do with his little trick of consuming the books. I'd thought about asking him to show me how it was done, but I didn't think I'd be able to do that to a book myself. Not the ones worth reading, anyway, and what was the point doing it with the ones not worth reading?

"I meant the play, not the character," I told him.

The Scholar frowned at me again, or maybe he was still frowning at me.

"I know everything about the play, of course," he said. "And all its variations. And its sequels. Why are you wasting my time with such silly questions? Aren't there seraphim that need slaying? Shouldn't you be bothering them?"

"Probably," I said. "But I'm not so much interested in *Hamlet* or its sequels as I am the play that came before it. You know, the one that Shakespeare stole to make *Hamlet*."

The Scholar sniffed. "It was entirely appropriate to use material from other works in that day," he said. "There were no concerns about copyright, and the cult of authorial voice had yet to—"

"He took the whole thing," I said.

The Scholar sighed at being cut off in mid-point, and a cloud of dust billowed about me. I held my breath for a few seconds.

"This is the trouble with your generation," the Scholar said. "You have no patience. No doubt modern life's distractions are to blame, what with all your telegrams and moving pictures and such."

"We haven't had telegrams since the war years," I said, although, to be honest, I couldn't remember the exact timeline of the rise and fall of the telegram.

"What war?" The Scholar asked.

"The Second World War," I guessed.

"There was a First World War?" he said, raising an eyebrow. "I *am* behind on my reading."

"The play," I pleaded.

"*Which* play?" he asked.

So I told him everything. Well, almost everything. I told him about the deaths and the Witches and Marlowe and the Forgotten Library. I told him how Will had brought the ghost from the other play to life with his ink. The only parts I left out were about Amelia and Morgana. Not because I thought he'd use them against me like others might have, but because I knew he wouldn't care. I also left out the part about Alice, because the Scholar and Alice really, really don't like each other. They had very different ideas about books and their uses.

"I have read rumours Shakespeare had found a way to the Forgotten Library," the Scholar said, gazing at the tomes around us as if those rumours were hidden away in them at this very moment. "But I had never dared believed those tales could be true. I was not even sure if the library even existed." He looked back at me. "You must take me there at once," he said.

"I need a break from getting killed for a while," I said. "And I'm pretty sure that's not the way you want to travel there. Plus, you seem to be missing the fact that it's haunted by a homicidal ghost."

"Surely there must be an alternate route if Shakespeare was able to make the voyage," he said, gritting his teeth at my obvious ignorance.

"Yeah, but there's no way we can ask him about the path he took," I said. "And Marlowe claims to not know anything more of the place than what he told me."

"Perhaps you should let me talk to Marlowe," the Scholar muttered. "I didn't even know he was alive."

"He isn't alive," I said. "Not really."

"Is he still writing?" The Scholar asked. "I would love to read more of his work."

"You're missing the point here," I said. "Do you know anything about the other play or not?"

"Of course," he snapped. "What kind of scholar would I be if I didn't know such things? Although personally I think you need to broaden your reading. I find the Jacobeans far more complex than Shakespeare. Now, take *The Duchess of Malfi*, for example. . . ."

I held up my hand to stop him before he entered full-blown lecture mode and someone complained to the librarians and security was called. I'd been through that chapter before.

"Please," I said. "I know all about the Jacobeans. I was there, remember? I just need to know about the ghost's play."

The Scholar took off his glasses again and polished them once more, to about the same effect as the first time.

"Very well," he said. "Let us discuss terms then."

I sighed. "You know, it would be nice if someday I asked a favour of someone and they told me what I needed to know out of the kindness of their heart."

"No doubt that day will be very lovely for you," the Scholar said. "But that day is not today. I haven't had a heart in centuries."

"I'm surprised to learn you had one at all," I said.

The Scholar placed his glasses back on his beak-like nose and turned his attention back to the book he'd been consuming.

"Well, perhaps you can find someone else to help you," he said. "Maybe that girl from the children's tale. I imagine she has all sorts of interesting things to say about *Hamlet*."

The Scholar was no fool. He knew I would have tried Alice first, and I was here only because there were no other options left to me. It was time to offer him an incentive. I took out the book Polonius had given me and showed it to him.

The Scholar studied the book like an owl studying a mouse. "What is that?" he asked.

"I don't know," I said. "All I know is a dead man in the Forgotten Library gave it to me."

The Scholar seized the book from my hands before I'd even finished speaking and he tore it open. The pages were still blank, but he ran his hand down one of them anyway. I expected nothing to happen, but words flowed up his arm from the blank page just like any other book, and his eyes filled with ink.

I recognized the words. They were in the same strange language as the words made of mist that came from the mouths of anyone who spoke in the Forgotten Library.

I grabbed the book back from the Scholar before he could consume another page. He stumbled toward me, reaching for it, and I had to push him back against the opposite shelf.

"What is it?" I asked him.

The Scholar stared at the book for a moment longer. He looked like an addict caught in the haze of a high. I snapped my fingers in front of his face to draw his attention back to me.

"Tell me what's in the book," I said.

The Scholar shook his head. "Nothing's in the book," he murmured.

"I saw you take the words," I said. "The same words that I saw in the Forgotten Library."

"They are no more real than that library," the Scholar said. "The words are a dream."

I looked down at the book in my hands. The pages inside were still blank. I ran my own hand down one of them, but nothing happened.

The Scholar licked his lips as he stared at the book. "Are there more texts like this there?" he asked.

"More than I could count," I said. I wasn't sure what was going on with the Scholar and the book, but it was clear that it was something valuable to him. "Tell me what you know about the play Will ransacked and I'll let you have this again. I may even bring you back another book the next time I'm in the Forgotten Library."

The Scholar's eyes drifted back to me. They were black with ink from the book. He considered me for a moment before answering.

"No one knows the name of the play that begat *Hamlet*. There have been many contenders, but even the scholars are uncertain. Perhaps a lost play by one of Shakespeare's contemporaries, perhaps an earlier play by a certain nobleman who did not wish to be known. Perhaps another text entirely that no one knows of." He scratched underneath his robes in a way that would have offended most polite company and gotten him arrested in certain countries.

"Can't you at least point me to a list of possible suspects?" I asked. "Give me the names of the authors of these other plays."

"Well, you know how writers are," the Scholar said. "Always lifting from other writers and claiming the stories as their own. One copies something and then another later writer copies that and just changes a few names or makes a tragedy a comedy and vice versa. Writer after writer takes elements from their predecessors."

"So you're saying writers are a bunch of thieves," I said. Which was a fair point, given the writers I'd known in my time.

"Bah, they are murderers," the Scholar said. He began to pace up and down the aisle now, spreading dust wherever he went. "Imagine it. One bard after another taking the story and killing the father text, hiding its body in the graveyard of obscurity and anonymity. Usurping the throne of literary greatness, until the next bard strikes, with quill and fresh parchment. Who's to say which one of those lost texts was the source for Shakespeare's greatest play?"

"You have no idea who wrote that other play, do you?" I said.

"The only one who can say for certain is Shakespeare himself," the Scholar said. "Oh, and the ghost, I suppose." He shook his head. "The Forgotten Library is no doubt full of contenders for Shakespeare's source material. Who knows how many plays have been lost to the ages and wound up there?"

I felt the last warmth coming through the window fade as the sun slipped below the buildings outside. If I didn't know anything about that other play or who its original author was, I'd never be able to learn anything about the ghost or where it had come from. I couldn't know any more than I already did, which wasn't enough.

I couldn't save Amelia from death.

I wondered if there were some way I could take her place in the play, so the ghost would come for me rather than her. But I knew Morgana. I knew she would enjoy refusing my sacrifice far more.

I didn't know what to do.

"Surely there must be some way to the Forgotten Library," the Scholar said, eyeing the book in my hands. "If we could find it, we could solve all your problems. And at last I would have access to a real library."

"How do you find a place that doesn't exist?" I said, shaking my head.

And then I knew how Shakespeare had managed to discover his entrance to the library. I'd known it all along, but I just hadn't realized it. To learn how to find an impossible place that didn't exist, I needed to talk to someone else that lived in an impossible place that didn't exist. But the idea of that appealed to me even less than the idea of talking to the Scholar.

"I owe you one," I said, turning to leave. "But you'll have to take a rain cheque."

The Scholar caught my arm. "I know a way to call it even," he said. "Take me with you."

"You don't even know where I'm going," I pointed out.

"I believe I do," he said.

I considered turning him down because I didn't think I could spend much more time in the company of the Scholar without murdering him. But I needed all the help I could get, and the Scholar could be a useful person to have around for what I was planning next. Maybe I could use him as a sacrificial victim, if nothing else.

"Let's get out of here before we're locked in for the night then," I said.

The Scholar came close to smiling. I wondered if the world was ending.

We went outside, to the parking lot, and the Scholar shivered against the cold, which I'm mortal enough to admit gave me some small sense of satisfaction.

"Quickly," the Scholar said, "which way to your horse and carriage?"

This just kept getting better and better.

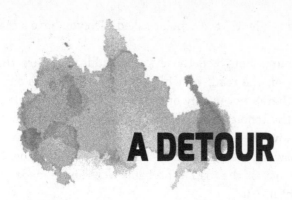

A DETOUR

It was night by the time we got on the motorway out of Oxford. A full moon rose on the horizon. The Scholar kept marvelling at the car—and all the other cars on the road—until I was tempted to make him sit in the back.

"I knew there were motor vehicles, of course," he said, "but I had no idea they were so advanced. Do we also have underwater submersibles like Jules Verne imagined?" Then he paused as a jet passed in front of the moon. "What on earth is that?" he asked.

I stepped on the gas and he sank back into his seat and turned pale as the edges of the road blurred. That was better. Now all I had to do was speed the entire way to our destination.

"Where exactly are we going?" he asked, as if reading my mind.

"Scotland," I said.

"Scotland?" the Scholar said. "Why would anyone ever want to go to Scotland?"

"How about you leave the whys up to me?" I said. "I don't really want to listen to questions the entire drive."

"Do you think the Forgotten Library is in Scotland?" the Scholar went on, ignoring me. "Imagine if the greatest English play of all time had its origins in Scotland." He chuckled until he choked. Maybe he didn't like the Royals any more than I did. It wasn't unreasonable. Most people who really knew the Royals didn't like them. Hell, most people who really knew the Royals didn't survive once they'd learned the truth about the Royals.

"I'm not taking us to the library," I said. "I'm taking us to the people that might be able to help us find it." Although "people" probably wasn't the best way of describing them.

"What do you mean, might?" the Scholar asked. "Do you have a plan or don't you?"

I didn't answer him, though, because I was suddenly aware that we were the lone car on the road. Which meant something was about to happen, because there's never only one car on the road in England. I started to slow and the Scholar looked around at the surrounding night.

"Are we there already?" he asked.

Before I could answer, a deer ran across the road in front of us. Or rather, it tried to run across the road. It probably would have made it if we hadn't driven right into it.

I managed to swerve enough that it went up on the hood and then over the side instead of through the windshield. And so I kept alive my winning streak of not being killed by a deer. The one thing I had going for me in all my lifetimes. I braked to a halt in the middle of the motorway because, as I've already pointed out, there was no one else on it. I got out of the car and looked around. Not even a set of headlights in sight. There was, however, the sound of a hunting horn in the woods bordering the road.

"Stay in the car," I told the Scholar.

"I don't even know how to extract myself from this device," he said.

"It's probably better we keep it that way," I said.

"Would you mind leaving me something to read?" the Scholar asked. "Perhaps that little book of yours? After all, it's of no interest to you given that its pages are blank."

I checked to make sure the book was securely in my pocket and then went around the front of the car to look at the deer.

It lay broken in the road, its head bent around at an angle it shouldn't have been able to bend at. Its dead eyes looked into my own. It resembled every other deer I'd seen that had been hit by a car, except for the fact it was wearing scraps of clothing: the remains of a shirt around its shoulders, a belt still wrapped around its torso. A black ring caught on one of its horns.

I sighed. I really just wanted to get out of this country.

I straightened up in time to greet the hunting party that burst out of the woods. They were a motley bunch: men in suits shredded by the branches of the forest, women in dresses stained with mud and with necklaces of brambles and thorns. They carried an assortment of weapons: spears, bows, arrows clutched in hands, even swords and axes. Some of them were on all fours, howling like dogs, maybe at the sight of the fallen deer, maybe at the pain of their bloodied hands and feet. I recognized them instantly. They were the fey.

They stopped at the sight of me and then stepped aside, to make room for Morgana and her entourage—Cobweb and Mustardseed and a few others whose faces I recognized but names I'd forgotten. The faerie were dressed in real hunting clothes—camouflage gear and facepaint—and rode horses. Like the deer, the horses wore scraps of clothing, and they were a little skittish, so I figured them for more fey. They rode up to me and stopped, and Morgana leaned forward and smiled at me.

"Darling," she said. "What a surprise meeting you here."

I resisted the impulse to step forward and kiss her muddy boot, but it took all my will. Instead, I scanned her entourage for Amelia. There she was at the back, dressed in the same hunting gear as the others. She didn't wear facepaint because her skin was already so grey. She studied me without blinking.

I looked around the road again, but there were still no other cars.

"I'm in the glamour," I said, stating the obvious.

"Of course you are, pet," Morgana said. And again I felt that sense of loss at not meaning more to her.

"Why am I in the glamour?" I asked.

She slipped to the ground from the horse and stepped over to the deer. She studied it while she talked to me.

"The question isn't why you're in the glamour," she said. "The question is where you're going."

I considered my answer, but I didn't see any point in hiding what I was doing from her.

"Scotland," I said.

"Why would you want to visit Scotland?" Morgana asked.

"That's what I said!" the Scholar shouted from the car, and Morgana looked at him, then raised an eyebrow at me.

"He's the last person I ever expected to see as a travelling companion for you," she said.

"It's a long story," I said.

"Well, you don't have much time, so you'd better get on with it," she said.

I looked around the scene. Nothing I saw there gave me much hope that things were going to get better for me anytime soon.

"I want to talk to the Witches," I said.

"The old crones?" Morgana said, raising both eyebrows now.

I didn't say anything. I didn't know how to explain my hunch that the only way to find a place that didn't exist might be to talk to the Witches, who lived in a place that didn't exist.

"Why not just visit the Globe again?" Morgana asked. "That seems easier than visiting Scotland. Or are you afraid that trick won't work twice?"

"I doubt that theatre is a safe place for me at the moment," I said. "I imagine the Royals will be watching it now. I imagine they're watching all of England right now."

Morgana looked down at the deer. She nudged it with a foot, but it didn't move. "The Royals have eyes in Scotland as well," she said. "No doubt they'll be watching the theatres there too."

"I'm not going to a theatre," I said.

"Of course you're not," Morgana said. "That would be too predictable for you."

I opted for the silence option again. I looked at Amelia and she looked back at me. It was just another typical father-daughter moment.

"You are traveling to Macbeth's Hillock," Morgana said, and I turned back to her. I wondered if maybe the ring I wore gave her the power to read my thoughts.

"Of course," she said. "The place where Macbeth met the Witches on his travels in the real world."

"*Macbeth* is just a story," I pointed out.

"All stories are birthed from life, are they not?" Morgana asked.

She was right. Macbeth's Hillock was my destination. It was the only other place besides Will's play where the Witches had lived. The only other place I knew about anyway. As such, it still had ties to them. At least I hoped it still had ties to them.

"What an interesting plot twist," Morgana said. "I believe we'll accompany you to see how this turns out."

"I don't think that's a good idea," I said, looking at the fey. I had a feeling this group would attract some attention, which might complicate my goal of travelling unnoticed.

"What you think is not of concern to me," Morgana said. She pulled a hunting knife from her belt and plunged it into the neck of the deer. Blood poured out and pooled around my feet.

"Let us continue the hunt," she said, and I had no doubt she was talking about the ghost.

She cleaned the knife on the rags of clothing still attached to the deer and then straightened up and whistled. Now headlights appeared down the road, followed quickly by the sounds of engines. I turned to watch the vehicles approach.

It was a faerie caravan. A trio of motorhomes chained together, with the roofs cut off to reveal what appeared to be a pub inside them. There were more fey and faerie, drinking wine from goblets and eating haunches of meat that I sincerely hoped were not from deer like the one at my feet. There was a band playing in the main area of one of the motorhomes, and fey dancing in another. Puck buzzed around the motorhomes on a motorcycle with a sidecar that held a woman with a donkey's head. A tanker truck followed the other vehicles, and I could tell from the smell that it was filled with faerie wine rather than fuel.

Yes, we wouldn't attract any attention at all.

I looked back at Amelia, but she was climbing into the motorhomes with the rest of the faerie and fey. The horses were gone now, replaced by men and women wearing rags and dazed expressions. It didn't look like there was room for them all, but they piled in until I was the only one left standing on the road, the dead deer still at my feet.

I considered the full moon for a moment and then walked back to the car. It started again despite the damage to its front end. I was almost disappointed.

"Are they coming with us?" the Scholar asked, frowning back at the faerie.

"It appears that way," I said.

"That doesn't strike me as wise," the Scholar said. "What if they were to do something to the books in the library?"

"I don't think they're interested in the books," I said.

The Scholar settled back into his seat. "Well, we shouldn't have any problems then," he said.

"What could possibly go wrong?" I agreed.

I put the car into gear and we headed for Scotland to find the Witches.

A SURPRISE APPEARANCE BY NEW PLAYERS

The drive to the north probably took as long as such trips normally take, but it felt longer thanks to having the Scholar as a passenger. We stayed on the highway despite the curious nature of our caravan. None of the drivers who passed us now that we were out of the glamour spared us a second glance, so I assumed Morgana had managed some sort of sleight to disguise our appearance. I wondered what we looked like. A long-distance lorry, perhaps? Or maybe just a row of weary travellers, looking for a place to rest their heads for the night.

The weather in the north was the same as it always is: dreary, with a chance of deepening gloom. We left the highway in favour of a series of ever-smaller roads, eventually finding ourselves on a pitted, one-lane strip of asphalt that was barely more than a walking trail. We cruised through farmers' fields until we reached our destination and then pulled over to the side as best we could.

Macbeth's Hillock was unremarkable, little more than a pleasant, grass-covered swelling of earth amid the fields. Most people wouldn't look twice at it if they drove past and didn't know what it was. In fact, most people probably wouldn't look twice at it if they drove past and *knew* what it was. But most people didn't know about all the blood that had been spilled on that hill.

"This is it?" the Scholar asked, unbelievingly. "It's rather unremarkable. The illustrations I've seen in books have made it seem much more dramatic."

"You don't really want to see it when it's dramatic," I said.

"There are variations in the illustrations, of course," the Scholar went on. "For instance, the Biltling Parchments show a craggy, almost cliff-like hill, complete with lightning, while the Encyclopedia Goblinus shows a warren of tunnels. . . ."

I got out of the car as quickly as I could and went over to join Morgana and the faerie as they disembarked from their vehicles.

"I've been thinking about all the losses from your court," I told Morgana. "You probably need a few replacements. You should take the Scholar."

Morgana smiled at me. "I wouldn't wish him on you, let alone my court," she said.

We looked at the hill. It was shrouded in mist and the area was getting gloomier by the second.

"Let's get on with it," I said, even though the Witches were among the last people I wanted to see at the moment.

So our merry company set across the field, singing and whistling and toasting each other with mugs and beer glasses and bottles. My shoes were soaked through almost immediately because of the wet ground, but I didn't bother complaining. I knew I'd have much more to complain about shortly.

That didn't stop the Scholar from expressing his irritation though.

"I say, is it always so dreary outside?" he said, frowning at the ground, the sky and everything in between. "I don't know why people ever bother to leave the library."

I quickened my pace and left him to mingle with the fey.

Morgana caught up to me as we neared the hill. "I would ask you your plan," she said, "but I know you better than that."

I smiled at her and then the smile faded from my face as we reached the bottom of the hill and the figures came over the other side.

They weren't the Witches. There were far too many of them for that—at least a dozen. And for the most part they resembled human beings even less than the Witches. There was Anubis and his staff, only the darkly glowing ankh was now a darkly glowing scythe blade. A bronze woman in a dress of metal plates, with four breasts and six arms, a sword in each hand. A stone man in a linen robe whose face bore an uncanny resemblance to the figures on Easter Island. Something that was either a sasquatch or a cross between a man and a bear, with long claws and even longer fangs. A man thing who seemed to be made entirely of red clay. A black woman who stood at least ten feet tall and wore ropes wrapped around her body and carried a bone spear. A creature with white fur who was surrounded by a dusting of snow that made it hard to see. I could go on, but it doesn't matter. The point is there were too many of them.

We stopped, and the rest of the faerie and fey stopped behind us. All except the Scholar, who came up to stand between Morgana and me.

"And who might these new players be?" he asked, scowling his fiercest welcome at them.

I looked around the field for a way out, but there wasn't one. The mist curled around us now, hiding us from the road. I sighed.

"The Black Guard," I said. I didn't bother introducing them. To speak the names of some of the Black Guard was to give them power. Also, I didn't even know all their names.

And then a skeleton pushed its way through the crowd on top of the hill to look down at us. The skull grinned at me and I shook my head as I recognized it.

"Just the man I've been looking for," Marlowe said.

Being hunted down by the Black Guard was a bad turn of events, even by my standards. The only thing that would have made it worse would have been if some of the Royals had come with the Black Guard. Thankfully, the Royals didn't like to stray too far from the castle and its catacombs these days. That's why they used the doppelgängers for the public appearances.

But this was still bad enough.

Morgana murmured something in the faerie tongue, and I heard her court go quiet behind me. Maybe she was telling them to get ready for a fight. Not that I held out much hope of the faerie being able to handle the Black Guard. They were tricksters, not warriors. Or maybe Morgana was just taking odds on what particular tortures were in store for me once the Black Guard spirited me back to the Royals' dungeons. I shuddered at that. One trip to the dungeons was bad enough. I didn't care to experience a second visit. Not in this lifetime or any of the others that would come after it.

The Black Guard came down the hill and circled us. Anubis stopped near me and I nodded at him. He didn't nod back. I didn't know who the others were specifically, but it didn't matter. They were all equally bad news in their own ways.

I shook my head at Morgana in case she was having suicidal thoughts about attacking. Then I turned my attention back to Marlowe as he clattered to a stop in front of me. Skeletons are a noisy lot when they move around. I doubted these were his original bones. Like I said earlier, even I didn't know where all the pieces of Marlowe had been hidden. But as Frankenstein had proven, you don't need the original pieces to make a body.

"So you're working for the Royal Family again," I said.

"I never stopped working for them," he said. "I had some peace in death, where they mostly left me alone. But then you raised me and put me back in their thrall again. And now here we are."

"So I have no one but myself to blame for this," I said, nodding. The same as it ever was.

"I'm sure it's just one regret in a lifetime of them," Marlowe said. "I imagine you'll forget it in a century or two."

I doubted that but kept my thoughts to myself. Clearly, I had to be careful what I said around him now.

"I didn't think the Royals would have this place under surveillance," I told him. "To be honest, I'm surprised the Witches allowed it."

Marlowe shrugged, which involved more clattering. "Where else would you go?" he asked. "It's clear you need the Witches to solve your little problem, and yes, every theatre in the kingdom is now under surveillance. That left you with only one option."

"It sounds like you know my thoughts better than I do," I said.

Marlowe tilted his skull in a way that made me think he was smiling. Or maybe grimacing. "I've known you for centuries. We are more alike than you realize, you and I."

I nodded my agreement. "It seems we're both monstrosities that can't ever truly be killed," I said.

"If you carry on like this, you might hurt my feelings," Marlowe said.

"I'll try to remember that when I'm in the dungeon," I said.

"Who said anything about dungeons?" Marlowe asked. "We are here to extend our hand in friendship."

I turned to Morgana. "You see these guys too, right?" I said. "I'm not just hallucinating them? Because what he said doesn't make any sense."

Marlowe took a step closer and held up his bony palms, as if to show he meant no harm. Or maybe to order an attack. It's hard to really read a skeleton's body language.

"The Royal Family wishes to put past quarrels aside for the moment and help you in your journey," Marlowe said.

I stared at him. Morgana stared at him. The faerie and fey stared at him.

"Splendid," the Scholar said. "Let us proceed then and get out of this miserable weather before I start to grow mould."

I gave him a look that deepened his scowl, then turned back to Marlowe.

"I have to confess I'm having trouble following this turn of events," I said.

"I have no doubt of that," Marlowe said, gazing out across the fields, which were almost entirely shrouded in mist now. "Perhaps it would make things clearer to remind you of how important Shakespeare is to the legacy and continued standing of England in the world. Obviously, any threat to Will's works, such as a haunting, is a threat to England itself. And the Royal Family cannot abide that. They're willing to bury the past to solve this problem."

For once, I didn't have a witty comeback.

"We'll provide assistance in your mission," Marlowe said, looking back at me. "Lead us to the ghost, and we will ensure it threatens no one ever again."

I willed myself not to look at Amelia. I was relatively certain I hadn't said anything to Marlowe about her, and I didn't want him thinking she was anything more than just another of the faerie.

"I don't imagine we can politely decline your offer of help?" I said, and Marlowe chuckled.

"Not politely or otherwise," he said. "Although I don't blame you for trying."

I eyed the Black Guard once more. They showed no signs of being any less fierce or deadly for all the talk of friendship. Anubis bared his teeth at me. The yeti thing seemed to have grown ice spikes all over its body as we'd been speaking. The refugee from Easter Island curled his hands into fists, with the sound of grating rocks.

"So what happens once we've made sure the world is safe for Shakespeare again?" I asked. "You'll just let me go on my merry way?"

Marlowe gave a rattling shrug. "Such decisions are not mine to make," he said. "We are merely the stars' tennis balls."

"Struck and banded which way please them," I said, finishing the line.

"Ah, Webster," the Scholar sighed, like he was dreaming about a long-forgotten meal.

I nodded at Marlowe. He'd done me a favour in a way by not lying about what was to come. He could have told me all was forgiven with the Royals. He could have told me it would be live and let live from now on. But he'd always had more integrity than that. I had no doubt his orders were to bring me in to the dungeons once the ghost problem was solved. At least he wasn't trying to hide that.

Well, one problem at a time.

"Let's get on with it then," I said. I didn't want any more surprises.

"One more thing," Marlowe said.

But of course there were always more surprises. Life wouldn't be what it is without surprises.

"We've brought along a little insurance," Marlowe said. "In case you attempt any trickery. Not that it's in your nature, of course. But if you should try anything. . . ."

He turned to look back up the hill. As if on cue, another of the Black Guard appeared, this one a spider-like creature around the size of a car. Alice sat on its back, wearing a little girl's dress and a top hat, and she waved at me. She wasn't bound or otherwise visibly confined, but she didn't look any too happy about the situation.

"She doesn't have anything to do with this," I told Marlowe.

"On the contrary," he said. "She's got everything to do with this. She's a friend of yours, and I know you are loyal to your friends. It's an admirable fault."

"There's really no reason to bring her along," the Scholar muttered, glowering at Alice. "She knows nothing. Less than nothing, in fact. Her knowledge is a dreadful mix of mistakes and outright fabrications." Like I said earlier, the Scholar and Alice don't get along. They argue a lot about books, if such a thing can be imagined.

"She would not be terribly missed then if something were to happen to her," Marlowe said, still looking at me. I didn't say anything.

The Scholar snorted and folded his arms across his chest, and dust billowed out over us. To his credit, though, he didn't agree with Marlowe. At least not audibly.

Marlowe offered his hand to me. "May you have a safe journey," he said. "And failing that, an honourable death."

I didn't really have any other choice, so I shook his hand.

"Here's to honourable deaths," I said.

At that, Marlowe nodded and the Black Guard started killing the fey.

THE FORGOTTEN LIBRARY

The Black Guard cut down, impaled or otherwise killed a dozen fey before I could even react. The woman with six arms was a whirlwind of blades. The stone man smashed his fist into a fey and a couple of men standing nearby fell as well from the shockwave. I couldn't see what the yeti thing did because a flurry of snow masked its movement, but it left bleeding bodies behind.

"Stop!" I cried. My hands instinctively reached for a weapon, but I had nothing. I was growing careless in my old age. Anubis assumed a fighting stance and readied his staff anyway as he remained close to me. The black scythe blade flared a bit, like a fire that had found fresh kindling.

I took a few steps toward Amelia, to shield her with my body, but the Black Guard had already stopped their killing before the word even escaped my mouth. They stepped back and assumed their guard positions again as the faerie and fey drew knives and sharpened sticks and even a few guns from beneath their own clothing. For all the good it would do them.

"What is the meaning of this?" Morgana cried, turning on Marlowe, and he took a step back. The power of the faerie queen is not to be tested lightly, even if you've got the Black Guard in your corner. I took the moment to glance at Amelia. She looked unmoved by everything that had just happened. She didn't even look at me. She just gazed off into the distance, as if thinking about something else.

"Unless I'm mistaken, you need blood to summon the Witches," Marlowe said. "Now you have blood."

"A thimble full would have sufficed," I said, looking back at him.

"Now you have extra in case something goes wrong," Marlowe said. I knew the deaths were also a message. If I tried any tricks, there'd be more deaths to follow.

But I didn't want to try any tricks. I didn't want any more dead faerie or fey on the ground. I didn't want Amelia or Alice or anyone else to join their ranks. And the truth was, I didn't mind the idea of Marlowe and the Black Guard tagging along with us now that they were here. We might need all the help we could get in dealing with the ghost problem. It was what happened after we dealt with the problem that I was concerned about.

I shrugged and put it out of my head for the moment. There'd be plenty of time for dealing with that later. I hoped.

I took another look at the bodies soaking the ground with their blood. Then I pushed past Anubis and walked up the hill to stand beside Alice and the giant spider thing. Alice smiled at me and the spider snapped its multiple sets of mandibles together and drooled some thick substance that melted the ground beneath it.

"Sorry I got you into this," I said to Alice.

"That's all right," she said, patting the spider thing on its back like it was some sort of pet. "I'm kind of curious about how this story ends anyway."

"You and me both," I said.

Then her eyes went wide and she looked all around. "What if it doesn't end?" she whispered.

I didn't want to think about that, so I took a few steps away from her and looked out into the mist. I said the words that summoned the Witches, low enough that hopefully no one else would hear. Despite the differences the Witches and I sometimes had, I didn't want other people bothering them. They were just being true to their nature when they did things like toss me into boiling cauldrons. I knew they couldn't help themselves.

I didn't bother trying to write the name of the play on a piece of paper or anything ritualistic like that this time. I figured there was no need in this place. I also didn't bother going down to the bodies for blood. There was enough blood in the air.

There must have been more than enough blood, because it didn't take long at all for the Witches to arrive. One minute it was just empty mist all around, the next the mist thickened into a dense fog and the Witches came out of it and circled me.

"Something wicked this way comes," one of the Witches breathed into my ear.

"A deed without a name," another of the Witches said.

"Double, double toil and trouble," the third Witch said.

"Let's skip the drama and get right down to it," I said. I took out the book and showed it to them. "I need to get back to the library where this came from," I said. "The only problem is it doesn't exist, at least not in our world. Kind of like the play you live in. But I think you know how to get there. You helped Shakespeare find it, didn't you?"

"Alas, poor Will," one of the Witches said.

"We knew him well," another said.

"We showed him the path to Hell," the third one said.

"We all make our own paths," I said. "Can you help us find the Forgotten Library or not?"

"Only one other has come to us to seek the way," one of the Witches said.

"One other who no longer looks upon the day," another one of the Witches said.

"One other who is dead to stay," the third Witch said.

So I'd been right about how Will had found the Forgotten Library. He always had been a crafty one.

"I'm going to take that as a yes," I said. "Name your price." I took a deep breath and waited. This part could get ugly.

Instead, the Witches drifted back away from me, disappearing into the mist again.

"Here is the way to an unknown land," one of the Witches said.

"Here is the way to a forgotten land," another of the Witches said.

"Here is the way to an unread land," the third Witch said.

Then they were gone, the only sign they'd ever been there a whisper drifting out of the mist.

"Come like shadows, so depart," they said.

Marlowe climbed the hill to stand at my side and look after the Witches.

"Did your little magic trick work?" he asked.

I stared into the mist. I couldn't see a thing. "I have no idea," I said. That had been my least painful experience with the Witches so far. It was almost like they were eager to fulfill my wish. So eager they hadn't even demanded anything in return. That didn't bode well.

I put the book back in my pocket and walked forward a bit. That was when I saw it. Another book lying in the grass. The copy of *Alice's Adventures Under Ground* that Alice had destroyed in the British Library.

"What is it?" the Scholar cried behind me. "You should probably let an expert examine it."

Marlowe stepped up to my side. "Indeed, what have you found?" he asked.

I looked deeper into the mist. I saw a couple more books lying there at the edge of my vision. One was charred almost to nothing. The other was so warped from the elements I couldn't make out anything on the cover.

"I think it's the way to the Forgotten Library," I said and started forward. "Don't let the Scholar touch anything," I added. "We might need those books to find our way back."

More books were scattered on the ground past the others. Some folios and what looked like ancient bibles and even a few confessionals. I thought I recognized a number of them from Baal's library, which had burned when I'd torched his home. They lay there as if someone had emptied out a box and simply walked away. Then there were even more as we went. A pile of them that rose to knee height on one side of us. Then another pile that rose to waist height on the other. Then stacks of them that formed walls on either side of us, rising slowly as we went, to chest height and then shoulder height and then towering over our heads. There were burning books in their midst, and others soaking wet or covered with mud or mould. More than a few were bloodstained.

"Where are we?" Morgana asked somewhere behind me.

"We are entering the Forgotten Library," I said. It was just like the other times I'd found myself in this place. Only this time I was alive. I hoped it would make a difference.

The ground gave way to a floor of books, and we walked upon their torn and faded covers. Then we passed through an arch made of books, and the sky on the other side was gone, replaced by more books.

"Why, truly this is Heaven," the Scholar sighed.

"Heaven is a library of the books that are," Alice said from somewhere distant. "Not the books that aren't."

"We are all far from Heaven," Marlowe muttered, and I was inclined to agree with him.

The hallway grew wider as we went, until it was like a great hall of the sort you would see in a palace. More hallways began to branch off from it, winding away in what looked like random paths. There were more books than I could count here. There were more books than I could imagine in the library.

"Perhaps we should split up and go our separate ways," the Scholar suggested. "To better explore this place."

"We'll stay together," Marlowe said, "until we find what we need."

I looked over my shoulder and saw the Black Guard forming a perimeter around the others, forcing them into the middle of the hall. The spider Alice rode was scuttling along the ceiling. She still sat on its back, but she was sitting upside down now. She waved at me and didn't seem to notice the Scholar glowering at her. I looked in front of us again and carried on.

"Which path do you think will lead us to our prize?" Marlowe asked.

"I suspect the only one who knows the answer to that is Will," I said. "We'll just have to find our way as best we can."

We came to what appeared to be a statue of a man reading a book in the middle of the hall. The statue was giant, twice the size of the largest Black Guard, and also made of books.

"There are more mysteries between heaven and hell than the mind can fathom," Marlowe said, gazing at the figure.

"If you don't mind, I'm not really in the mood to talk philosophy," I said as I went past the statue.

Marlowe chuckled. "What form of conversation shall we pass the time with then?" he asked.

"I've been thinking things over," I said.

"I suspected you would be," Marlowe said. "Although I'll tell you now it will change nothing."

"I don't think you came up with the idea that I would travel to Macbeth's Hillock to seek out the Witches all on your own," I said. "I think you were waiting for us because someone must have tipped you off."

Marlowe grinned that skullish grin of his at me and nodded. "It's true," he said. "We never would have found you on our own. Whatever remains of our friendship compels me to tell you that you have a spy in your midst."

I looked over my shoulder at the Scholar, and the Scholar scowled back at me. "I'm sure the Royal Family has many fine texts to tempt me," he said, "but even they do not have a collection like this library. I would not have risked my chance to explore it by turning you over to the fate you no doubt deserve."

"Not him," Marlowe said to me, wisely ignoring the Scholar. "Him."

I followed the direction he pointed with his bony finger, looking past the Scholar and into the crowd of faerie and fey.

Puck.

Puck grinned and shrugged as everyone stopped to stare at him.

"Sorry, but I couldn't help myself," he said.

"In his defence, I believe the sprite tells the truth," Marlowe said. "He's a creature of pure mischief and could no more pass up the opportunity to sow chaos than you could to steal grace from an angel."

"I'm no sprite!" Puck said indignantly.

"Not yet," Morgana said in a hard tone of voice she usually reserved for me. I felt suddenly and strangely jealous of Puck. "Put him in irons."

Cobweb and Mustardseed and a few other faerie fell upon him, and within seconds Puck was shackled and on his knees.

"It's in my nature!" he protested. "You know that."

"I know, my pet, I know," Morgana said, her voice back to normal, as if her mood had already passed. "Now hush." She nodded at the woman with the donkey's head, who stepped close and pulled a needle and thread from her purse. The donkey woman sewed Puck's mouth shut so quickly her hands were a blur. And then Puck had nothing to say at all.

Morgana looked at me, but I turned away and kept on walking. What else was there to do, after all?

We went past a tree made of books and then what looked like a fountain of books frozen in mid-splash. The architect, if there was one, had classic tastes.

The Scholar sidled up to Marlowe as we went down the hall. He whistled a tuneless tune, then cleared his throat several times.

"What is it?" Marlowe sighed.

"I must admit I am curious about the rumours of your collaboration with Shakespeare," the Scholar said to him.

"There was no collaboration," Marlowe said, looking back at the passage of books in front of us.

"Of course, of course," the Scholar said, nodding. "I would have known if such a text had been written. But discussions of the possible text, on the other hand—"

"There were no discussions of a collaboration either," Marlowe said.

"I understand," the Scholar said, rubbing his hands together and engulfing us in a cloud of dust. "Such important playwrights as yourselves couldn't be seen in formal discussions regarding a matter like that. Everyone knows the treaties it would violate."

I didn't know anything about those treaties but I refrained from commenting. Let Marlowe suffer.

"There were no discussions, formal or informal," Marlowe said, grinding his teeth together. "Will and I never had any interest in working together."

The Scholar didn't say anything for a moment, and I thought maybe Marlowe had got off lucky. But his peace didn't last any longer than mine where the Scholar was involved.

"But surely, from time to time, you imagined what a play written with him might be like," the Scholar said.

"No," Marlowe said.

"No, no, of course not," the Scholar said, nodding again, this time so hard his entire body shook. "No artist wants to admit being influenced by another."

Marlowe looked around as if searching for help. I stared straight ahead and didn't meet his gaze. He'd earned this for betraying me.

"So perhaps you could imagine *now* what a collaboration with Shakespeare might have been like?" the Scholar said.

Marlowe even looked to the heavens, but we both knew there was nothing there that would save him.

The Scholar reached beneath his coat and pulled out a piece of crumpled paper and a tooth-marked pencil. The paper looked like a page torn from one of the books in the Oxford library.

"It would be best for you to write down your ideas," the Scholar told Marlowe. "So you don't forget them."

Marlowe strode past us, leading the way now, but the Scholar just followed him, still holding out the pencil and paper.

"Yes, we really should find someplace private to sit down and discuss your ideas in detail," he said.

I used the moment to drop back to Morgana's side and I walked with her for a time.

"It appears we're entering our final act," she said, as we gazed at some picture frames made of books on the walls. The frames held jumbles of more books, of course.

"You don't have to be," I said. "Why don't you take your court back into the glamour?"

"What would that solve?" she asked.

"It would keep you alive," I pointed out.

She shook her head. "You mortals are so limited in your thinking," she said. "Besides, we would miss all the fun if we did that."

"You must be enjoying this," I said.

"It does have its entertaining diversions," she said, "but I would prefer our entertainment to be of the non-haunted variety."

"I meant you must be enjoying my suffering," I said. I gestured at the Black Guard and the strange stacks of books that surrounded us. Then I looked at Amelia. "I have to admit, you could not have inflicted a worse punishment upon me than to raise her and make me lose her once more."

"If you think I birthed Amelia to punish you, then you are as dimwitted as Puck," Morgana said.

I glanced back at Puck, who was clearly within earshot. He capered along behind us, not seeming to mind the insult.

"If I'd wished to punish you, I would have made you one of the fey," Morgana said. "As I did. If I'd wished to punish you, I would have made you love me. As I did. If I'd wished to punish you, I would have claimed your soul as mine. As I did. But I did not birth Amelia to punish you."

I looked at her now. She looked more fiery than usual. Something I'd said had upset her. I wanted to fall to my knees and beg for forgiveness.

"If you must name it, call it a favour and not a punishment," Morgana said. "A favour for the favour you did me."

I tried to remember what I could possibly have done to help Morgana, but I couldn't recall a single thing.

"I don't have a clue what you're talking about," I admitted.

She suddenly turned on me and just like that there was a knife at my throat.

"You could have left me at the mercy of Arthur, but you didn't," she said.

I glanced around and saw the Black Guard watching, but they made no move to intervene. Up ahead of us, Marlowe had turned to watch, too. The Scholar babbled on in his ear about something, but I could not make out the words from here. It didn't seem as if Marlowe was listening anyway.

"You stopped Arthur from slaying me," Morgana went on, digging the blade of the knife into my throat. "You saved my life. Unlike the rest of those louts, you had the conscience of a true knight. Even when drunk."

"So birthing Amelia from the dead was your way of repaying me?"

I said. Faerie logic is a struggle to understand at the best of times, but this was a new one.

Morgana hissed at me and then shook her head and stormed after Marlowe and the Scholar. She didn't put the knife back in its sheath.

I couldn't help but follow. I wanted her to keep talking to me, even if it meant a knife at my throat. I wanted to keep hearing her voice. But then we came across the burning chamber.

The hallway entered a room where every book that made up the walls and floor and ceiling was burning. In the centre of the room rose what looked like an altar of flaming books, and on top of this a single tome blazed away, its fire raging more intensely than the others'. The flames didn't stop me from recognizing it.

"Are you seeing what I'm seeing?" I asked Marlowe, who had stopped in the entrance to the room and was staring at the book burning atop the other books.

"The Nameless Book," he whispered.

So this is where it had gone after we'd burned it that night in London. An impossible book in an impossible place.

"I really need to stop getting involved in other people's problems," I sighed.

The hallway continued on the other side of the room, but obviously I wasn't eager to step into the flames. I wondered if Will had come this way and what he had done if so.

Marlowe kept staring at The Nameless Book, like he wanted to go in there and start reading it amid the flames. If I were a true friend of his, I'd have dragged him away. But he'd shown me the state of our friendship, so I left him there and walked back a bit to join the others, who had stopped at a wise distance.

Which is how I found myself standing beside Amelia, unwatched by Marlowe or the Black Guard, who were all fixated by The Nameless Book.

"I'm sorry," I said to her. I rubbed the spot on my throat where Morgana had pressed her knife. My fingers came away with a bit of blood on them. "I don't really know what else to say." There were so many things I had to apologize for, after all.

Amelia just looked at me with that dead gaze of hers.

"Tell me about my mother," she said.

"Your mother," I said.

"My flesh-and-blood mother," she said. "Not my birth mother."

I thought about how to answer that. But there was no real way to tell her the things I knew she wanted to hear.

"She was my grace," I said, and my voice broke on the words. That was all I could really say about that.

After a moment, Amelia nodded like she understood.

"You couldn't have saved us," she said.

"I could have tried if I'd known what was coming," I said, although I didn't really believe that. Not anymore. How could I have foreseen the death that would claim Penelope and Amelia? No one ever sees death coming until after it's already arrived.

"What would you have done?" she asked.

"I don't know," I said. "Something. Anything."

"The only thing that could have saved us from the grave is a god," she said. "But you aren't a god anymore."

"I never was," I said. There was so much more to talk about with her, but this was neither the time nor the place, so I changed the subject.

"How has your life been with the faerie?" I asked.

Amelia considered that for a moment before answering. "Have you ever lived in the glamour?" she asked.

"Not as long as you," I said. I decided not to tell her about the time Morgana had enslaved me and kept me in the glamour like her plaything. There are some things you just don't discuss with your daughter.

"It's like a dream that never ends," Amelia said. "Or at least I imagine it's what a dream is like. I've never had one."

I registered that in silence and let her go on.

"It is tolerable enough in its own way," she said. "Morgana is kind to me. She treats me as well as she treats any of the faerie. As well as she could treat any child, I suppose. And they accept me as one of their own. I am more faerie now than human. Perhaps I have always been such."

I looked away, then back at her. I remained silent.

"I would like to wake," Amelia said. "I would like to live."

I wanted to hug her then, to tell her I would die to make sure she lived if I needed to. But I didn't want to give anything away in case any of the Black Guard were watching. I didn't want Marlowe or the Royals to know how important Amelia was to me. So I did nothing.

They say being a father is hard. They have no idea.

I went back to Marlowe. He was still staring at The Nameless Book. He had taken a few steps forward and was standing in the burning room now. He didn't seem to notice the fires, but they didn't appear to be harming him. They only seemed to burn on the books. It was that kind of place.

"We should keep moving," I told him. "This is not what we came for."

"Perhaps we should take it with us," Marlowe murmured.

I looked at the book, then away before it could catch my eye.

"I don't think that's a good idea," I said. "That book has gotten us into enough trouble already."

"We were so much younger then," Marlowe said.

"And we're so much wiser now," I said. "Or something, anyway."

"Imagine its power if we could learn how to use it properly," Marlowe said.

"That's exactly what I'm talking about," I said.

"It could be a formidable weapon indeed," he said.

"I think we have enough weapons," I said, glancing around at the Black Guard.

"We don't know what we will face when we find the ghost," Marlowe said.

"I think that book is the kind of weapon that will destroy us all if we use it," I said. "I think we probably got off lucky last time."

He didn't say anything to that, but he didn't exactly look discouraged either.

"Perhaps it would destroy us," he said. "At least we'd all be free then."

I gave him another moment, and then I started walking. I stepped into the burning room and carried on. The flames licked at my feet but I felt nothing at their touch. I gave The Nameless Book a wide berth and didn't look at it again. I crossed over to the hallway on the other side.

I didn't say anything else to Marlowe. He'd follow me with the Black Guard or he wouldn't. It was his choice. And to be honest, I didn't really see how it made any difference one way or another.

The Scholar was the next to follow. He came to my side and looked down the hallway.

"Are we close then?" he asked. "I am not fond of all this walking."

I looked at him. "How come you're not interested in that book like the others?" I said, nodding my head in the direction of The Nameless Book. It was definitely one a kind, after all. The sort of thing the Scholar usually coveted.

The Scholar didn't even glance behind us. "That thing? That's not a book," he said.

"What is it then if not a book?" I asked.

He shrugged. "I have no idea," he said. "There's books and there are the things that aren't books. Why would anyone care about the things that aren't books?"

Words of wisdom, I reflected, as I started walking again.

One by one, the others followed me through the burning room and into the hall on the other side. Even Marlowe, although he was the last.

YOU ARE NAUGHT

We continued down the hallway, to who knew where. Eventually Marlowe made his way back up to my side. His experience in the burning room must have made him thoughtful, because he started spilling his conscience to me.

"You're no doubt wondering why I returned to the Royals' service after you raised me instead of hiding in some secret part of the world," he said. He looked around us. "Some place like this, maybe."

"It's what I would have done," I said. "Hiding, I mean. But then I never would have been in their service."

"And I never would have done many of the things you have," Marlowe said. He knew me better than most, and I had to admit his words stung a bit.

"You have me there," I said. "But I thought we had a better relationship than this. The number of times I've saved your life. The wine and women and everything else we've shared." I shook my head. "I should have known better. Everyone has their price." I'd died enough times at the hands of so-called friends to learn that.

"Not everyone has your free will," Marlowe said.

"I'm not exactly doing anything of my free will these days," I said.

We passed under a stairway of books that ended several feet in the air above our heads. There was no doorway at its end, but we kept an eye on it anyway, just in case.

"You had the choice to just walk away from the Royal Family all those years ago," he said. "So what if they swore to have their vengeance on you? It doesn't matter. What happens if they capture you? They'll eventually grow tired of torturing you in some dungeon somewhere. It might take hundreds of years, but we both know that is nothing to eternity. And you have all eternity to wait. One day you'll figure out how to escape."

You'll be free again. You'll always be free again. I never will be. I had to go back to the Royals. I am bound to be their servant. You have your curse. That is mine."

I shrugged. "Doesn't mean you had to turn me in," I pointed out.

"True," he said, laughing that rattling laugh of his.

"So what's your reward for doing it then?" I asked.

The hallway opened into another chamber ahead of us, and we slowed so we could finish our pleasant conversation before we encountered something else that should not be.

"Any reward I get won't be for locating you," Marlowe said. "My reward will be for stopping the ghost before it starts to haunt other productions outside of the faerie court. Will's legacy must be preserved for the good of England."

"Frankly, I can't see what interest you'd have in keeping Will's work alive and in performance," I said. "Especially if he didn't even write it in the first place. Your reputation would only stand to gain if theatres had to abandon his work because it was too risky to stage. They'd seek other plays from the same time. Like yours."

And then I understood Marlowe's motivation. I stopped and looked at him.

"So the Royals are going to give your work a greater role in the world in return for this little mission," I said. "What's it going to be, some sort of festival?"

Marlowe stopped as well, although he kept his eyes on the room ahead instead of looking at me. "Nothing like that," he said. "They have promised me nothing."

"I doubt very much you're in this for nothing," I said. "Not unless death truly has changed you."

"Nothing but a little ink," Marlowe said and continued forward again.

"Ah," I said. I had no choice but to follow.

"As you pointed out earlier, Will left his ink pot behind in this library when the ghost scared him away," Marlowe said. "The sole remaining supply of that ink anywhere, even in the impossible places. I do not know how much is left, but perhaps there will be enough for one more play."

"And how would the world learn of a new Marlowe play?" I asked. "After all, you've been dead for some time. It's not like you can just suddenly publish it."

"I imagine a scholar will stumble across it in a library somewhere," he said. "With a little help, of course. It will be the find of the century."

"Just don't let our Scholar find it," I said. I glanced back at the Scholar, who was muttering to himself while eyeing all the books around him. "Or it will be the loss of the century."

"Think of it," he went on. "A renaissance in Marlowe."

"I wish I could see that," I said, and I was telling the truth. I'd always admired Marlowe's work, and the truth be told, I thought him a superior playwright to Will in many ways even before I'd learned the truth about *Hamlet*. He could have delivered many more classic plays if he'd been given the chance. But few people are ever given the chance to live to their fullest potential.

Maybe we would have gone on spilling our souls to each other like that, but then we reached the next chamber. Thankfully, it wasn't burning, although enough books blazed here and there to illuminate the space. It was the room I'd woken in those other times I'd visited the Forgotten Library. There were the tables and chairs made of books, and there was the ink pot on its side and the quill, among the scattering of papers and other books Will had left behind.

I didn't see any sign of Polonius or Peaseblossom, though. The secret places where they'd erupted into the room from before had been covered with books again, so they just looked like the wall and floor once more. I decided to keep what I knew about those hiding places to myself. If everyone in our little group was going to have secrets, then I needed some of my own.

We came to a halt just inside the room and surveyed the scene. The Black Guard fanned out along the edges. I didn't know if it was to protect us or keep us imprisoned. The spider scuttled along the walls, Alice giggling on its back.

"Well, this looks like a place of some import," Marlowe said. His gaze settled on the ink pot. "Perhaps even the very spot *Hamlet* was written."

"Stolen, you mean," I said.

Marlowe ignored me as he went over to the table and picked up the ink pot. He looked inside it for a moment. He shook it and then upended it. Nothing flowed from it. He brought it to his lips like a bottle, but still nothing issued from it. The ink pot was empty.

"I guess it must have all spilled out when the ghost startled Will and he fled," I said. "That's a shame." I looked at the other books on the table. Who knew what else Will's ink had brought to life?

Morgana strode into the room and looked around. "Show yourself, ghost!" she cried. "Come out and face a queen more powerful than any king!"

"She's not much of one for subtleties, is she?" Marlowe observed, dropping the ink pot back to the table with a sigh.

"I think subtlety is an insult to the faerie," I said.

The ghost did not show itself, though. The dead, if they were here, stayed hidden and nothing possessed us.

Marlowe picked up the quill next, and I shook my head at him.

"As I also told you earlier, it's not the Black Quill," I said.

But as I watched, the quill began to darken in Marlowe's grip, turning from white to grey and then to a black as deep as night.

I thought again of Will's words that he would hide the Black Quill away in some place no one would ever find it upon his death. A place like the Forgotten Library.

"The Black Quill needs souls like you need grace," Marlowe said, staring down at the quill. "The life force of its user is its ink. When that ink runs dry, it is just another quill. Until it finds a new soul. One who can put it to the uses to which it was intended."

"Is a little bit of ink really worth your soul?" I asked.

"It depends on what you write with that ink," Marlowe said.

"No wonder there's a ghost haunting the play," Morgana said. "Magic ink. Soul-stealing quills. Frankly, I'm surprised a ghost is the only problem we have."

"But where is the ghost?" Marlowe asked, tearing his gaze away from the quill.

"That I don't know," I said. "I was dead the other times I visited here. Maybe that made the difference."

"Perhaps it is like the Witches then and needs a blood sacrifice," Marlowe said, nodding.

But he wasn't nodding at me. He was nodding at Morgana.

Anubis lunged at her back with his staff. The scythe was the black blade of a spear now. Morgana didn't even see the strike coming. But I did.

I threw myself in between them. And Anubis's staff sank into my chest as easily as if it were a blade.

I felt a great pain that filled every space within me and then turned into a lightness that lifted me up into the air. Anubis held me up on his staff, the glowing blade of it buried inside me and doing who knew what to my insides. He looked at me with those black eyes of his. I spat blood at him. Something like this happened every time we met.

Marlowe came over to gaze up at me suspended on the staff. "I suppose one soul is as good as another when it comes to sacrifice," he said. "My orders were to bring you back dead or alive, but I imagine it will be easier if you're dead."

I looked around at the others. The Scholar stumbled back, looking paler than usual. Murder wasn't his type of thing. The fey stared in confusion. The faerie looked on curiously, except for Puck, who appeared to be smiling despite his mouth being sewn shut. The Black Guard watched impassively. It was just another day at the office for them.

I don't want to tell you about the expression on Amelia's face.

And Morgana? I didn't know how to read her look as she stared at me on Anubis's staff. There was a black glow pulsing out of my chest now, in time with my heartbeat.

"It was the ring that made me do it," I said, spitting up blood.

"No it wasn't," Morgana said softly, and she was right. The ring made me love her and probably would have wanted me to save her. But it wasn't what had made me throw myself in between Anubis and her. I'd done it because of her words.

Because she'd told me she'd birthed Amelia as a favour to me.

"This is all very lovely but we must move things along," Marlowe said. "Your service will be remembered, but your friendship even more."

"This is treachery," Morgana said, and the softness was gone from her voice now.

"True," Marlowe said, glancing at her. "But no worse than what the faerie might do."

"Our nature leads us to trickery, not treachery," she said.

"You may wish to have this discussion with your dear sprite," Marlowe said, looking down at the Black Quill in his hand again. "For it concerns me not at all."

"You are naught," Amelia said, looking at me. "You are naught." I thought maybe she had lost her mind at the sight of my impending death.

Then there were sounds in the walls, of things stirring. The books shook and dust puffed out here and there, as if the walls were threatening to collapse.

"Ready yourselves for whatever may come!" Marlowe cried, and the Black Guard drew their weapons and bared their fangs and flexed their claws and so on. Marlowe grabbed one of the papers from the table and poised the quill over it.

"Promise me something," I managed to say to Morgana. I so desperately wanted to slide off the staff and into welcome death, to collapse to the floor and into the deepest of all sleeps. But I couldn't. I needed a few more seconds.

"Save your breath," Morgana said, her eyes locked on mine.

"I have nothing to save my breath for," I said. "I will be going away for a time. I want you to look after Amelia while I am gone."

Books began to fall from the walls and ceiling. More books erupted up from the floor.

"I do believe we are in the presence of a ghost," Marlowe said, sounding pleased with himself. He clapped me on the shoulder like we were friends again.

"I understand now you are the closest thing to family she has left," I said to Morgana.

Morgana didn't say anything, which was a first, so I carried on despite the black pulses from my chest spreading to my vision. I didn't have much time left.

"If you won't do it, at least find her a home—" I said, but now Morgana finally interrupted me.

"If she survives what is to come, I will look after her like she is one of my own," she said. And that was as much as I could ask from the queen of the faerie, I suppose.

My eyelids started to flutter shut despite my best efforts to keep them open. I wondered where I'd wake next. The dungeon underneath the Royals' palace? Or someplace worse? If there was someplace worse. Yeah, there was probably someplace worse. There was always someplace worse.

Then Amelia stepped forward, into my line of sight.

"I'll mark the play," she said.

Marlowe glanced at her. "What are you carrying on about, girl?" he asked.

Now I understood what she was doing. She was speaking lines from *Hamlet*. She was trying to save me, the only way she could. The only way anyone could now.

By turning my death into a scene from the play.

I put all my energy into speaking, and I spat more blood with the words. Black, black blood.

"Is this a prologue, or the posy of a ring?" I said, answering her with another line from *Hamlet*.

"Tis brief, my lord," Amelia said, softly.

And then the walls collapsed in a shower of books and the dead stumbled into the room from their hiding places. The bodies of men and women, faerie and fey, marked with the ugly slashes of swords or the mottled skin of poison or the burned flesh of fires. I saw Peaseblossom among their number, and Polonius. And all the dead from the theatre in Berlin. They stumbled forward and milled around us, as more erupted from secret graves in the floor or fell from the ceiling in showers of books.

"Mark me!" they all cried. "Mark me!" And the mist with its strange words came from their mouths.

Anubis shoved me off his staff with a foot to free up the weapon, and then I was gone.

But not before I grabbed Marlowe's skull as I fell and ripped it from his skeleton.

THE PLAY'S THE THING

I woke lying on books. I sat up and looked around. I was still in the same room. No more than seconds could have passed, because little had changed. There was a bloody, blackened hole in my chest, although it didn't hurt anymore. The dead were still emerging from their hiding places, the Black Guard were still readying their weapons, the Scholar was still screaming like a little girl. Marlowe's body had slumped to its knees but remained there, headless, the Black Quill useless in its hand. Morgana stared at me, speechless. I dared not look at Amelia to see what she thought.

"The devil take thy soul!" said a voice from my hand. I looked down to see I was holding Marlowe's skull, wreathed in fading letters.

"Whatever my fate, we're going to share it," I said to Marlowe. That is, that's what I tried to say. But the lines that came out of my mouth were entirely different once again.

"Take thy fingers from my throat," I said, "and hold off thy hand." And now the mist came out of my mouth as well. I didn't even bother trying to decipher the words it formed.

Then I cast Marlowe's skull from me, across the room. Or rather, some force took control of my body again and made me throw the skull across the room. It clattered on the ground and came to a rest, glaring back at me. I was possessed once more.

"What is the reason that you used me thus?" I said to Marlowe. Or rather, the ghost forced me to say. "I loved you ever, but it is no matter."

"Tis almost against my conscience," Marlowe said. More lines from *Hamlet*. He was being forced to say them as well.

So we were both possessed. I hadn't been sure if my little trick of grabbing Marlowe's skull would work or not. Whenever I'd died in the play before, I'd wound up here in the power of the ghost. When Amelia had started the play with me, I figured the same thing would probably happen again. I'd grabbed Marlowe because I thought maybe the possession would extend to anything that I was holding. The book Polonius had given me on that first visit here had travelled back with me, after all. And Marlowe was kind of dead to begin with anyway, so it was a bit of a two-for-one for the ghost.

Peaseblossom staggered up to us out of the crowd of the dead. "I am but hurt," he said.

The Black Guard with all the arms struck out with one of her blades and separated Peaseblossom's head from his body. The head fell to the ground and rolled across the books, staining them with its blood.

"To be or not to be," Peaseblossom's head said. "Aye, that is the question."

That seemed to trigger something with the Black Guard. They fell upon the dead in the room then. They struck them down with their blades and claws and massive stone fists. The dead fell, some of them in pieces, but didn't seem to notice their attackers. And they certainly didn't die again. They spouted more lines from the play even as they fell.

"I have to admit, this is delightful," Morgana said. Then she threw herself at Anubis with her knife and the room erupted into true chaos as the faerie court leapt into battle with the Black Guard.

I stared, powerless, as Peaseblossom's body walked over to Marlowe's skull and picked it up. The body shoved it onto the gushing stump of its neck and then turned to me.

"Mark me," Marlowe said. I could almost see him straining to look about for the quill. But it remained useless in the hand of his abandoned skeleton.

"I will," I said.

And then someone tossed rapiers from the melee, and we each caught one, even though I desperately didn't want to catch mine. The ghost threw us at each other, and our blades met.

"Mark me!" Marlowe roared again.

"Mark me!" I roared back at him.

All around us in the crowd, the dead uttered their own lines from the play.

"Things standing thus unknown, shall live!"

"Read on this book!"

"I have no life to breathe!"

I was able to manage a glance around the room, and I saw the Black Guard striking down not only scores of the dead, but also the faerie and the fey. Anubis and Morgana were involved in a leaping, whirling dance with their weapons, and then Amelia came out of the fray and threw herself onto Anubis's back, sinking a knife deep into his neck. Beyond her, Mustardseed ducked under the fists of the stone creature and lashed out with two blades dripping a foul-looking green substance, scoring sizzling gashes in the stone.

"I am dead," I said, words issuing from my mouth and circling my head.

"Never believe it," Marlowe said to me, hacking through those words at my head with the rapier blade. I had a feeling he wasn't fighting his possession now. In fact, I had a feeling he was encouraging the ghost to kill me. I dodged the blow and went for his stomach with my blade, but he blocked it. I wanted to hurry to Amelia's side to help her, but I could not. I had mostly lost control of my body with my death.

Anubis lashed backward with his staff, but Amelia ducked underneath it, supernaturally fast. It seemed she'd picked up a trick or two during her time in the faerie court. Morgana used the opportunity to dart in and slash Anubis on his snout and he howled at her. The sound threatened to shatter my eardrums.

"Thou livest," Marlowe said to me. "Report me and my cause."

"Tell my story," I said.

"Tell my story!" the dead all cried. And now the faerie and fey that the Black Guard had struck down were rising again. They joined the chorus of the dead, all of us shouting lines from *Hamlet*. The words came in no order or consistency, though. We all spoke the words of different characters, and different scenes. It was as if whatever possessed us was mad.

And we were powerless to do anything about it. We were as helpless as the ghosts I'd seen in the Tower of London, who were forced to play their roles over and over for the rest of eternity, unaware of the world around them.

And then I finally understood what was happening.

There was no ghost from the forgotten play haunting the faerie productions of *Hamlet*. The ghost was the forgotten play itself. Will's ink and maybe even the Black Quill had given life to the play, not merely one of its characters. And now the play was using the dead it killed in the faerie productions to act itself out again—to live! It was collecting a cast and audience for itself.

What was it the ghost at the Drury Lane theatre had said? *As long as I have my role, I am no more dead than you.*

Of course, that knowledge did me little good, as I was now trapped in the ghost play along with all the other dead. Unlike the other dead, though, I had one saving grace.

Marlowe and I came together a few more times, trading blows, and then I had my opportunity. Our blades crossed in a parry and we strained against each other, chest to chest, face to face. I still couldn't take control of my body back, but I didn't need it. All I needed was to touch him. And lo and behold, the back of my hand holding the rapier grazed his jawbone. It was all I needed.

I used that second to draw the grace back out of him, the grace that I'd used to grant him life back in that theatre props room. I wasn't doing anything that seemed to go against the stage directions of the play, so whatever was possessing me didn't appear to notice.

Marlowe, though, he definitely noticed. His eye sockets seemed to grow wider, as if he realized what was happening.

"O, I am undone," he cried.

And then the grace was within me and I resurrected.

THE FINAL ACT

I stumbled away from Marlowe atop Peaseblossom's body as life surged back into me.

"Here I lie, never to rise again," Marlowe sighed. He turned and waved his rapier at another of the dead, who seemed more than happy to engage him in battle.

"Mark me!" the dead all cried again.

I looked down at my chest and saw the wound Anubis had given me had already healed. But I couldn't afford to die again. I had no more grace left after I had drained Marlowe. If I died this time, I'd be trapped in the ghost play along with the other dead, for who knew how long.

I turned and saw Anubis reach back and grab hold of Amelia's arm. He threw her from him, into the midst of the battling faerie. A pile of them fell to the ground and Anubis rushed forward to finish her off, ignoring the bleeding wound in his neck Amelia had given him. But then Morgana was in his path, her knife in one hand and a newfound sword in the other.

"You will not have her," she said. "Not as long as any of my court remain!"

Anubis slashed at her head with the staff, and she brought the sword up to parry the strike. But the move was just a feint, as Anubis snapped at her arm with his jackal's jaws. She cried out as his teeth bit deep, and then he let out another eardrum-shattering howl and released her as I ran him through from behind with the rapier.

"You'll not have either of them," I said. "Not as long as I live!"

Anubis spun around to face me, ripping the rapier from my grip. Now I was weaponless. But then Morgana tossed me her sword and I caught it. She grabbed hold of my rapier and pulled it free of Anubis's back as he came at me with the staff that he'd already used to kill me once.

Her wound didn't seem to be slowing her down any, even though I could see black bone gleaming through the tears in her skin.

"I knew you'd return to me," Morgana said. "It takes more than death to stop you."

Her words of praise gave me heart, and I parried a half dozen blows from Anubis with cheer. That warm feeling inside me quickly faded when I took a look around to see how the battle was going, though.

The Black Guard were slaughtering everything in the room. They had struck down a good number of the faerie and fey now, but the dead just rose again, in the thrall of the play. The Black Guard were striking down the dead, too, but the wounds didn't seem to make any difference to the fallen.

I saw Polonius a few feet away, missing an arm. With the hand of his other arm, he held Marlowe's skull.

"I knew him!" he cried.

"To what base uses we may return," Marlowe said.

The headless body of Peaseblossom was wandering about, as if in search of its missing part, which I had lost track of. Others among the dead were acting out different scenes from *Hamlet*. None of them fought back against the Black Guard. It was as if the ghost possessing them wasn't aware of the Black Guard or didn't care about them. And why should it? The Black Guard were only giving the ghost a greater blood sacrifice and adding more cast members for it to use.

I resolved that if I ever got out of here I was going to have to do something to help the dead escape their fate. And then I'd figure out how to help the ghosts of the Tower rest at last, for this was not something anyone should have to endure.

Except for maybe Will. He had a lot to answer for.

Anubis snapped at me with his jaws, but I just slipped to the side, putting the dead Polonius in between us. I took the moment to deliver a kick to the headless body of Marlowe. I meant to break some of those bones, but they were made of sturdier stuff than that. The body just tumbled back into the melee, taking the Black Quill with it. I hoped no one else knew the quill for what it was.

"I still don't understand something," I said to Morgana. "You say you birthed Amelia to thank me for saving you. But I'll be the first to admit there were other times when I was not so charitable."

"Like the time you abandoned me in the goblins' caverns?" she asked.

She stabbed Anubis in the back with the rapier again, rather viciously I thought. He barely seemed to notice it this time, he was so intent on me.

"I knew you'd find your way out before they caught up to you," I said, backing up some more. I didn't have anywhere to go, but I needed to buy some time so I could figure out a plan of action that might yet save us. "Besides, you were going to do the same to me."

Anubis came after me but hesitated when the skull of Marlowe rolled out of the fray and into his path.

"How long will a man lie i' the earth ere he rot?" Marlowe cried.

Morgana pulled the rapier from Anubis's back once more, and this time he just swung the staff in a casual arc behind him to make her dance out of range. She bumped up against Mustardseed, who was backing away from the sasquatch thing with its claws dripping blood. Mustardseed had lost one of his blades and was clutching his side, but he was grinning like he was having the time of his life. I lost track of him when Anubis stepped around Marlowe's skull and came after me again.

I kept backing up because that elusive plan of action wasn't showing itself. But things were getting worse by the second. We didn't seem to be able to harm the Black Guard with our weapons, which didn't bode well for us escaping here alive, let alone putting an end to the haunting.

Then Cobweb somersaulted through the scene, blowing a handful of spider's silk at Anubis. The web covered his face and Anubis stumbled blindly to the side, clawing at himself in an attempt to see again. Cobweb flashed a smile at us and leapt back into the battle.

Polonius wandered after him, stopping briefly to pick up Marlowe again with his remaining hand.

Morgana strode up to me and waved the knife in my face. "Or do you mean the time you invited the dwarves to visit our court?" she asked, carrying on our conversation.

"To be fair, I didn't really know much about them then," I said. "I just thought they liked to drink."

A blade stabbed at her back from somewhere in the crowd, but she knocked it aside with the rapier without looking. I saw a veil of cobwebs covered the wound where Anubis had bit her on the arm.

"Or perhaps you mean the time you brought us the holy wine as a gift?" she asked.

"I didn't know it was holy wine," I said. "Just because I found it in an angel's lair—"

"And the other angels came looking for it," she said. "Is that one of those times you mean?"

"Yes," I said. "After all those . . . let's say misunderstandings, why would you still want to grant me any favours?"

She smiled at me. "Because you were almost faerie in those moments," she said, "and I couldn't help but feel some affection for you because of that."

I shook my head. "I don't know whether that's an insult or a compliment," I said.

I looked for Amelia again. She had risen from the ground and stood at the edge of a small group of surviving faerie and fey. The Scholar was among them, trying to bury himself under a pile of books. Puck was there too, unfortunately, and the woman with the donkey's head. I looked around for Alice and saw her still on the spider. It was clinging to one of the walls, seemingly entranced by the bubbles Alice was blowing from her mouth. Wherever they hit books they burst and the books crumbled into dust. There were more books behind them, though.

"Why do you continue to torment me then?" I said. "Why all the business with my soul and the ring and everything else?"

Morgana laughed. "I am still the queen of the faerie," she said. "I cannot help my nature any more than Puck can help his."

The Black Guard with all the arms came at us then, slashing at me with one sword and hacking at Morgana with another. We both dodged the blows, throwing ourselves backward. The Black Guard struck off Polonius's other arm with a third of its many blades, and Marlowe's skull fell to the floor again.

"O, I am slain," Polonius said, and wandered away. Marlowe just let out a long-suffering sigh.

"Well, I hope the fact that I died for you means we're even again," I said to Morgana. I jumped over a cut at my feet and then ducked a hack at my head a second later. The Black Guard hissed at me but I just nodded at her. I'd been on a battlefield or two in my lives, and it wasn't the first time I'd fought someone with an extra set of arms.

"Perhaps," Morgana said. "Until the next time." She turned her body sideways to slide nimbly between a double thrust from the Black Guard. Morgana slashed down with her knife and cut the wrist of one of the arms, and blood sprayed all over the three of us. The Black Guard dropped the sword from that hand and Morgana danced back again, smiling that evil smile.

I saw Mustardseed and Cobweb stagger out of the dead and into the remainder of the faerie court. Mustardseed was weaponless now and sporting a slash down one side of his face to match the wound in his side. Cobweb was missing his right hand. They both had mad grins on their faces, though.

I kicked the Black Guard's sword away while dodging another cut aimed at my head and parrying the thrust at my stomach. I glanced at Anubis but he was still struggling with the web.

"This is not going well," Morgana remarked, rather unnecessarily I thought.

"No," I agreed.

"If we are going to die, we should at least die at our daughter's side," she said.

"That sounds like as good a plan as any," I said. This time I didn't try to argue that Amelia wasn't her daughter. I figured she'd earned the right to say that.

I feinted at the Black Guard's throat and she brought up two blades in a double parry. But I just wanted those blades out of the way so I could dart past her, to the group of remaining faerie and fey. The Black Guard spun after me, and Morgana came around the other side, sliding under the Black Guard's other blades. We joined Amelia and the others at the same time. I gave Amelia a once-over to make sure she wasn't wounded. She had a few minor cuts, but nothing more serious than that. Still, that didn't matter much if we couldn't find a way out of here.

The Black Guard closed in on us in a tightening circle, smashing the dead out of the way as they came. So far we hadn't managed to kill one of them. They didn't even seem inconvenienced by the wounds we had given them. And now Anubis had freed himself of the web again. He came at me, growling. It was a sound that shook the room.

"I really hate these guys," I sighed.

"The book!" the Scholar cried from under the pile of books he'd made to hide himself. "Give me the book before it's too late!"

"You'll have plenty of time to read when we're all dead," I said. But his words gave me an idea. "Alice!" I cried. "I need you!"

Alice slipped off the spider's back and slid down the wall to the floor. The spider remained where it was, still entranced by all the bubbles floating around it, as Alice skipped through the crowd to us. She went through the legs of the yeti thing that was surrounded with all the snow. It smashed its hands down at her, and there was a shower of ice and blood.

"Alice!" I screamed.

But then she came out of the snow, jumping on one foot in some invisible game of hopscotch. The Black Guard stared down at what it had struck. It was the remains of a snowman that had been wearing identical clothes to Alice. The Black Guard was now surrounded by a ring of snowmen, all in the form of Alice, all wearing the same identical clothes.

Alice hopped to a stop in front of us and curtseyed. "This story is very exciting!" she said. "I don't know how it's going to end. I don't think the author even knows how it's going to end!"

"Why don't you be the author and end it for us?" I said.

Alice clapped her hands. "I know just what it needs!" she said. "More books!"

Morgana shook her head and raised her blades to the oncoming Black Guard, who were almost within range now. "This is just like that time with the giants," she said.

"I told you before, I didn't know you guys had a history," I said.

I pulled Alice close, so none of the Black Guard could reach her with their weapons.

"Alice, you know how you travel between libraries?" I said.

She nodded. "I remember it," she said. "It's like walking, only I'm walking between books instead of places."

"How incredibly whimsical," Morgana said, flipping the knife in her hand as she waited for the inevitable rush by the Black Guard.

I ignored her and stayed focused on Alice.

"Can you reverse it?" I asked.

"You mean go back to libraries I've been to before?" she said. "But there are so many interesting ones I haven't been to yet."

"No, I mean can you bring a library to you?" I said. "Or at least one book?"

"The book," the Scholar moaned from under his pile.

Alice smiled and nodded. "Oh yes, I do that all the time," she said. "But sometimes I have trouble putting the books back. They usually wind up out of place."

THE DEAD HAMLETS

Maybe that was how I was always able to find Alice by using books that had been mis-shelved in libraries, I thought, then shook my head to clear it. This was not the moment to be thinking about that sort of thing. We had only seconds before we were all about to join the ghost play, and I had a feeling that this time it would be a permanent stay.

As if reading my mind, Cobweb flung his remaining hand out in a flourish. A silk web sprang from it like a fisherman's net in all directions and entangled the limbs of the Black Guard.

"That was all I had left," Cobweb said, sinking to his knees in exhaustion or blood loss or maybe both. "Whatever you have planned, you had best make haste with it."

If he thought I had a plan, he clearly didn't know me. Still, I had to try to find a way to save us all.

"Alice," I said, "I need you to bring us The Nameless Book."

"You would fight the Black Guard with a greater madness?" Morgana asked.

"The Nameless Book isn't really a book," Alice said to me, frowning. "It's just things stuck in another thing."

"It looks like a book and we're calling it a book," I said. "That's good enough for me."

All around us, the Black Guard tore and slashed and bit at their web bindings. They were almost free now.

"The sooner the better," I added.

A section of the wall suddenly burst into flame in the shape of a doorway. The books burned away in seconds, but the fire didn't stop. I looked through the flames and saw the room with The Nameless Book on the other side.

"I don't know how you do it, but thanks," I said to Alice.

"It wasn't hard," she said. "It really wants to come to you."

"Do what you can for Amelia," I said to Morgana. "I'll return when I'm able, but I don't know when that will be."

I turned to Amelia and smiled at her and she smiled back. We said nothing, because there was nothing to say.

Then I started toward The Nameless Book, only to have Morgana stop me with a hand on my arm.

"You will unleash chaos if you read the words of that book," she said.

"Hopefully that chaos will be stuck in this place and won't be able to find a way out to the world," I said.

"And if you're wrong?" she asked.

I shook my head. "Please," I said. "One problem at a time."

I turned back to The Nameless Book but Morgana didn't take her hand away.

"There is another who will read it in your place," she said.

"Thanks, but I won't ask that of you," I said. "And I won't let you make Amelia do it either."

"That is not who I meant," she said and turned to Puck.

He sprang forward and Morgana slit the threads binding his mouth with her knife. The irons fell from his limbs at the same time.

"Here is your chance to redeem yourself, my pet," she said. "Read from the book and unleash the greatest chaos the world has ever known."

Puck cackled with delight and darted forward, past the Black Guard, who were freeing themselves of the last of the web now. He ran through the flames and grabbed The Nameless Book from its burning altar. He quickly flipped it open and started reading the words inscribed on the first page. I dare not repeat them here, for if I did this tale would end right now. Let me just say the world stopped for a second as a sound like the very heavens ripping open echoed throughout the library. The Black Guard even paused to look around and find the source of it.

But the source found them. A thing, a very indescribable thing, threw itself out of The Nameless Book and into our room. It was too large for the doorway, so it burst through the wall of books, and fiery texts flew everywhere. It fell upon Anubis, and his staff meant nothing to it. There was a spray of blood and flesh and black beetles and foul things I didn't recognize at all. I felt some small sense of satisfaction.

The thing from The Nameless Book wasn't the demon I'd bound into it all those centuries ago in Marlowe's theatre. It was something far worse than that. Why it left Puck and the rest of us alone, I don't know. Perhaps because we were the ones who had opened the book. Perhaps because it was saving us for last.

The other Black Guard turned their attention away from us and swarmed the creature, which I still can't picture clearly in my memory. And suddenly there was a gap in the ring around us. I didn't even have to yell at anyone to move. We ran into the room with The Nameless Book, through the flames to the hall on the other side. I knocked The Nameless Book from Puck's hand before he could summon anything else from it.

He stuck his tongue out at me in disappointment, but he ran along with the rest of us.

"From this time forth, my thoughts be bloody," Marlowe cried from somewhere in the melee, "or be nothing worth!"

The dead continued to act out the play behind us, oblivious to the horror in their midst, or perhaps just uncaring. We left them behind as we fled through the Forgotten Library. We ran back the way we'd come in, but that turned into a dead end when we reached a section of the hall where the ceiling had collapsed. A wall of books lay in our path. We scrambled to pull them aside, but there were too many. An inhuman scream sounded somewhere behind us, and hundreds more books fell from the ceiling upon us.

"We need to find another way out," Morgana said, and I was forced to agree with her. We ran back a bit to the nearest intersection. I thought about trying to summon the Witches again to show us the way out, but I had a feeling they wouldn't answer my call this time. Or if they did, they'd bring the things from the Nameless Book to us and then toss what remained of our bodies and souls into their cauldron.

"Alice, any ideas?" I asked.

"Oh yes," she said. "My head is full of ideas. They buzz around there like bees in a hive. Sometimes they get so noisy I have to put my head somewhere else until they quiet down."

"Left it is then," I said, and we ran blindly down that hallway.

The Scholar was suddenly at my side, trying to take the book Polonius had given me from my pocket. I swatted his hands away, but not before he managed to slide a finger in between the pages. More words ran up his arm for a second, forming incomprehensible jumbles on his skin much like the words in the mist, and I finally saw what I had been missing all along. The final piece of the puzzle. I pushed the Scholar away—far away—and kept running. Now I just needed the time to put all the pieces together in the proper order.

I looked around at what remained of Morgana's court and was relieved to find Amelia still among us. But it was a bittersweet sense of relief. There were only a handful of others left: Morgana, Puck and the woman with the donkey's head, Mustardseed carrying the unconscious Cobweb, and, unfortunately, the Scholar. The Black Guard had taken their toll.

Something screamed behind us again, but closer this time. Something not of this world.

And then we came across the raven. It sat on a shelf of books that jutted from one wall, looking at us. I saw the name Poe on the spine of one of the books.

"What is that thing doing here?" Morgana asked.

"It's being a pretty bird, of course," Alice said, and she stopped running and waved at the raven.

"Ravens never forget an enemy," I said, remembering the Raven Master's words. "And they never forget a friend." The raven croaked at me as if it were agreeing.

"Bah! It's just a common scavenger!" the Scholar said. "A regular nuisance they are, always stealing pages from books to line their nests—"

"Shut up!" the rest of us shouted in unison and, finally, the Scholar shut up.

I nodded at the raven. "All right, old friend," I said. "Show us the way out of here."

I expected the bird to take flight, but instead it just pecked at the Poe book and croaked at us again.

"Perhaps it just wanted to witness your end," Morgana said.

I ignored her and grabbed the Poe book from the shelf. I figured the raven was drawing attention to it for a purpose. As soon as I removed the book, the other books on the shelf collapsed, taking down part of the wall with them. Behind them was a door made of more ancient books, all folios like the kind I carried with me. The handle and hinges were made of shreds of paper. The raven took flight and circled over our heads.

"Do you think it's safe to take such a door in a place like this?" the Scholar asked.

"Probably not," I said and opened the door.

There was another hallway behind the door, but this one was made of pages instead of books. The words on them were handwritten rather than typed, and the paper yellowed and crumbling, so they must have been old pages indeed. We ran down this new hallway, the raven leading the way. I didn't bother closing the door behind us. I knew it wouldn't stop the thing on our trail.

We only ran for a minute or so before we reached the end of the hallway. It terminated in a curtain rather than another door. The curtain was made of more pages. We burst through it, and suddenly the pages flew everywhere, a whirlwind of them surrounding us. For a second, I thought our pursuer had caught up to us. Then the papers all fell to the floor and I saw where we were. The stage of a theatre. We looked out onto the empty seats of the audience, dimly visible thanks to the glow of the spotlights trained on the stage. I spun around to look behind us, but there was only a closed curtain at the midstage mark. The creature chasing us gave another cry, but it faded away into some distance we couldn't see. Then there was only the sounds of our merry crew gasping for breath.

I stepped back to the curtain and looked through it. There was only empty stage on the other side. We had escaped. I looked down at the pages littering the floor and saw they were all blank now. Many of them were already crumbling away to little more than dust.

The raven circled the auditorium, croaking some more at us. Maybe that was its version of applause.

"Would someone care to explain what just happened?" Morgana said.

"All the world's a stage," I said and laughed.

I turned in a circle, making sure there were no threats anywhere else, and that's when I recognized the theatre. We were back in Berlin, on the stage where it had all started. I nodded at the raven.

"Someday you're going to have to show me your tricks," I said.

The raven just made a noise that sounded suspiciously like a chuckle. It flew off into the shadows at the rear of the audience and disappeared.

"That's it," the Scholar said behind me. "I want to go back to the library."

"Which library?" Alice asked.

"I don't care," the Scholar said. "Any library."

"They're not just places, you know," Alice said. "They have feelings. How would you like it if some library said it didn't care what kind of scholar it had in it?"

"I'll be happy to take you back to the library," I said, trying to cut off the conversation before it got out of hand. I checked the wings at each side of the stage. No nameless horrors, no Marlowe, no Black Guard. That was enough for me at the moment.

"What happened to the thing from the book?" Puck asked, looking around the theatre. He seemed disappointed that whatever had been following us through the Forgotten Library hadn't made it out to our world.

"I don't know," I said. "I guess it's still back there with the Black Guard. It's probably looking for us right now."

"Do you think it'll ever be able to escape?" he asked.

"Maybe," I said. "I imagine it's got all eternity to discover a way out."

That thought seemed to cheer him and he grinned as he headed for one of the exits at the other end of the audience. The woman with the donkey's head joined him and they held hands as they went.

"That was certainly a distracting little adventure," Morgana said, narrowing her eyes as she looked at me. "But I can't think of anything we did to rid ourselves of the ghost."

"I think we've had the secret to getting rid of the ghost all along," I said and held up the book Polonius had given me. "Haven't we?" I said, turning to the Scholar.

He stared at the book and licked his lips, then grinned at me in what he no doubt assumed was a friendly fashion but instead looked more a death grimace.

"What is one book when you could have a library?" he said.

"What are you talking about?" Morgana asked. "There are no secrets in that book. All the pages are blank."

"Blank to us, maybe," I said. "But not to him. Am I right?" I asked the Scholar.

"Your illiteracy is not my fault," the Scholar said.

"You knew from the moment you saw this book that it was the play that Shakespeare stole, didn't you?" I said. "You just didn't want to tell me because you wanted to find the Forgotten Library. You thought I'd have no need to go there if I knew I already had the play."

"It is the greatest library ever known," the Scholar said. "What scholar could resist that temptation?"

In case you were wondering, it was moments like this that made me reluctant to turn to the Scholar for help.

"We almost all died because of you," I said.

"Me?" he protested. "You were the one who raised that hack Marlowe from the dead!"

"You might redeem yourself yet," I said, ignoring the point he'd made. I went to hand him the book and he snatched it from me before I could even finish the motion.

"Blank pages," Morgana said again. "Am I the only one seeing that?"

"Just because they're blank doesn't mean they're empty," I said. I nodded at the Scholar. He opened the book and ran his hand down a page. Words flowed up his arm and danced across his eyes. The same indecipherable words that floated out of the mouths of everyone dead and trapped in the play.

"Beautiful," the Scholar whispered. "The language, it is full of grace. Poetry in a tongue that no longer exists."

"What is it?" Morgana asked, staring at the Scholar.

"It's the ghost play," I said. "Or all that remains of it, anyway. The one that Will stole and called his own. The one that he brought to life with his ink, for it was the ghost of the play itself that was haunting your productions."

"The father text to *Hamlet*," the Scholar said, nodding. "The story that began it all."

"Polonius must have given it to me in the hope I could use it to figure out what was causing the haunting," I said. And so I had, for all the good that it had done the dead now trapped in the play.

"What use is the text to us?" Morgana asked, shaking her head in exasperation. "We should burn the thing and send it back to the Forgotten Library."

"We must do the opposite," I said. "The play wants to live again. It's like Frankenstein, assembling itself out of the dead. We must give it a helping hand."

"I think all your recent deaths may have made you mad," Morgana said, staring at me.

I looked out over the empty seats. "If we can bring the play back from the Forgotten Library, then maybe it will no longer be a ghost," I said. "And if it is not a ghost, then perhaps it will release the dead it has now."

"And just how do we do that if the play has already been lost forever?" she asked.

I looked back at the Scholar. "You remember what you take from books, right?" I asked him.

He snorted as if the question was an insult. "I remember every word I've ever read," he said. "I am a Scholar, not some half-witted student."

"Find a few ancient books that have been forgotten in libraries," I said. "Books that are meaningless for scholarship. And write the words from this book in them. On blank pages or in the margins. Wherever you can.

Just make it look as if those words have been there all along. Then leave the books somewhere they will be easily discovered."

"I am also not some mindless scribe," the Scholar grumbled, glaring at me as he consumed another page.

"Do it and I'll let you finish reading the book," I said, nodding at the text in his hands.

He scowled at me in a less disagreeable fashion than usual. I took that to be a sign of his assent. "It will be the find of the century for some lucky academics," he said. "The original *Hamlet* discovered."

"Scholars everywhere will want to read it," I said. "Actors everywhere will want to perform it."

"I'm the only Scholar of worth," the Scholar muttered, but I did my best to ignore him.

"We will bring the play back to true life," I said, stepping to the front of the stage and looking out into the auditorium. "And when it lives again, the haunting will stop because it won't be a ghost anymore." I turned back to Morgana. "Just try not to put on any more productions of the play until that happens. We don't need it to keep spreading in the meantime."

"I swear we will never stage that play again," she said.

Then she stepped up to me and kissed me, and I felt warmth and peace fill me at her touch.

"I swear it on your soul," she said, breaking away from me. And that feeling of peace stayed with me even though she no longer touched me. For the first time in a long while, I felt whole again. And I realized then from her words that she had given me back possession of my soul.

She stepped over to Amelia and looked at her for a moment. She took her by the hands and smiled, but it wasn't that usual cruel, mocking smile. It was something else entirely. I'd never seen it on Morgana's face before.

"If you need me, I will always respond to your call," she said.

Then she drew her hands away, and I saw her slip the black ring off Amelia's finger.

She turned from Amelia and gave me that same strange, unfamiliar smile. Then she went down the steps at the side of the stage and up the aisle to the exit. Mustardseed gave us a grin and followed after her, still carrying the unconscious Cobweb.

Amelia didn't follow them. She stayed with the Scholar and me, watching Morgana and the others go.

"I guess you're free now," I said. I could barely believe it. I never actually thought Morgana would release Amelia.

"So are you," Amelia said.

It took me a second to understand what she meant. I looked down at my hand and saw the black ring was loose on my finger now instead of fused to it. I slipped it off and stared at it in my palm. Morgana had freed me as well. So why did I still feel such a longing for her?

It had to be an after-effect of the ring, I decided. Some sort of emotional residue that would take time to fade. I thought about throwing the ring off into the shadows, but I didn't. I slipped it into my pocket instead for safekeeping. I didn't want someone else to find it and cause problems for themselves. That's what I told myself, anyway.

Now it was just the four of us in the theatre: Alice, the Scholar, Amelia and me.

"It's a long journey back to the library, isn't it?" the Scholar said with a sigh. "And I'll have to ride in one of those horseless carriages again, won't I?"

"What are you talking about, you silly old man?" Alice said to him. "You're holding a library in your hand."

"I don't know your children's tricks," the Scholar grumbled, clutching the book to his chest protectively.

"There's a lot you don't know," Alice said, folding her arms across her chest and pouting.

"Ha! I've *forgotten* more about books than you'll ever know," the Scholar said.

Alice cocked her head at him. "I thought you didn't forget anything you read," she said.

The Scholar spluttered and I looked away to hide my smile. The pages on the floor suddenly sprang up around us in another whirlwind. This time they did all crumble into dust. When the dust blew away and settled into the corners of the stage, Alice and the Scholar were gone, and the book with them. Alice had done me a huge favour by taking the Scholar with her. I'm sure it would cost me dearly in the future. But for now, it was just Amelia and me alone on the stage.

I shook my head. "Those two are either going to kill each other or become best friends," I said.

"Maybe they'll do both," Amelia said.

I nodded and looked around some more, but there was nothing else to see in the theatre. Finally I had to look back at her. She smiled at me.

"I don't know what to say to you," I admitted.

"Tell me about your life," she said.

"My life," I said. I mulled that over. Where to begin? I felt a great heaviness start to weigh down my body. Maybe it was the exhaustion from the battle finally catching up to me. Maybe it was something else.

"I've never had a father before," she said. "I'd like to know all about you."

"It's a long story," I said. "Several long stories, in fact."

"I think I have the time," she said.

She reached out her hand and I took it. She was still cold with death, but I swore to myself then that I would do everything I could to warm her with life.

"Let me tell you about when I met your mother," I said, and we walked off the stage together.

NOTES

1. The idea of a ghost play was inspired by the scholarly notion of an Ur-Hamlet—a play that existed before Hamlet and informed Shakespeare's classic. Some believe the Ur-Hamlet was an earlier play written by another playwright, perhaps Thomas Kyd. Others believe the Ur-Hamlet was simply an earlier draft of Hamlet written by Shakespeare. Obviously, I took the idea and ran with it.

2. There are a number of references to John Webster in this book. If you haven't experienced a Webster play, I suggest you seek one out in your local library. You'll probably have a hard time finding one staged near you. He was that kind of playwright. Very few of his plays have survived to this day, unless traces of them linger in other plays.

3. The song Frankenstein sings is "I Remember I Remember" by Thomas Hood (1828).

4. The sonnet Cross finds in Spenser's tomb is Shakespeare's Sonnet 55. It is about immortality, among other things.

ACKNOWLEDGEMENTS

I'd like to extend thanks to my agents, Anne McDermid and Monica Pacheco, for continuing to believe in me, no matter what crazy thing I do.

I'd also like to express my appreciation for Kelsi Morris, the editor of *The Dead Hamlets* and *The Mona Lisa Sacrifice*, for her keen eye and patience. The successes of the Cross books can largely be attributed to her, while any failures are mine and mine alone.

While I'm at it, I'd like to thank all the good people at ChiZine for publishing the Nameless Books of our time. The world is a far more interesting place thanks to ChiZine, even if it is a less safe place to live.

I must of course thank my family for continuing to put up with my frequent absences and prolonged arguments with imaginary people. While you may not always come first when it comes to time in the day, rest assured you always come first in my heart.

Finally, I wish to thank you, the reader of this book, for continuing to follow the adventures of Cross. Without you, this book would be nothing but the ghost of an idea.

Turn the page
to read an excerpt from
the next exciting book
in the Cross series,
The Apocalypse Ark!

Out in January 2016 from ChiZine Publications.

NOAH HAD A LITTLE ARK

The one and only time I met Noah in person was when he wrecked the Spanish Armada back in the 1600s trying to capture me. He nearly succeeded.

I'd hired myself out as a mercenary to the Spaniards during one of their many misadventures on the continent. I wasn't a sailor, just a soldier in the Spanish army when they were happily sacking places like Flanders and Antwerp. Like most good soldiers, I didn't really care about the politics behind it all. The Spanish paid more than their rivals, and that was all the reason I needed. Also, they had the best wine. If you don't think that's important, then you've probably never been a soldier in the 1600s. When the Spanish decided to invade England, I was so drunk I barely registered the news.

I sobered up quickly when the British caught our fleet at anchor in a port I can't even remember the name of now. They sent in the fire ships, blazing wrecks designed to light our own vessels on fire. Most of our captains panicked and cut themselves free of their anchors to escape. Hard to blame them. There's little more terrifying to a seaman than watching a burning ship bearing down on his own ship—except, perhaps, for that burning ship to be loaded with gunpowder. And just like that, we were scattered and on the run.

A good admiral like Nelson might have been able to turn the tide. Hell, a good captain like Drake probably could have done it. He did it against us on more than one occasion, after all. But we were led by some duke or another who had probably never set foot on a ship before this particular misadventure. Things went from bad to worse faster than I could sober up. As a wiser man than me once said, so it goes.

Somehow our ship and a few others wound up sailing along the coast of Ireland to get home to Spain. Don't ask me how that came about. Maybe it was some tactical decision, or maybe it had something to do with ocean currents. I don't really know. I wasn't any more of a sailor then than I am now. I can't even recall the name of the ship I sailed on, which is a major form of heresy among the sailors I've known. It's like not remembering the name of your mother. In fact, I imagine more sailors know the names of their ships than the names of their mothers.

It was off Ireland that Noah came for us. The first sign was the clouds on the horizon. We thought them only a storm, and we weren't too worried. The worst a storm could do to us was scatter the fleet and sink a few ships, and we were already scattered and missing a few ships.

But the clouds came at us with unnatural speed, and our ship started to rise and fall on the waves. And then the lookout shouted down that he saw other vessels hiding in the clouds. When the captain called up to ask if they were galleons or merchant ships, the lookout didn't say anything else, just crossed himself several times. Like that has ever helped anything.

We crowded the gunwales and watched the storm come. As it neared us, we saw the clouds stretched all the way down to the waves themselves. They were black as night, and lightning flashed in the constantly rolling mass. The water in front of the storm churned and swelled in directions that didn't make sense, as if something massive was twisting and writhing just under the surface. It was unlike any other storm I'd ever seen.

And the ships within it were unlike any vessels I'd ever seen.

Or rather, I'd seen them all before, but never like this.

There were English men of war ships much like the ones that had been harrying us along the coast. There were also Roman triremes and Chinese junks. There were longboats and fishing boats. There were even wooden rafts. They were all clustered in a large mass, tied together with ropes or joined with suspension bridges that ran between them. One giant vessel that bent and warped in many directions as it rode the waves.

And in the centre was the ark.

It was a vast wooden ship, only the bow emerging out of the churning clouds. It towered above the largest galleons in what was left of our armada, but it was covered with barnacles and starfish all the way up to the deck, as if the ship spent most of the time underwater.

THE APOCALYPSE ARK

Barnacles and starfish and bones. Skeletons hung from the bow like forgotten decorations. It was the sort of thing you saw on pirate ships from time to time, but on pirate ships the skeletons tended to be human in nature. Not so on the ark. There was something that looked like the shell and bones of a giant crab, only it had long arms like tentacles instead of claws. There was a man's skeleton that ended in what looked like fins at the hands and feet, and a skull that looked more like a frog's than a man's. And there was the skeleton of a man with wings, which I took to be an angel. I wasn't sure, though, as angels normally just faded away to wherever it is dead angels go when I killed them. But there was nothing normal about the vision in front of me.

I didn't dwell on the bones anyway. I was too distracted by the living crew of the ships.

They were unlike anything I'd ever seen, and most of them I haven't seen since. A creature like a black octopus with mouths all over its body that swung from rope to rope in the torn rigging of a galleon. A woman with six arms and no legs who scuttled along the gunwales of the ark like a spider, stopping every now and then to wave a pair of swords at us. A half dozen men who looked like Vikings with horned helmets, until the ark drew near enough we could see the horns grew from their heads.

"What manner of abomination is this?" one of the soldiers beside me said, as the captain of our ship shouted the orders for us to turn and ready our cannons for a full broadside. I would have shouted the same orders in the captain's place, but I suspected they wouldn't make a difference.

"It is the worst of abominations," I said to the other soldier. "It's Noah and his ark."

I didn't bother to tell him how I knew. We weren't that close, after all. Besides, men on ships were always telling each other outrageous things. You had to do something to pass the time.

"Has it come to save us from the British?" the other soldier asked.

I didn't answer him. I knew what Noah wanted. He was hunting for abominations, and he must have sensed me.

The captain shouted the order to fire, and our gunners delivered a full broadside into the ark itself. Shattered pieces of wood and bone flew from it, and our crew gave a cheer. A cheer that quickly died in our throats when the six-armed woman scurried to the bow and waved her swords at us.

Then Noah himself came out on deck.

He was a giant the size of three men. He wore a white robe stained with blood. His long beard was also white and just as stained. Despite the distance, I could see his eyes were as black as the clouds. He dragged a trio of angels along behind him with a chain he had wrapped around one hand. The chain ran through collars on the angels' necks. The three of them carried a bound book, struggling with its weight even though it was no larger than any other bound book of the time. Its colour was perhaps black, but that's not quite right either. It seemed to have no colour at all. I had to look away from it, for it made my mind uneasy.

"Find the thing that should not be and bring it back to the ark," he bellowed, raking our ship with his gaze. "The one who delivers it I will reward with death!"

The captain shouted at the gunners to reload, his voice barely audible over the sounds of the rain hammering down on us, but I knew another broadside wouldn't do any good. The ark was too large, and too close. I looked around for some escape, but we were on a ship at sea, and the water didn't strike me as much safer than the ship, given the present circumstances.

There was, of course, the coast in the distance. We had turned in its general direction to deliver the broadside, but we were too far away to reach it before the ark fully overtook us. The monstrous vessel moved too quickly. But perhaps with a little help. . . .

I expended a breath of grace to change the direction of the wind and fill our sails. The ship surged toward shore.

And then the rain came down even harder. It fell upon us like the very sky had collapsed, like we had sailed into a waterfall. It battered us and knocked men to the deck. I caught sight of the lookout falling past, into the sea, and then he was gone. The rain tore open the sails and the ship slowed, and men who were veterans of many a bloody battle cried out in fear at the madness engulfing us.

And then the madness really began.

Noah roared something unintelligible, at least to my ears, and yanked the angels forward on their chains. They stumbled past him and to the bow of the ark. They moved like they had been broken in every possible way. They opened the book as one and began to chant words they read in it, but I couldn't make out what they were saying.

Something heard them, though.

Tentacles lashed out from under the waves and caught on to our ship. The limbs of some great beast whose body remained out of sight. I knew what it was from the legends anyway. The kraken. I didn't really want to see the rest of it, given the horrors of the tentacles themselves. There were things stuck in them. Bits of wood and rope from other ships. Swords and axes that must have once been used in a vain attempt to repel boarders. And the bodies of men. They were half buried in the tentacles, like they were being absorbed into them. And then I saw they weren't bodies at all. The men were still alive. They turned their faces to us as the tentacles smashed down onto our ship, seizing it, and they cried out in different tongues. English, Spanish, Greek, Mayan. They all screamed the same thing.

"Kill me!"

The tentacles curled around the mast, caught on to the sides of the ship, even the wheel itself, knocking the man there aside. And then they pulled us toward the ark.

The captain of our ship didn't need to shout orders. The soldiers and sailors around me drew their weapons and hacked away at the tentacles. The limbs of the great creature bled like any other being cut open with a sword, but they bled black sludge. The men caught in the tentacles wailed like an unholy choir.

I looked around to see if the other ships of our battered armada were in the same plight as us, but they were lost in the deluge. I couldn't see them, and I couldn't see the shore anymore. All I could see was the ark and its fleet closing in on us.

And the boarders.

They came along the tentacles to our ship. The spider woman running down one thrashing limb like it wasn't even moving. The men with horns in their heads swinging along another, chopping handholds into the tentacle with their axes to stop from falling into the sea below. A jellyfish thing on bone stilts running across the water. I knew we could no more repel these creatures than we could repel nightmares in our sleep.

I laid my hand on the shoulder of the man beside me. "I'm sorry, but they seek you," I said.

He stared at me. "What madness do you speak of?" he asked.

"You're dead anyway," I said. "At least I will have a chance to escape."

I let some of my grace flow through my hand and into him. Enough that Noah would be able to sense it, if the grace was how he had found us. The other man's eyes widened as he tasted Heaven for the first time in his life. And the last.

And then I performed a couple of quick sleights. One to make me look like him. And one to make him look like me, just in case Noah somehow had my description. I even added a bit of glow to the other man's skin to attract attention.

Then I ran for the bow of the ship and threw myself into the water.

I dove under and swam as far as I could, kicking against the strange and sudden surges that threw me one way and then another under the surface. The water was colder than I had expected. It was colder than I had ever remembered it. I waited for one of those tentacles to grab on to me, but they never did.

When I finally came up for air, the ship was a good three lengths behind me and barely visible through the rain. I saw the impossible shapes of Noah's crew swarm onto it and converge on the glowing figure on the deck. I tried not to listen to the cries of the men and other things.

I dove back under and swam as hard as I could for land. When I reached it some time later, staggering up onto a rocky shore, the storm covered the sea behind me. More lightning flashed within the clouds here and there. And then a roar rent the clouds themselves, opening them up to reveal the ark once more. I caught sight of Noah again, standing on the deck of the ark. He held something glowing in his hands, something that he tore into little pieces and then tossed aside.

I ran when he turned to look in my direction. I ran from the beach and up into the green hills of Ireland beyond. I ran until I could no longer see the ocean and the ocean could no longer see me.

EMB
RACE
THE
ODD

THE MONA LISA SACRIFICE
PETER ROMAN

For thousands of years, Cross has wandered the earth, a mortal soul trapped in the undying body left behind by Christ. He's been a thief, a con man, a soldier and a drunkard. He's fought as a slave in the Colosseum and as a knight at King Arthur's side. But now he must play the part of reluctant hero, as an angel comes to him for help finding the Mona Lisa—the real Mona Lisa that inspired the painting. Cross's quest takes him into a secret world within our own, populated by characters just as strange and wondrous as he is: gorgons and dead gods hidden away in museums; faeries that live in countryside pubs, trapping and enslaving unwary travellers; and super-rich collectors who trade magical artifacts among themselves. He's haunted by memories of Penelope, the only woman he truly loved, and he wants to avenge her death at the hands of his ancient enemy, Judas, a forgotten god from an ancient time. The angel promises to deliver Judas to Cross, but nothing is ever what it seems when Judas is involved, and when a group of renegade angels looking for a new holy war show up, things truly go to hell.

AVAILABLE NOW
ISBN 978-1-77148-145-8

THE HOUSE OF WAR AND WITNESS
MIKE CAREY, LINDA CAREY & LOUISE CAREY

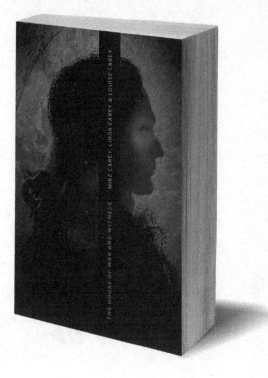

Prussia, 1740. With the whole of Europe balanced on the brink of war, an Austrian regiment is sent to the farthest frontier of the empire to hold the border against the might of Prussia. Their garrison—the ancient house called Pokoj, inhabited by ghosts only Drozde, the quartermaster's mistress, can see. They tell her stories of Pokoj's past, and a looming menace in its future . . . a grim discovery that both Drozde and the humourless lieutenant Klaes are about to stumble upon. It will mean the end of villagers and soldiers alike, and a catastrophe that only the restless dead can prevent. . . .

AVAILABLE NOW
ISBN 978-177148-312-4

THE YELLOW WOOD
MELANIE TEM

For Alexandra Kove, the path of her life took her far from the claustrophobic forest where her father raised her. She believed that she had to escape, that her only road was away from the family and circumstances of her birth. Now, her road has turned back, converged with the paths of the family she thought was safely in her past.

AVAILABLE NOW
ISBN 978-177148-314-8

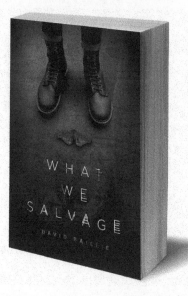

PROBABLY MONSTERS
RAY CLULEY

From British Fantasy Award-winning author Ray Cluley comes Probably Monsters—a collection of dark, weird, literary horror stories. Sometimes the monsters are bloodsucking fiends with fleshy wings. Sometimes they're shambling dead things that won't rest, or simply creatures red in tooth and claw. But often they're worse than any of these. They're the things that make us howl in the darkness, hoping no one hears. These are the monsters we make ourselves, and they can find us anywhere . . .

AVAILABLE NOW
978-1-77148-334-6

ANGELS & EXILES
YVES MEYNARD

In these twelve sombre tales, ranging from baroque science fiction to bleak fantasy, Yves Meynard brings to life wonders and horrors. From space travellers who must rid themselves of the sins their souls accumulate in transit, to a young man whose love transcends time; from refugees in a frozen hold at the end of space, to a city drowning under the weight of its architectural prayer; from an alien Jerusalem that has corrupted the Earth, to a land still bleeding from the scars of a supernatural war; here are windows opened onto astonishing vistas, stories written with a scientist's laser focus alloyed with a poet's sensibilities.

AVAILABLE NOW
978-1-77148-308-7